D0360566

WOMEN AND APPLETREES

WOMEN AND APPLETREES

Moa Martinson

TRANSLATED AND WITH AN AFTERWORD BY

Margaret S. Lacy

THE FEMINIST PRESS
Old Westbury, New York

This translation is dedicated to my mother, Adina,
and to the memory of my husband, Edgar.

© 1973, 1983 by the Estate of Moa Martinson
Afterword © 1985 by The Feminist Press
All rights reserved. Published in 1985.
Printed in the United States of America.
89 88 87 86 85   6 5 4 3 2 1

This translation of *Women and Appletrees (Kvinnor och Äppelträd)*
is published by agreement with Bokförlaget Legenda AB, Stockholm.
First Feminist Press edition

Library of Congress Cataloging in Publication Data

Martinson, Moa, 1890–1964.
    Women and appletrees.

    Translation of: Kvinnor och äppelträd.
    I. Title.
PT9875.M39K7913   1985   839.7'372   85–6898
ISBN 0–935312–38–2 (pbk.)

Cover and text design: Gilda Hannah
Cover art: Mary Cassatt, "Baby Reaching for an Apple," 1893. Reproduced
courtesy of the Virginia Museum of Fine Arts, Richmond, Virginia
Typesetting: Com Com
Manufacturing: Haddon Craftsmen, Inc.

Contents

A Note from the Publisher

When we asked Scandinavian scholar Cheri Register several years ago to identify Moa Martinson for us, she said, thinking of The Feminist Press's emphasis on "lost" literature by and about working-class women, "Martinson might be described as 'the Agnes Smedley of Sweden.'" Like Smedley, Martinson was dirt-poor, self-taught, a journalist before she became a novelist, a woman who never forgot her roots, and who spent her life not only writing, but engaging in social causes. The two were also as different as one might expect women to be across national borders.

Like many first novels, Smedley's *Daughter of Earth* and Martinson's *Women and Appletrees,* are partly autobiographical. Both writers begin with memories of strong grandmothers, follow the difficult lives of mothers, and the mixed triumphs of daughters. In Smedley's novel, the heroine is a loner who has to reject mothering and motherhood in order to survive. In Martinson's novel, mothering is central, as is the strong intimacy between women. Martinson provides a rare glimpse for us into the lives of heterosexual women who are woman-centered, whose friends and comrades are not the men they have married, or the men who have fathered their children, but the women they have bonded with. The men in this novel are lonelier than the women, who, as Martinson makes clear, always have each other:

Children can live in the same city, have the same birthday, play on the same garbage dump, eat the same cheap bread, hear the same oaths—man's whisky-bass, woman's falsetto, go to the same school, and still not feel attachment or sympathy. But when the time is ripe, they meet and are friends until death.

So it was with Sally and Ellen.

The Feminist Press is pleased to be Moa Martinson's American publisher, and to be publishing Margaret Lacy's rich translation of *Women and Appletrees* as the first volume in our new international series of feminist classics.

Mother Bathes

Tonight Mother bathes.

It's a long time since Mother Sofi and Fredrika began their bathing, but even so the whole farm gets tense when they do. The whole farm, the whole neighborhood, nearly the whole parish.

Two middle-aged women, both of them nearly fifty, one with fifteen children, if you count the first, born before the marriage and long since disappeared in the world, a farmed-out illegitimate. The one with fourteen children, the other childless, married to a half-blind, crippled old man, who had a little land, much too little, but the most money in the parish according to persistent rumors. Every parish in the country has a mysterious old man like that who is said to have lots of money, an old man or woman, whichever it happens to be.

Two middle-aged women who bathe every week. Nobody had ever heard of anything like that in the parish, nor in neighboring parishes either. Hired men and maids, sons and daughters, once in the summer maybe, but married women? And year round!

It began ten years ago, one autumn after flax threshing. Full of straw, black with dust like a charcoal stack, and after days of hard work with the flax, Mother Sofi walked heavy and tired in the dusk beside her helper and wanted to get clean. It was when she was carrying the fourteenth, that's to say, the fifteenth, and she was forty years old. "I don't think

I'll go up in the morning. I fall down so easily. When I had the last one, I was still dirty with scutch. I'm not up to washing myself tonight either. I just don't care. I think I'll crawl up in the hayloft, that'll do all right. I had my first one there. Remember that, Fredrika? I had my first in the hayloft, but, *ja,* there's a new thing now, a midwife. Midwife? What's the use of that, you're the one's got to give birth anyways. In the old days a neighbor just came and wrapped the baby. The cow calves best alone, you know. I'll just go in now and go to bed."

"We'll go to the washhouse and bathe ourselves," Fredrika said, and so it began.

The whole countryside called Sofi "Mother," not because of all the children, but because she was married to the farmer who owned the most land. It was usual in that region. Everyone liked Mother Sofi, and when she married the owner of the farm where she worked, the biggest farm in the parish, but even so the least respected, everyone said, "She's too good for him." But Sofi had an illegitimate child as her only dowry.

The farmer, however, had his own mother. For ten years she had lain paralyzed in the shabby, unkempt best room of the farmhouse. There she lay, quarreling and ordering and ruling, with all the money in a big leather purse under her pillow. Every öre that could be scraped together was put in the old woman's leather purse, and once there, none came out.

The farmer himself went with a leather apron on, everyday as well as Sunday, not as is usual for the sake of simplicity or for any old custom, but because of his incurable rupture. He was commonly called the leather-apron farmer or *"skroiga"** farmer. And he had never worked. He couldn't. He was born ruptured, it was said. His hands

*A dialectical word for a scrotal hernia.

2

looked withered, looked strange with that big body, with the leather apron, with everything he held. Never do you see hands, withered and soft like that, on a farm.

It was a big farm with poor soil. Tough, that soil was, contrary as old women or as horses hard beaten. Soil that lay there, mossy and miry and matted, and only spited you. Soil that pliantly spread itself out for birch roots and useless wilderness, but set itself perversely against the ploughshare, against the spade and hoe, like a woman in bed who hates her man.

And when the farmer with those soft hands married his lively young maid, everyone said, "She's too good for him." But she had an illegitimate child. "Think over what you're doing," Sofi's father said. He was a Frenchman, who as a young man had to leave his homeland during a revolt. He had married a Swede, a half-gypsy, who long since had left him and two children behind. He supported himself by tailoring, and he could also "stick" pigs and cats as his gypsy father-in-law had taught him.

"I'll be rich, and I'll get to keep the baby," Sofi answered, and she married the leather-apron farmer.

But Sofi didn't become rich, and she didn't get to keep her baby. When she was bearing the farmer's first one, his paralyzed mother took out her leather purse one day and said to her son, "Now you farm out the maid's kid."

And the illegitimate child was farmed out. Sofi never saw her firstborn again, the one born in the hayloft. Rumor gave the father's name to more than one. Many said it was the farmer's own but that he didn't dare to admit it to his mother, who was a strict reader of the Bible and bigoted, rejoicing that Hagar was driven out in the desert.

And now Mother Sofi is forty years old, and stands there, tired and heavy, beside Fredrika, who also married "to get rich." "We'll go to the washhouse and bathe ourselves."

Every week after that evening, except for the week Sofi

lay in bed after her fifteenth child, the two women bathed in the washhouse. Every Friday. "We must have a definite day," Fredrika said.

At first no one noticed.

Each had his work, each child who could walk and understand an order was forced to work. For father couldn't, of course, work.

"Your father is *skroig*," the tenant farmer's Sven said to Mother Sofi's oldest on the way to school. "Your father is *skroig*, leather-apron farmer's kids," taunted the children who turned off at the pauper's house.

And the farmer, clumping around in his leather apron, with heavy steps comes into the barn where his young sons are winnowing the grain. "Haven't you got any farther?" It was always "Haven't you got any farther?" "You are *skroig*," they muttered after him sometimes. One day one of the younger ones tied a sack around his belly like an apron and walked straddle-legged back and forth, "Now I'm *skroig*, now I'm *skroig*."

"Take off the sack, you'll ruin it," the farmer said.

"Can't you see I'm *skroig*?" the little one asked.

Leather-apron farmer, everyone said.

On that big, mismanaged farm, the children grow up in fear that any of them will need to go on errands to the neighbors. They are always home, building their own kingdom with their ideas and views, and all of them look with revulsion at a pair of soft hands hanging from a pair of long, thick arms. And when the oldest son, stooped from heavy work and thin from watching and worrying, comes in to Mother Sofi to look at the fourteenth newborn, he sits bowed like an old man by the bed and looks at her, looks at the red little face poking out of the blanket beside her. He looks down at his big calloused hands, hands sixteen years old with every trace of childhood gone, looks at Mother Sofi and says, "Father is *skroig*, how can there be so many children?" His big blue eyes, so like her own, stare tiredly and perplexedly into hers. And she stares back, cannot answer. He sits there awhile. "What is it this time?"

"A boy." Then Mother Sofi begins to cry.

Her son strokes her hair with his roughened man's hands, the knuckles knobby from work, and he asks, "Was it very bad this time, Mother?"

"No, I'm no worse now than usual. Have you got your meals?"

"*Ja,* Fredrika is here so there's always food. Why are you crying, Mother? Don't mind about what I said." But then Mother Sofi cries still more. "Has Father been in to see you?"

"No, not yet. He never comes in when I'm sick, you know."

"*Ja,* I know that. I have to go now, it's chore time. Don't get up too soon." He stoops over, looks intently at the baby's face, and presses his mother's hand. "He looks like you, Mother." Then he goes, slowly thinking things over, like a man who now has another mouth to feed.

Mother Sofi bathed every week.

At first no one paid any attention to it. The bath went unnoticed with all the washing and butchering, making potato flour, washing the wool, dying the carpet rags. The washhouse was always fired up one day in the week, and the bakehouse was inside it. The baking began early for Christmas, rye bread, which would stretch to the next seedtime, rusks, which would last until Easter. Fredrika was always there to help, the only help Mother Sofi wanted to have. Fredrika, who married to get rich, but who hardly got food from her "rich" man, because, when it came down to it, she could never make herself go to bed with him. "If he were only bleary-eyed and old. He isn't so terribly old, barely sixty, but his legs have running sores. I didn't know that. I can never lie with him." And the man became crazy and stingy, even begrudging her food, although she worked all

5

she could on his little farm. They could have only one cow, though the man had ten thousand *riksdalrar*,* so everyone said. That was why she married him. Fredrika had to go out as help in order to "get clothes on my back," as she put it.

The two women bathed undisturbed through Christmas. On Friday, the third of January, light could be seen in the washhouse and smoke from the chimney. The farmer pulled on his winter cap, took his cane, and stomped out. The washhouse was latched from inside. He pounded on the door.

"Who is it?"

"What are you doing in the washhouse at this time of day and this time of year?"

"We are bathing."

He stands there silently a long time, wondering, considering whether to turn back. The situation is way over his head. Then, suddenly enraged, he shrieks, "Get out of there!"

"We are bathing," Fredrika says.

"Ja, we are bathing," Mother Sofi says.

"You're acting like damned whores! Stop it or I'll show you! The washhouse is mine."

"What did he say?" Mother Sofi asks.

"He called us whores because we want to wash ourselves," Fredrika says loudly, and the farmer hears her and yells, *"Ja,* you are real whores, going there to bathe the same time you're celebrating Christmas, but it's my washhouse."

Then Fredrika opens the washhouse door. She stands naked outside the doorway while the cold air whirls around her like a cloud. Big and stately and white, she shimmers ghostlike against the dark January sky, and the farmer stands frozen, doesn't know what to think. Never before has he beheld a naked woman. It is cold, the middle of winter, Fredrika and Sofi, all this goes round in his head, has he gone

*Rixdollar, a silver coin worth about a dollar.

crazy! Fredrika has a big scoop of hot lye ashes, and emptying it right over him, she says, "Here, take this for calling us whores. I've known ever since we went to school what a wretch you are and why you couldn't get any girls. And you never even could learn your lessons. You just ate, carried your big bellyful around, and just ate. Clear off now, or I'll baptize every inch of you. And you leave us alone. We only wash the dirt off us once a week."

And Mother Sofi and Fredrika got to bathe in peace.

But the rumor got around.

A man can't go in to his children and say, "Your mother bathes, stands naked in the washhouse." No, that he can't do.

He doesn't believe much in the Bible, never goes to church, he's got money in the bank, but to go in to the children and say, "Your mother bathes, and they've thrown lye on me." No! He stumbles into the barn, wipes the ashes off his cap with hay, stands for a long time, wondering. "Bathing, why in . . . why in the name of Jesus," he shrieks, "why do they bathe?" And he goes into the big house and lies on his bed, brooding, thinking that this, too, will pass. Everything passes, Mother lay paralyzed for ten years, lay paralyzed, and only nagged and quarreled, but then she died, everything passes.

But soon the whole farm knew that Mother Sofi bathed, then the next village knew it, and in a year the whole parish knew it. It became common knowledge. The sons and daughters grew up, and everyone knew that now the oldest daughter also bathed every Friday with Mother Sofi and Fredrika. The sons, too, went gladly to the washhouse, not on Fridays, of course, but people didn't know that.

Tonight Mother bathes.

It's soon ten years since she began to bathe. Her oldest son has become a man. His stooped back has straightened, his muscles developed, the place has a farmer now who can and will work.

There are many on the farm who can work. The youngest is nine years old already. But he's not going to work, the oldest has made up his mind about that. He's going to go properly to school, and then he's going to be a priest, a priest in the family makes up for a lot.

Nowadays no one talks about Father, no one's concerned about him in the least. Now they talk about Mother, for people have to talk. There's a young farmer on the place now, and Mother Sofi is also young, and though her daughters and sons are young and can work, no one can work as hard as Mother Sofi, herself. She buys and sells in her own right, and the oldest and the next oldest also buy and sell. No one asks anymore about Father. He lies in his bed in the big house. He's old, soon seventy. And he doesn't care anymore, not even about Mother's bath any longer, as often as he stood outside the washhouse.

The young farmer is twenty-six years old and knows a few things. He knows that Mother hasn't lain with Father for nearly ten years, and that's good, he gets out of more mouths to feed. But people talk about Mother. Now she isn't so well liked anymore. She's disgraced in some way, disgraced because she bathes. He's young and strong and wise, and he has to laugh. How can a mother be disgraced because she bathes?

But his sisters' suitors are somehow bolder up here at the Big Farm than down in the valley. Down in the valley, they go always in the darkness, always at night. No one knows who it is who dawdles outside the girls' windows in the valley. He, himself, has gone courting in the valley, always going at night, but up here at the Big Farm his sisters' suitors have come on Sunday afternoons, in broad daylight, and even before the last hymn's been played in church.

At a big dedication dance there was a parish fight because of Mother's bath. A half-drunk farmer from a neighboring village, emboldened by drink and wanting to show off, taunted, "Your mother bathes, and your father, old *skroiga,* has to lie in the sheepfold. Your sister, *ja,* she's also one of those like your mother." A fight broke out. Then came the district court session, and the Big Farm's oldest son and his brothers had to pay a large sum for physical damages, assault and battery.

The youngest brother is going to be a priest; that he had said to the girl in the valley. She also had asked about Mother Sofi's bath, and he had answered that Mother was from another district, even more that her father was from a foreign land where bathing like that was customary. (He couldn't very well know about things like that, but he had to say something for Mother's sake, and she must bathe even if the whole country came with warrants. She would get to bathe as long as she wanted to, soap and water were cheap, and besides, he liked it, there was nothing wrong with it, just the opposite. *Ja,* people said something terribly dumb about Fredrika, something they certainly themselves didn't understand, but people . . . and though he didn't know if country people bathed in France, still for Mother's sake they did, and no one from France ever came here.) And the girl in the valley was satisfied, and when people there talked about Mother Sofi, she said that's what French people do and that Mother Sofi's youngest son was going to be a priest.

The gossip about Mother Sofi came from a new quarter.

Like a stubbornly persistent dandelion, the September moon shone, steadily following the young farmer on his way to the girl in the valley. Before he went, he saw the familiar shadows, his sisters' suitors, by the mossy green apple trees. The smoke from the washhouse rose long and thin, straight up to the moon. It is Friday, Mother Sofi bathes.

The smoke from the washhouse chimney soars toward the moon, but doesn't get any farther than the branches of the big whitebeam tree that stands back of the washhouse. There it becomes suspended, as all smoke before it became suspended, as it tries to rise toward the moon. The little stream, commonly called a river, flows freely from the fall rains, and the big sloping bleachfield lies virgin since the beginning of time. It just exists, has never felt a ploughshare, not even the hooves of cows or pigs, for the bleachfield must always be kept clean. Only the horses get to go there sometimes when the plums have ripened behind the stables and lie in masses on the ground. The children and the grown-ups can't possibly eat all of the big, juicy plums, and the cows get sick from them. When the horses have eaten their fill of the fruit, they usually go out and roll over in the bleachfield and graze in the grass until the woven material is put out the next spring.

Mother Sofi and her oldest daughter are getting undressed when Fredrika knocks on the door to the washhouse. "Tonight there's a dung-heap of a man standing by every single apple tree," she greets them.

The other women only nod. They look with interest at the package Fredrika carries, and naked, they follow her into the bakehouse, still warm from the week's baking. Cups and all the things for a coffee party are set out. From her package, Fredrika takes out a saffron bread twist, a cone of candies, and a large, fine soap that scents the warm room. "Now you must have got a nice sum from him," Mother Sofi says, drawing the skirt which she had been holding in her hand around her thin body, and taking the soap, she holds it eagerly under her nose.

"Ja, he's not quite so stingy anymore, though he's crazy enough. Old as he is, he pays five whole kronor just to get to see my thighs, and to get money from him in any other way is impossible." Followed by the others, Fredrika goes into the washhouse and begins to undress. The hot water steams from the big washtub, and after ten years of work, stopping up the chinks and rat holes, the old washhouse is warm and comfortable. A big load of the best birch logs is stacked against the wall, the sons always keep it well sup-

10

plied, and the oldest son has chopped enough wood chips for a year. He's thinking of putting on a new roof.

Soon Fredrika stands there in all her fifty-year-old white plumpness. Mother Sofi's daughter is like a reed beside the big woman, and Mother Sofi, little and thin, would look like a pitiful plucked hen if it weren't for her sparkling eyes and curly, light hair. Her mouth is sunken, and the wrinkles beginning to show in her energetic, firm little face. Her breasts hang like two small, loose sacks from having nursed so many eager little mouths. The touchingly thin body, which was like a girl's, was more graceful than any of her daughters' when she wore a dress. It resembled a curious living rune stone when her clothes came off. Her stomach was one single scar, knot against knot, scar against scar, with big, broad, shimmering streaks here and there. "Terribly ruptured blood vessels, you have," the neighbor used to say at Sofi's childbirths.

Mother Sofi often stared at her stomach during the bath nights. Like a skinny woman Buddah she sat there, gazing down on the scarred knots, her mouth tightening, and sometimes tears fell, dropping on her poor belly, and sometimes she said bitterly, "Such a miserable scrap heap." Fredrika would never say anything then, just busied herself making coffee and hummed a tune.

The first time the daughter saw her mother naked, saw her stomach, she burst into tears. "What is it, Mother, what's the matter with your stomach?"

"Childbearing scars," Mother Sofi answers harshly.

Her daughter only stares, tries to say something but can't find the words, sitting there naked in her young beauty, glancing at her own smooth stomach, at her white breasts, fuller and bigger than her mother's ever were. At last she asks, "Were we so heavy?"

"No, but you were too many." And Mother Sofi soaps the scarred knots as if she thought she could wash them away.

11

"What does Father say?" the daughter asks. "What does he say about your stomach? Isn't he afraid?"

"He hasn't seen her stomach," Fredrika answers. "Don't ask such dumb things." Mother Sofi only nods.

And the daughter silently scrubs her young body. She knows, knows very well, there are men enough who want to see, see and caress and kiss hers, and forgetting her mother's sadness and scars, she soaps her shoulders and breasts, her eyes happily shimmering.

Outside the moon drifts higher and higher over the farms and villages, over the hills and valleys. Out in the Big Farm's overgrown gardens, young womanhearts sing the eternally new song, hard workworn womanhands tightly hold coarse manhands and the backs of their young brown necks. Down to the valley the young brothers hurry to go courting.

But in the big house father lies with his leather apron on, thinking, "Everything passes, Mother died at last." He pulls his fur cap down over his ears, for he is very cold, turns toward the wall, sleeps, wakes, and sleeps again. The moon shines, it's like daylight. He doesn't know if it's morning or night; the moon is full and shines all night.

Maybe it's morning, maybe his sons are already in the barn, he should get up and look. With difficulty he gets up and goes out. The drifting moon seems to glare scornfully at him: the crazy old fool, what's he doing out here at midnight, night's for the young.

The barn is locked, the horses thumping their hooves as usual at night, the cows swishing their tails. A sheep baas sleepily at the sound of his step. He plods along through the plum orchard, the fruit shines silvery-gray from the dew, and bending down, he gathers some up. They are pecked by the magpies or rotten. Wiping the dew from a half-eaten one, he eats the plum the magpie left.

By the bleachfield he stops, it no longer smokes from the washhouse. He walks toward it, then right up to it, and as so many times before, stands under the whitebeam tree and listens. Fredrika is talking. "Now she went, that daughter of yours, to Albert from Moss. Don't you think he'll get her in trouble, he's fathered one kid already."

"I don't know and I don't care. No one can escape the consequences of one's desires," Sofi answers.

"We'll have another cup before we go," Fredrika says.

The old farmer remains under the whitebeam tree. He sees his wife walking from the washhouse over the bleachfield with Fredrika's arm around her waist, and he broods, as he's done so many other nights, on that dreadful mystery: two women who bathe and don't care about their men. Then he thinks, it's not late, she doesn't matter, and he goes to the washhouse, picking the lock as usual. He stomps around in the darkness, smelling the sweet-scented soap. He goes on into the bakehouse, and knowing where to go, he gropes around for the sugar, the cream, and the bread, takes some cream from the jug and a slice of Fredrika's bread twist, sits down, eats, and drinks, enjoying the warmth and the good smell of the soap. It isn't the first time he has helped himself to the party's leftovers. But more often he falls asleep, then sleeps too long, though now this last time, he slept all Friday so he could wake up in the night.

It's so strange and so utterly pleasant, for here it smells good and is warm, and there's always good bread and coffee; if he doesn't come too late, the coffee's warm, and then— Fredrika, for the leather-apron farmer has never forgotten Fredrika's naked white body standing there against a dark January sky ten years ago.

Fredrika has bathed here, here where he has sat and drunk coffee like a thief on his own farm. Bathed that white, plump body that he has visions of even at seventy years. He sits until it gets quite cold, then stumbles back over the bleachfield and plum orchard, and nearly runs into his oldest son coming home from the girl in the valley. "Go in, Father, it's one o'clock. Mother has finished bathing long ago." He pushes the old man into the big house and slams the door so that it thunders through the whole place. Mother Sofi and the children sleep in the so-called second house. Mother Sofi lies in a room where the pensioned old woman lived both long and well before she died, so old no one knew for sure when she came to the farm, and she wasn't even related to the leather-apron farmer. There Mother Sofi and her nine-year-old boy, still the youngest, slept. The oldest daughter often slept there, too, when she came home too late at night.

But at last, as the climax of passing years, the malice became too great and sin hung like a cloudwall around the parish. Then God's people began to cry out to the Lord for mercy. One Saturday evening in November, all the devotions in the meetinghouse were dedicated to offering prayers for the sinful Mother Sofi from the Big Farm, for her oldest daughter, and for Fredrika.

It was one of the country's first meetinghouses. The zeal was great; everyone thought he was morally superior to the parish priest himself, who let his flock fend for itself. Everyone shrieked and prayed and sang and portrayed the sinful women, their bathing, their orgies with men, and everyone offered special prayers for the young daughter.

Two days later after a search, Mother Sofi was pulled from the river. She was dead.

It is a sunny November day. The leaves are still on the whitebeam, shimmering in their colors, colors nearly as brilliant as the rag strips Mother Sofi used to dye with stuff from roots and bark.

Now she lies on the bleachfield, drowned. The sun dries the hair by her temples and it begins to curl. The sun shines on her face; she looks as young as one of her young daughters. It shines on her sons and daughters and on an old farmer who understands nothing, who can't even understand that now there's again an end, now another end has come. It shines on a tall, stately woman who stands on the bleachfield and swears, vowing vengeance. "They will be

14

burned," she cries, "their damned house will be burned up, I'll do it, now, today, I'll set it on fire! It was because of them she did it. They prayed for her, they yelled, those madmen, that she was sinful, that she ruined her children because she washed off the dirt she never could get off herself when she was bearing the children." The big woman sobs and howls at the sun.

The oldest son steps forward, looks at his mother's face, sees how peaceful and young she looks, sees how the clothes cling to her little figure, the nimble little figure he has seen in the fields and cellar, in the barn and sheepfold; he has seen her most often with a little one at her breast or her stomach swollen with child. "I will never marry, Mother, be at peace. I will not marry, I will take care of everything as before."

No one hears what he mumbles, for all are crying, grieving. Fourteen children, a farmer, and a woman who howls at the sun. But off in the plum orchard, the magpies are laughing as usual.

"We'll carry her to the washhouse," Fredrika says. "I'll wash her myself." And the oldest son and Fredrika gently lift the small body, carrying her in to the white-scrubbed washbench.

The next day when the oldest daughter and Fredrika are doing the last deed of love that can be done for a person, washing and dressing her for the last journey, Fredrika says, "Now there'll be talk that we didn't have Corpse Mary here to wash her, but she'll get her two kronor from me anyway. I didn't want her going around gossiping about Mother Sofi's childbearing scars; you know how she describes the corpses she washes so she can get her drop of coffee in all the houses."

Mother Sofi was buried outside the old churchyard wall, the burying place for suicides.

All her children and Fredrika followed her casket to the grave, and the trembling, white-haired priest, foolish with old age and sermonizing, read the ritual of suicides for Mother Sofi.

The old farmer, Father, lay at home, lay unmoving in his bed in the big house; the family sickness, his mother's sickness, had struck him. "Everything passes," he mumbled, "everything passes, one dies at last. . . ."

But at the grave outside the churchyard wall, a heavy, tall woman stood beside the little priest, and glancing scornfully at him, she said with a loud voice, "Mother Sofi! Your children and I know that Jesus Christ will awaken you on the last day and lead you into God's blessedness."

And the rumor spread widely that Fredrika, herself, said the prayers at her friend's grave, and that Mother Sofi's illegitimate firstborn child came to her mother's burial.

The Third and Fourth Generations

ONE

Sally and Ellen

"We're going to move, my dad's taken a job in the country!" Sally nods her head importantly from side to side of her listeners.

"So you'll be a farm girl now?" asks a little boy in a coarse voice, spitting like a man. Sally sticks her tongue out at him. Her girl friends follow her to the veal butcher's, everyone's gathering place for urgent news, to get the details about the move, as fast that is, as Sally can snap them up from her folks there in the attic of the barrack's general store.

Sally's mother sits on a battered iron bed in the "cubbyhole" (that's what the storekeeper and everyone else called it), and endlessly questions her husband, "What do you mean, do you think we can move to the country with an iron bed and an empty suitcase, to the country where folks have their places crammed with heaps of stuff? What did you have to do with that damned strike? Fifty öre a day, what's that, and everything in hock; do you think we can move to a manor house with what we've got, and be ridiculed by their help and tenants? How many was it you said, three pairs of draft horses, three pairs coming to get this that isn't even a load for one? Are you completely crazy? And then we're to sit and ride with three pairs on the highway for eighteen miles with this? *Ja,* you're crazy for sure. And

17

what'll you do there anyway? You can't be a farmhand; you can't even hold on to the reins. You've been at the factory your whole life. What did you have to do with the strike committee? Got kicked out, that's what you got. *Ja,* I'll not be going to your farm. I should milk, maybe, and feed the pigs, no thanks! I'd rather stay at the factory till I starve to death. An iron bed and a suitcase! And three pairs coming to get that. There's never a dull moment in this place. What'll those farmers think? Or do they think we have cows and pigs and looms here in this south suburb, and a coop with hens maybe since they're coming with three pairs? You're really crazy."

Sally's mother has to catch her breath, and the man butts in, "Quit jawing and listen to this! On Friday we're being evicted, on Monday the wagons come, and we're off. When you're evicted, it's just as well your best stuff's in hock, it'd only get ruined in the rain. You rant about weaving looms, some bits of that junk we can gather together. What do you say about taking my mother along? It'd keep her from the poorhouse awhile, and she still hasn't had an auction though Father's been dead three years. God knows what the poor wretch lives on. She's got at least four loads of junk—I'm sure of it."

"Your mother won't put up with you, you know that."

"*Ja,* but if you go out to Norrtull and talk her into it. Stop being so damned mad. We've got to try something. Don't think I'm that crazy about oxen and cows and pitchforks exactly."

Sally's father had never failed in winning over his wife when he took that good tone, and just now he had to take it, for the future looked more than cloudy. He had been a little too aggressive, obligated himself too dangerously in the last strike; every bit they had scraped together the past seven years was at the pawnbroker's, and they had to live in the cubbyhole, the worst place in the whole southern suburb. Now they were being evicted even from there.

18

Never had anyone been evicted from the cubbyhole, the rent was ridiculously low, seventy-five öre a month. The cup couldn't be more bitter. Something had to be done; even Sally's mother took that in, and she couldn't deny that she almost admired her man a little because he had found a way out of the labyrinth they had got into. It wouldn't pay for him to look for work anywhere in this whole factory city, that much she knew. And throwing her fringed shawl over her shoulders, she hurried out to Sally's grandma in Norr-tull, Grandma who knew everything about the country; she had lived there nearly her whole life.

The barracks buzzed with talk.

This was news, Svenssons in the cubbyhole going to the country. They knew Svensson only too well, one like him who only wanted to take it easy and get mixed up with strikes and devil work. Now that he's been kicked out, he's got to fork manure. *Ja,* poor Mrs. Svensson, all she has in the world in hock, and the kid always having to move. Poor child, she certainly doesn't have proper parents.

Sally has seen a lot of dwelling places in her seven years. She's never lived for as long as a year in one place. Here in the southern suburb, she's already lived in three places. She knew everyone in the barracks before she moved in.

All the women are nice, she thinks, the kids, too, the men are usually drunk, of course, but the women are really nice. "Here, you can have this," says the woman on the ground floor, the veal butcher, "Take this, your mother's always bleeding." And Sally gets a big chunk of liver sausage that tastes so good that she smells liver sausage as soon as she's hungry. The woman butchers calves in a woodshed of the barracks and makes sausage to sell at the military training school nearby.

"Here's a sandwich for you," another woman says, "I feel sorry for you, your dad lies with others, and your mother's always sick."

19

Often the women stand talking at the veal butcher's, talking about Dad or Mother, or about miscarriages or whores, this one or that one they call a whore, or about the "English sickness," it's impossible to keep track of it all no matter how hard she tries, for it's terribly interesting when the women talk all at once; but the main thing is the liver sausage, for Mother is often sick and Dad is almost never home.

Best of all is Beda, she'll be the hardest to leave—think, to leave. Ride a long ways off—Dad isn't so bad after all. But how will that go with Beda? Sally almost cries, poor Beda, who has the "innocent's sickness," a terrible sickness. "She's never had a fellow," all the women say, agreeing about that. That's why she's sick and has sores over her whole body, sores that smell bad. Poor Beda, her face is so beautiful, so white with her wavy black hair. Sally knows no one as beautiful as Beda who has the innocent's sickness.

Just now Sally sits on the lowest step outside Beda's door. She wants to go in but doesn't dare to, feels she must sit here awhile. Beda will be so sad when she hears about her leaving. Sally hears Beda's brother arguing about something behind the door, Beda's brother with his black hair and angry eyes; he's handsome, all the women say that, and he doesn't care about any girls; he's standoffish, they say, but just wait, that'll go, he's still so young. Now he yells, and Sally hears every word, "We have to get a real doctor. Can't you see she'll croak, you with your damned innocent's sickness. When I get a hold of that quack salve peddler from Barnö, I'll wring his neck!"

Croak. Sally knew that meant folks died; maybe Beda was going to die now. *Ja,* she's probably dead, for it's very quiet now in there. All the women in the barracks have said that Beda could die anytime; they knew of many who died of the innocent's sickness.

A few days before, Sally had made paper flowers, flowers of red, green, and white paper; there was always plenty of paper, she could just take it from the factory. She had decorated the whole porch outside Beda's door with paper flowers. "Come and see, Beda," she had called, "look, it's so beautiful." And Beda thought it was, too, but the women ordered Sally to take down the flowers that instant. "You're decorating for the dead, you crazy kid," they scolded, "it's bad luck, take them down at once, do you want to send a person right to the grave?" "A person," that was, of course, Beda, but Sally thought they looked scared, as if they were afraid of the grave themselves; they really thought they could die of any old thing just because she had decorated a bit with paper flowers. But none of them was as sick as Beda. Sometimes she lay nearly unconscious. Then her mother fell on her knees and prayed, begged God to take Beda home, she certainly wanted Beda to die. Beda's mother believed in God; Sally's didn't, nor the other women either, of course. They scurried around, bumping into each other, dabbing water on Beda, giving her drops, maybe even pulling her through, but Beda could only stand upright or lie, she couldn't sit. The innocent's sickness was incurable.

"No, only if they force themselves and get a fiancé, can it go away," the woman who makes the sausage said. But Beda couldn't force herself, she was so pale and beautiful, Sally certainly understood that Beda couldn't move in with a guy and quarrel and fight like Dad and Mother, or like the other women with their drunk men.

Not even the doctor from Barnö could cure Beda although she'd drunk many bottles of his medicine. He had made all the women in the barracks well; Mother had drunk many bottles for her bleeding, and Sally had sold those bottles later at the store, buying a special cookie with the money, a big brown ginger snap, baked from old cookies freshened up with new dough.

Now Beda's brother shouts again, "You've got money! We must damn well get the doctor or she'll die."

Sally realizes that Beda is now very sick, beautiful Beda,

who gave her öre so often and kissed her and told her stories, sewed a doll for her now and then. Think if she died. That would be almost good; she wouldn't need to tell her then about moving, and Beda couldn't get to like any of the other girls, give them money or kiss them. "Dear Beda, get really well now, so you can marry some rich, sweet guy, or die now, before I move, so you won't like any other girl than me," Sally prays, not to any special god, for she hasn't begun school yet. She's heard stories about Jesus in Sunday school, but since she'd been there only twice and that was at Eastertime, she'd got the idea that Jesus had enough worries of his own. She prayed to Beda instead. "Sweet Beda, get well now and marry, or die now when I'm leaving, so you won't like anyone else but me."

The door hastily opens. "Hey, you're sitting here, that's good." It is Beda's brother who looks as if he'd been crying.

"*Ja*, I want to say good-bye, we're moving away now." (Sally has a week to say good-bye in, but she's forgotten that.)

He doesn't hear her. "Sally, you're not dumb. Can you get a doctor here from the city? A good doctor, ask a policeman, he'll show you. Tell the doctor to take a cab, you can ride back with him. You'll get this money when you come back." He holds up a fifty-öre piece.

Without any unnecessary questions, Sally answers, "I'll run all the way. I'll be back with the doctor in half an hour."

She dashes off. It's a quarter of an hour into the city. The telephone is nearly everywhere, but it's not yet in the southern suburb; people there had to send for the doctor themselves. Sally didn't need to ask any policeman, knowing well enough where a doctor could be found; she had the city at her fingertips.

Surprisingly, the doctor was home, for he was in great demand in the poor quarters of the city. "Sick call," a girl announces into the room where Sally rings.

"*Ja*, thanks, what is it?"

"Aunt Beda in our house is sick, she has the innocent's sickness, she's going to die now, you, doctor, must come at once." The words ran like peas from her little red mouth. Astonished, the doctor stops in the middle of the room.

"What did you say? What does the woman have?"

"She has the innocent's sickness, and now she's going to die, for she won't have any guy. I get to ride back in your cab. Come, dear doctor, now at once, otherwise she'll die. They have money, her brother has work," she adds. She's seen a lot and knows where the shoe pinches. And the doctor has also seen a lot; he knew well how idiotically the gossiping women carried on in most of these workers' barracks. Even in better-off homes he had heard curious things, and even there they were used to knowing how much their neighbors made, what sickness they had, and so forth. But this was in any case the first time in his practice that a little girl had come and summoned him for a woman who suffered from the innocent's sickness, whatever that could be, maybe measles. Dirt, damp rooms, cold, undernourishment or starvation were so natural, so wholly imbued in their consciousness that boils, rashes, and such must absolutely depend on sexual restraint.

When they sat in the old horse-cab, for cars hadn't yet made their appearance in traffic, even if one heard tales about them or someone's injuries from those wonderful machines, the doctor asks, "Do you know if they've had any doctor there before?"

"The doctor from Barnö," Sally answers offhand. She's riding in a cab for the first time in her life and doesn't want to be distracted with anything so ordinary and banal as sickness and death. She's nearly forgotten Beda; now she's riding in a cab, soon she'll be traveling far away, eighteen miles, the world is wonderful.

Arriving at the shabbiest of the suburb's barracks, they stop at its run-down entrance, where, to Sally's indescribable joy, all the children of her quarter are lined up. The doctor gives her twenty-five öre. "Thank you, you're a bright girl."

Beda's brother takes charge, showing the doctor up the stairs. "The door straight ahead," he says, and giving Sally the fifty-öre piece and patting her on the cheek, he follows the doctor in. Everyone in the yard has talked about his never looking at girls. The little girls look nearly with worship at Sally when she joyously dances past them and up the three flights to the cubbyhole. No one is home, the key hangs on the nail. Sally takes it down and steps in.

Sally's mother has gone to persuade Grandma in Norrtull to follow them to the country, for she thinks, you certainly can't move with that bed you couldn't even sell and a couple of empty suitcases. Grandma can't understand her son for his stupidity in wanting to set himself over gentlemen. *Ja,* reasons Sally's mother, it's certainly idiotic, gentlemen always get to set themselves over one no matter how they behave. Well, she wasn't so pleased with her mother-in-law either; she never rinsed out her dishcloth but let it lie there and sour. Though Grandma was house-proud and sharp-eyed enough, of course. But those endless miscarriages got on your nerves, and one must not put up with any filthiness, the poor must have things clean, nice and clean, she was strict about that. Although that strike certainly ruined the little they'd owned; there was nothing even left to scrub. Well, she'd promised that she'd talk to Grandma and defend her son; the old woman would soon be eighty years old, so it should surely go to win her over. Two wagons of furniture you had to have these days when you moved.

Sally, of course, didn't know about that. In her excitement and happiness she walked around, waiting for someone to talk to. Next to Beda, Mother was still the best to talk things over with, and the best one of all to show the fifty-öre piece to.

Three pairs of oxen in front of three hay wagons! Sally is so ashamed she could die. Never for a moment had she imagined anything other than horses, three pairs of splendid horses dancing and prancing through the suburb's streets, coming for her, and Dad and Mother, of course, and the iron bed and the two suitcases. Dad had said three pairs, and Sally in turn had told the children that.

Oxen, big and heavy, certainly, but oxen, and they had lain down in the muddy yard to boot. They were tired, their drivers said; they had walked eighteen miles during the night. Now they've lain here since four o'clock this morning. The woman who made the sausage had a bad stomach and often ran out to the privy at night. Sally remembered how she told Mother that she was out there twenty-three times a night when she began taking the doctor from Barnö's medicine—"I thought I would die," she had said, "I lay right on the floor out there at the end, but it was good, of course, that the medicine worked like that, the doctor from Barnö said," and she had got better then. Now early this morning she had rushed out in her big clopping shoes to get there in time, shrieking and bellowing like a madwoman when she caught sight of the oxen, the whites of their eyes shining in the light of the lantern she'd carried.

Sally is furious. Why did that woman have to wake up everyone? The sausage woman who butchers calves, buying pitiful half-dead calves at the market and wheeling them home in a barrow, and butchering them in the woodshed, and making sausage from them—she could surely recognize an ox without howling and acting like a fool. Sally had many times wheeled the barrow for her.

Now all the kids in the barracks are standing in a ring around the oxen, although it's barely dawn, for in October the light comes late in the mornings and early in the evenings. The drivers of the oxen are eating in the cubbyhole, and Dad, uncorking a bottle of brandy, offers it to them. Mother is in Norrtull with Grandma.

It's a long way out to Norrtull, but Sally, putting on the old coat she's sick of, and pulling on a curious homemade cap that resembles an English bishop's, a fashionable style then, sneaks out while the men drink. "Ugh! booze, never think of anything else"—the words tumble out like a lesson learned by heart when she gropes her way down the stairs. It was her mother's habitual comment, and however worn-out the words were then, they were no less true. No one knew that any better than a wife and daughter in a suburb barracks.

Concealed by the porch, Sally waits awhile, trying to see who the children are playing around the oxen, but she can't distinguish any special one, hearing only the oxen's heavy panting, smelling their warm rank bodies. Then she hears her best friend of only yesterday sneer, "Sally-farm-girl rides behind oxen, and she thought she was so impor-tant!"

"*Ja*, but they're strong. Feel that horn!" Triumphantly holding onto the horns of a tired and patient ox, a boy now sits astride one. Sally is forgotten. The children straddle the oxen's backs. Oh, joy of joys, a living creature under one, a big strong colossus that lies still and lets itself be kicked and abused. Never has one had so much fun, such kingly fun. The big oxen only lie and chew. When they sometimes stir themselves, then the children sit still, uncertain. Maybe? Maybe the oxen will get up, become angry? But no, they don't get up, and the play continues. The children, never fierce themselves, quickly change the oxen into wild mus-tangs, honoring them with fine names. They sneak in and swipe sugar and bits of bread from scanty cupboards; though the oxen won't eat the sugar, that doesn't spoil the game—the mustangs get the bread and their own always greedy mouths get the sugar.

Sally dodges past the children and the oxen without saying good-bye. Is there anyone, for that matter, to say good-bye to? Those mean kids? It's a good thing she's leaving, even if it means being pulled by oxen. Beda was dead. The rooms where she lived were empty. The place had been scoured and smoked. Beda had had syphilis, the women said and bad-mouthed her now, of course. The doctor had laid down the law something terrible, had examined Sally, and had ordered all the women in the barracks to scrub and sterilize. The whole yard and the privy had been sprayed with disinfectant. And Beda's folks had been forced to move. The manager had acted like a madman, and Beda's brother had beaten him up—Dad had helped him, and had cursed all the women. The doctor had said that they'd all get the innocent's sickness in the end, and the doctor from Barnö had been taken to jail. And now the yard is full of oxen that had come to move her, Sally. "Dear Beda, everything's so awful for me," she prays as she hurries through the dark streets. "Dear Beda, if you are maybe in heaven, think of me; your mother said you would go to heaven, for you were innocent. It's so awful for me. I'm alone and now I'm leaving. Good-bye, Beda, I'm saying good-bye only to you, only you."

When she is well into the city, she slows down. Lanterns shine one after another, the cabs already driving out in long rows, the women hurrying to work at the factories, the men going home from the night shifts. Some of them jokingly shout at the little figure—kids so young shouldn't be out at this early hour, but Sally just trots along, looking longingly at the closed stores. Twenty-five öre she has that no one knows about, the doctor's twenty-five öre, but the stores aren't open yet. She had hidden the money the whole week, planning to buy candy to take along to the country.

Grandma's house is a ramshackle one outside the tollgates. For thirty years she had been a farm worker's wife. Now she's been a widow for three years, somehow managing not to have an auction and go to the poorhouse, which was customary for one in her shoes. Her only son was no one to depend on; he had wasted himself, but yet it was nearly unthinkable to her, in spite of her seventy-nine years, to sell everything she'd accumulated. Not one thing had been bought new, of course, but still. Grandma had been a weaver, had worked one of the very first awkward looms that had been imported, but she couldn't make enough as a weaver. She'd had to marry, or she would have starved to death, although there wasn't much to live on after that, for that matter, she was used to saying. That she got to live here was because the "old gentleman" liked her, people said, although the "old gentleman" had been dead for twenty years, and Grandma had never seen him. But people talked—those that are "kept" women for gentlemen, such bad women, always take care of themselves well enough, they said.

Today Grandma is cheery and talkative; she has nothing against starting afresh, and she's glad that she didn't have an auction. She knows just how it will be out in the country, rejoicing that her son is going there. "They're coming with oxen, then that's a real farm," she says when Sally's mother, angry and tired, complains about the oxen and country ways. And when Sally comes, Grandma tells her how much more fun it is to move with oxen than with horses, for the trip goes slower. "The time comes soon enough for toil and moil," she adds, and supporting herself on her cane, she shuffles across the rotted floor to warm a drop of coffee for Sally. "Do you think they'll soon come?" she asks Sally, while Mother rummages in Grandma's junk.

"Dad was offering them brandy when I left," Sally answers.

"*Ja*, one is so poor that one lies to get a few coffee beans and rusks on credit, but one has, of course, brandy to offer," Mother says, furious with anger.

An old highway. Ancient, tramped on once by herds of deer and goats, who knows? Tramped on by countless feet and hooves. Here once the first monks wandered, sent to a cold barbaric land with orders to master and bring up its inhabitants. Here the king's slaughter-cattle hobbled, followed by serfs chained together, serfs like animals, intended for sacrifices to the gods, for the king and luck in war. Here God's knights rode, for once upon a time God needed such men. Here the king's army, farmers, tramps, robbers, murderers, astrologers, witches, beautiful women, and poets rode.

Oceans of dreams, hopes, thoughts, decisions streamed through hundreds of years over the road that became more open, broader, getting fields and ditches around it mile after mile.

The old road seemed like a billowing wave of dreams, oaths, prayers, songs, psalms. The air over it seemed to tremble from millions of questions and replies. Travelers nowadays are made anxious by its monotonous desolateness, by its endless twisting route, and by the fields alongside, a thousand years old, which look as worn and gray in the spring as in the fall. Aging grayness symbolized the air, the thousand years' exploitation of the fields, and the worn-out road itself, where prayers, oaths, and dreams through the ages seemed to stretch over the road's staked markers, hanging there, graying like ghosts. And travelers are made afraid and seek shortcuts through forests and pastures. The old road lay still and desolate.

It is Monday night. For a thousand years that night has always been the quietest on the road. Storms can rage over it, day in and day out, Monday like Sunday, but people always rested on Monday night. He who would die didn't want to do it on the road, waiting until he came to some other meaningless place. Nor did she who would give birth want to do so on the road. Everyone hurried on the road, even the beggars, but on Monday night people rested.

Thus the country's oldest highway lies deserted, and three ox-carts rumble slowly forward without needing to stop and get out of the way for either man or beast. Sally sits curled up in the bobbin of Grandma's old loom, rocking back and forth to sleep with the oxen's quiet plodding and the even sound from the slowly rotating wheels. Suddenly she's wide awake. A giant moon rises from a large surface of water, a lake. The road goes a long way by the edge of the lake, winding six miles nearly around it, and Sally stares at the moon until she thinks the ox-cart is being carried away over the lake. It is like a year since morning with the six oxen in the yard. Far away are the barracks, the old women, the kids. She is quite certain that the whole southern suburb of Stockholm is right under the moonlake, and that she and Mother and Dad, Grandma, the furniture, oxen, and carts are moving right over it now, moving over it, and rubbing it out in some way, but Beda can't be rubbed out, she is dead and is up in heaven, for she was innocent her mother said.

And the youngest ox driver, who has the same curly hair as Sally, smiles toothlessly at her and asks if she's hungry, and she gets a thick chunk of cheese and an enormous piece of sour home-baked rye bread. Sally shares this with Grandma, who sits in her Gustavian bed, and Grandma says, "It wasn't yesterday that I ate such good rye bread." And Grandma tells the best story Sally knows, the one about Grandma's mother, Mother Sofi, whom Grandma never remembered seeing alive, for Grandma was illegitimate and couldn't stay with her mother who ruled over the Big Farm, far away in the country, where plums lay in heaps in the autumn and no one minded if the apples were taken. "You are like my mother. I saw her when she was dead; she had drowned. It is strange how much you are like her, Sally. You have the same hair, and your face is exactly like hers." And Grandma tells about sorrows and hardships, and poverty and injustice, and about the farm with all those many children who had scattered in every direction after Mother Sofi was buried.

As the moon glided over the lake, it seemed only yesterday that the smoke from the washhouse hung in an old whitebeam tree, and the shining moon enchanted and puzzled the child of the third generation, the descendant of Sofi's illegitimate, for the moon has its own chosen ones here on earth, who are always set off from others in whatever house or hut they are born.

Nowadays no one is left uncounted in statistics for being illegitimate. First and second class, even to the seventh class, one is counted. An illegitimate is counted "second class" in statistics; a child is born second class outside of marriage. A child who is born within marriage is better, the statisticians mean and write "first class," for they have to maintain their statistics.

If a traveling Englishman, German, Frenchman, or Bengalese met the ox-carts by the moonlake that night, he might have been enticed by the picturesque sight, stopped them, questioned them, interviewed them, and then made a small contribution to the statistics. He might have traveled back to England, Germany, France, or Bengal, and written in the big book of statistics bound in calfskin the following:

> During a journey in Sweden in the year 1907, I found that the country's farm workers had an excellent economy. With a touching piety for his forefather's handmade cupboards and looms, a farm worker who moves owns three ox-carts filled with household furnishings. Farm workers' children in Sweden are wide awake and lively, and of that blonde and beautiful type, which is singular to the land in question.

Statistics are very undependable, but the Frenchman or German or Bengalese couldn't know, of course, that Grandma was illegitimate, that the junk in the carts was hers and not the former paper factory worker's, now a farm worker, who got kicked out because he had been a member of a strike committee, or that Swedish children were more often dark and thin as gypsies, or that a farm worker in Sweden, in 1907, often didn't have a bed to lie in.

How could he know that? How could he have time to find out that, if he stuck to statistics? Statistics make everything in life and literature into robots.

What Sally remembered

It is an evening at dusk outside Norrtull, a year before the journey by the moonlake. Sally has been staying with Grandma for two days.

In the next house the "poor family" lives. Not even the poorest people in the southern suburb or in Norrtull accept them as equal. The mother in that family politely addresses Grandma "Madam," for Grandma has so much furniture and is said to have money in the bank, two hundred, Dad once said. Grandma gets a little dole, of course, five kronor a month, but the poor family says "Madam" to Grandma, and they don't dare to use the familiar "you" to Sally.*

There's nothing unusual really about the poor family; it's only that the mother was in jail for three years because she had murdered a child. And the poor family gets some dole, too, of course, for the father sells rags in the winter and helps on farms in the summer. The children have such strange clothes and are so nice. They never swear or dare to steal apples from the old women at the market, or trespass anyplace. The four children always stand off to the side and watch the other children playing if they're by chance at another place.

Sally has been playing with the poor family's children for two days and is now worshipped just like a princess. Snot-nosed and shivering, they follow all her orders, expectantly wait while she is in eating breakfast and dinner, for she is good-hearted and gets to take out a whole loaf of

*The Swedish singular "du" form of the pronoun, you, is not familiarly, but this practice is changing.

bread—Grandma isn't stingy with her only grandchild. Silently, greedily, they eat the bread, staring at Sally, waiting for her to find some new game, for she never runs out of things to do. She has learned a lot in all the different places she's lived, and she has a lively imagination. In her apron pocket she has the only fine plaything the poor family's children have ever owned, a glass stopper for a carafe. The oldest boy, who's eight, had given it to her the first day Sally had come. "Play with us," he had whispered, hoarse with eagerness, "play with us and you'll get to borrow this. So many colors come if you look through it; the house becomes so fine when you look at it through this, and the hills, too." Flat-topped bare hills surround Norrtull, and in the distance the ridge of the garbage dump is visible. The sun had shone that short fall day, and Sally had seen all the colors of the spectrum play in that wonderful glass stopper.

Sally has played hopscotch, danced, made playhouses, and was quite beyond tiredness when night came, and Grandma squintingly examined her clothes, for the poor family has vermin, of course. But now Sally is going home, Mother's coming late tonight to get her, and the four outcasts stand in a knot, shivering with cold, trying to brighten the time for Sally so she'll come again soon.

"Here's your stopper," she says. Silently the boy takes it. He would gladly give it to her, but it's the only thing he has, and when he's enrolled in school, Jesus, school, that terrifying place that everyone scares him about, he has to have something then; he'll have the stopper there with him. But Sally is the best for sure that he knows, and he stands there, thumbing the beautiful, gleaming bit of glass. In school there will be no one as fine as Sally, who can play and sing, and has such beautiful hair.

Sally feels listless, tired of all the worship the ragged little outcasts have given her. She stares at the sky, hanging red and murky, darkening more and more over the low hills.

People who walked on the road out there a long way off looked like ghostly trolls against the hills and sky. "See, they look like spooks, see that?" she asks.

"Naw," they don't.

"I'm going back in the house now. Good-bye all of you."

"Do you think this'll not break if it's banged on a stone?" the boy asks, holding up the stopper. Despairingly he longs for something that can awaken interest in his first love.

Sally is interested. Glass that is so fragile, think, if there were glass that didn't break if it were struck against stone; that would be amazing. This stopper is so thick, surely it can't break. "Certainly it won't break if it's banged on a stone; it won't break if it's banged on an iron floor!" The boy believes her at once, and Sally, herself, confidently believes what she's said. Slowly the boy raises his arm and then powerfully strikes the glass on a large stone in front of Grandma's house. The stopper breaks into bits.

The world becomes desolate and dark.

The poor family's oldest son thinks that his fair princess is, *ja,* he knows only the word that Father always says to Mother, an ass. The four children begin to howl and sob in the dismal, gloomy world, where the low-crowned hills lie around them. Sally is beside herself. She can't understand why she feels so miserable. An old bottle stopper! But that's no excuse. The boy has treasured it. *Ja,* and she knows so well that they never before have owned anything so splendid; well, if she wants to be honest, she's never owned anything that fine either. Think though! Those poor wretches don't dare to do anything, don't say anything either, just hunch themselves over, bawling, saying nothing! Sally is nearly wild, nor can she go in. "I'll give you another one, I'll buy one for you!" No one listens to her; they only cry, and it becomes even darker.

Their mother now comes out. "What are you bawling

about? Can't you be good when Sally is so nice and plays with you?"

"The stopper . . . the stopper," they sob, "the glass stopper's broken."

"I told him to do it, and he broke it," Sally explains with no frills. She is always direct.

"*Ja*, it's your own fault then, you crybaby," the mother says, hitting him. "Be quiet now. Sally's only joking with you, and you know her Grandma's rich."

And the children stand there, wiping their noses, and Sally becomes more and more confused; she knows that something is quite wrong. A terrible injustice is being done, for she, Sally, is being backed up. They are the woman's own children, and even so, she's supporting Sally, though it *is* Sally's fault that the stopper broke. Sally had believed it would *not*, although she knows, of course, that glass always breaks when it's struck against stone. And there stand the four children in their cast-off rags and don't talk to her, only wipe their noses, and not even their own mother sticks up for them.

Sally goes in to Grandma. "I'm leaving now, Grandma, I'm going home. I know where we've moved. I can find it, and Mother won't need to come for me. She's not feeling so well either. She was sick when I came here."

But Sally isn't seven years old yet, and Grandma says firmly, "You must be good and wait until your mother comes. Eat now."

"I don't want anything," Sally says, "I can't eat anything, and I must go, I *must*, dear Grandma. I can't stay here any longer." And Sally runs out in the darkness.

The poor family's children had gone in.

Whimpering, she stumbles on the road into the city, finds her way through the streets southward, and comes right to the new place where Mother has already got things in order. She is just going to leave when Sally appears. "I walked home, so you wouldn't need to drive out," Sally says, exactly as Dad used to say to Mother when they got on and everything was well and good.

"Do you want something to eat?" Dad asks, who is very pleased with his daughter, although he never has time for her because of his preoccupation with the workers' cause.

No, Sally is not hungry, she is tired. For two days she is sick. "My head aches," she replies when Mother asks. Her head doesn't ache in fact; she is trying to work out a problem that is worse than a headache. She has got caught in a quagmire of undeserved praise, and it sickens her. And she can't understand the children's mother. The crying children and the broken beautiful glass stopper hang like a nightmare over Sally, day and night, and she is nauseated just at the smell of food. If Mother had not needed to scrub at a place where Sally knows she can look not only at picture books, but also at herself in mirrors that go from floor to ceiling, she would have been dangerously sick. Now early one morning she trots, pale and subdued, beside her mother on a new adventure.

Children can live in the same city, have the same birthday, play on the same garbage dump, eat the same cheap bread, hear the same oaths—man's whisky-bass, woman's falsetto, go to the same school, and still not feel attachment or sympathy. But when the time is ripe, they meet and are friends until death.

So it was with Sally and Ellen.

Sally lived most of the time just outside of the tollgates. Only one time as a child did she live in the country, the time she rode in an ox-cart by the moonlake. Ellen lived all her childhood in the city's slums. Until she was grown, she knew only streets and alleys, and the thin, trampled grass by the tollgates and the dump.

Ellen is six years old and lives in an alley. She often moves from one alley to another, and they are always alike, no trees, no flowers, only a yard with many rats, most often a little yard where the trash cans take up the whole space.

Uncle's yard is big and sinister, full of holes and trash, with a forest of stakes pointing toward a sky that hung like a roof, a strange gray roof in the dusk, and oxen and horses, harnessed to wagons, wait for their drivers there.

The yard is a land of horrors for the little girl when it is dark and her stomach knots and Aunt yells, "Go on now, a big girl like you doesn't need anyone to go with her!" Oh, the cramps that always come as soon as it gets dark. A child's stomach often reacts against incessant coffee, bread, and herring, but Aunt gets less than nine kronor a week to manage with, and Ellen's mother can only pay four for her illegitimate child's food and care. The factories pay very little for compensation, for it's not their concern, the foreman has said.

Ellen's stomach pinches and aches, and her heart pounds wildly as she stands on the porch. Despairingly she looks at the forest of stakes that stretch to the sooty sky roof, hears the panting of the animals, takes a few steps, looks up at the house whose windowlight makes the yard still darker, filling it with shadows and shapes, with all the murderers Uncle reads about in the newspapers, and with all the spooks and ghosts the women in the yard talk about. Like the old woman with cancer (a dangerous sickness that everyone is scared of), who went to the hospital where they killed her, and now she stands here in the yard every night, crying and screaming at her man who forced her to go to the hospital—that's what Mrs. Broberg has said. The terrible cramps come again; she has to go across the yard, must, must get to the other side to the privy; in spite of spooks and dead old women, she must get to the other side, where rats, so big no cat dares fight them, shuffle over her feet in the dark, help, it's so black-dark, and then the high seat, and think if she falls in it, she closes her eyes in horror.

Whimpering, she patters along a few steps, then stumbling into a hay-cart that she hasn't seen in the darkness, she stops, stiffens, is quiet. The porch door bangs; that is Broberg going to the drivers' depot, the drivers that Uncle is the groom for. Her stomach then twists with pain, doubling her over. Now the dreaded thing has happened that she gets the stick for and no dinner, gets beaten and shamed before the big stable grooms who always pinch her in the seat or chin and say things the grown-ups laugh at but little ones don't get to say.

All around the doors bang; the grown-ups, so strange

they are, always swear although they're not angry. She hears Mrs. Broberg swear at the cat. Why does she swear at the cat? Oh, if the cat comes here to her in the darkness, she will never dare to get up again. She begins to cry aloud. She must stay here until something happens, until she dies. Then, that voice: "Dear child, why are you here in the dark, crying, and no coat?" It is Mama, pale, sweet, quiet Mama that Aunt and Mrs. Broberg talk bad about, Mama that Aunt is always nice to on Friday nights when it's payday at the factory.

"Mama! Mama, I'll never dare to go to Aunt's again, never, never. . . ."

But Mama went to Aunt, who was her own sister, and in a few days Ellen moved to another alley.

So many strange things happen in the city's slums.

Ellen sees so much that's incomprehensible, for who in the alleys and in the streets is embarrassed in front of a six-year-old? Ellen's days are filled with strange, confusing events. Mama never has time—the factory, the rent. . . . When she comes at night, always at night, Ellen hangs on her neck, curls up in her lap, quiet, happy, gets sleepy, tries not to sleep, but sleeps anyway, and wakes, huddled up, freezing, someplace on the floor, far from the bed, which is always on the floor; no matter how often Mama changes alleys, Ellen's bed is always on the floor. She crawls over to the bed, whimpering a little—Mama—sleeps again. Mama, of course, has to go to another alley nearer the factory, where her bed is also on the floor but where there is no place for a child. Ellen's new "aunt" isn't used to coping with another bed on the floor in front of the stove in the mornings, however. When the alarm clock rings, "Uncle" will go to the docks, and "Aunt" will be off to scrub a school, for two kronor is good to have to be sure; and in the new alley where there's room only for trash cans, and where the children play in the street or in the yard next door, which is bigger, "Aunt" says, "Out with you to the other kids where you belong!"

"Aunt" goes, leaving the key under the doormat. When Ellen gets tired and hungry from playing in the alley, she goes in and has bread and milk, for the new "aunt" is modern and doesn't give children coffee, or sugar either, for it's harmful to teeth. Ellen hunts for the sugar bowl, for the sugar sack. It's locked up, and she goes out again to play.

Now "Uncle" comes, ugh, he comes too early, walks unsteadily. Ellen has to run ahead and get the key under the mat and open up, "Aunt" has said. "Uncle" lies down on the sofa, snores, smells awful. Ellen sits, looking at his mouth, brown with snuff, studying the curious lines around his nose and forehead. Amusing herself with the lines, she nearly steals over to follow them with her finger to see where they end—it's almost like the maze in a magazine, but catches herself, stopped by the smell of snuff and whisky. She doesn't dare to leave, for he could wake up, and he's dangerous if he wakes up, will beat up whoever wakes him, "Aunt" has said. She sits there, wondering aloud "now where" and quite unconsciously, walks over, nearer, nearer, trying to see where the line from his chin to his ear leads. . . . Finally "Aunt" comes, "Out with you to the other kids where you belong!"

Sometimes it rains, and she's alone with the doll Mama bought, the doll that never became the great joy she thought it would when Mama came with it, for it can never be taken outside and shown in the alley. "Aunt" is a proper person, and when a fool of a mother goes out and buys a doll for her illegitimate kid who could better use a shirt, well, at least the doll shouldn't be ruined.

Ellen sits alone with the doll on her knees, playing mama who works at the factory and buys a doll for her child, when the door carefully opens, and the clockmaker on the lower floor comes in. A little old man with a white beard, wearing slippers and a blue apron. He has candy, the best candy in the world, brown, wavy cough drops, "King of Denmark" ones.

He talks softly and pleasantly about the doll, about a sweet little girl, about candy, about more candies, many more, and then he folds back his apron and wants her to hold something there, hold the thing that drunk guys take out when they pee in the alley, and the police catch them. It creaks in the stair landing, and the old man sits on the sofa, innocent, nice, trembling a little. Then he sneaks out, planning to come back another rainy day when Ellen is there alone, playing mama who works at the factory; then he'll come again with his King of Denmark candy. Maybe, but Ellen tells "Aunt" that the clockmaker's been up, and she's a proper "aunt" who makes a terrible row about the perils of life on porches and stairlandings, and the old white-bearded man had to go to jail.

Grown-ups are very strange.

And the days go by and weeks and months. Spring comes with sun and stench from the alleys and yards. Small caravans go in a procession on the road out to the tollgates to the sparsely grassed hills, where anchovy cans and egg-shells bear witness to the grown-ups' longing for the country. Sometimes expeditions of children wander on the road far out to the city's garbage dump, the dump where the foxes go on bitter winter nights, where young men often lie curled up among rags and trash and catch rats, rats that yield ten öre apiece. The children act out the world's pageantry on the garbage dump, performing weddings, playing marriage, furnishing rooms, setting up stores; they're policemen, drunk men, and frightened women; they're drunk women who pull up their skirts and pat their seats and yell the worst words of the alley, while the sun shines over the giant garbage dump and their eyes gleam. All too soon the darkness comes, the double darkness. The quiet, tired children wander first in the giant shadow from the garbage dump, a kilometer long, to the tollgates, then in the swarming darkness of the alleys, which pads and whispers all around while they hurry to their doors.

The new "aunt" is a proper one. "You surely haven't been near the garbage dump?"

"Oh, no, 'Aunt'," and the milk and bread disappear as Ellen eagerly eats while her lashes droop tiredly against her cheeks.

One day heaven comes, heaven which Ellen has heard so much about from the Salvation Army. Only much better, much lovelier is the heaven that comes one day directly to Ellen. Mama doesn't work at the factory any longer. New coat, new dress, new shoes, Ellen got all of them on the same day. It's magic, more unbelievable than when the old organ-grinder Stramen conjured up two öre from his monkey's apron pocket.

And "Aunt" is nice and pleasant every day and often says to "Uncle," "The main thing is that you take care of yourself. Let people gossip. No one is any better than anybody else." But "Uncle" talks loudly about devilish whores, and whore's kids, and about "bad folks" while he drinks his beer and takes his pinch of snuff.

Mama comes for Ellen in the middle of a shining day, at noon, and they walk away from the alleys, away from that part of the city, walk through a big park, stop on a wide street, a street with trees, climb three flights of stairs, open a door, and step in. It's a big light room with two windows overlooking the park they've just crossed; there are rugs, curtains, a fine bed, one single finely made bed, not bed against bed, sofa against sofa, like that in the alley, and flowers. No rubbishy plants with some scentless stalks in moldy clay pots, but real flowers. White lilies, red tulips, a whole bunch in a vase on Mama's table. A whole bunch just of flowers, no sprigs or leaves to fill it out with, and it is still winter. A little girl from the slums quietly, intensely enjoys herself, as if never anyone in the world had enjoyed herself before.

But in the evening Mama takes her to the alley again.

"Aunt" isn't so happy any longer, and the new coat is at the pawn shop. Mama has been in the hospital a month, and "Aunt" doesn't get paid any more. But "Aunt" is a proper person and she says to anyone who'll listen, "The kid's mama has given me so many presents that I ought to keep her a year for nothing."

Now "Aunt" though is so poor that she can't any longer, and "Uncle" drinks his beer and takes his snuff and asks how long he should take care of whore's kids free, but "Aunt" isn't afraid of "Uncle." She gives him a cuff, two, three, and he roars, and "Aunt" screams, and the neighbors come, and the police, and though "Uncle" is drunk, the police can't take him, for he's home, but the police say, "Watch yourself, Karlberg, you're headed for real trouble." Then "Uncle" goes off and doesn't come home for several days, and Ellen gets to go with "Aunt" to scrub in a building.

"Aunt" says that Mama is dead, but Ellen doesn't think that sounds dangerous. People say, "Now you won't get to see your mama anymore," but the grown-ups have lied so often that she doesn't pay any attention to them; of course she'll see Mama again. . . .

One day her real aunt comes.

"Now I have to take the kid again," she says, "I have to since things went that way with my sister; that's how it goes when you sin against the sixth commandment."

Ellen suddenly becomes very white, a big dark yard with a forest of stakes, rats, coffee, bread, beatings, bad-mouthing Mama. But "Aunt" says, "How dare you! Sixth commandment, you idiot, go to hell!"

Ellen is six years old, doesn't understand much, but some things she understands, and she is happy over that "go to hell." Her real aunt is the worst person she knows. And she climbs up in "Aunt's" lap, and "Aunt" is nice, and she cries a little and says, "I'll take care of you if I have to do it for nothing, but tomorrow I'll go to the poor relief board."

But "Aunt" didn't go to the poor relief board. "Uncle" and "Aunt" quarreled that night, and when "Uncle" pushed "Aunt" down the stairs, "Aunt" broke her leg, and Ellen was sent by the city's poor relief board to a shoemaker who has a cafe.

She comes into a big room and a heavy woman asks, "What's your name?"

"Little Ellen," she answers.

"Just Ellen, we'll say," the new "aunt" says. "Little Ellen is too long with the rush we're always in here."

Ellen gets a big cup of coffee and a plate of buns, soft buns with sugar. There are only tables and chairs in the room, and a flowering tree and high windows with gold drapes. She bites the bun, looks at the flowering tree, the high windows, remembers a new coat, new shoes, and a room with flowers, red tulips, white lilies. "Mama, Mama," and tears run down into the coffee, and the good bun falls on the floor. "Mama, Mama, come, where are you, come, Mama!"

"Haven't they told the pitiful child that her mother is dead," the new "aunt" says, and Ellen sits in the lap of a new "aunt" again, who says, crying a little, "Dear child, your mother is dead, didn't you know that?"

She quits crying then, and "Aunt" dips a new bun in the cooling coffee. Taking a good bite and after swallowing it, Ellen says, "You say that Mama is dead. What is it to be dead?"

"Eat first," "Aunt" says. "Hurry up, it's soon full of people here."

Ellen hurriedly dips the good bun, and after eating it asks again, "Why is Mama dead? What is dead?"

And "Aunt" answers, "I don't know for sure. We'll understand sometime. Be a good girl now."

Grown-ups are very strange. And they never know anything.

44

TWO

One year goes, then two. It isn't dull to be at the cafe Ellen
thinks, who is eight now. The days are no longer lonely and
isolated. It is work—yelling, swearing, corkpopping, going
to school, running errands, making quick movements to
avoid drunk men's embraces. All the swear words, all the
raw words, words always alluding to things sober people
never mentioned out loud, she just takes for granted now.
It's just when people are drunk that they swear and talk like
that. No, not all the time, not at all. It's a strange world
anyplace, luring one, coming abruptly, compelling one to
think and be on guard.

The mystery, life's mystery, brushes against a six-year-
old, an eight-year-old, against children. And the children
think, one this way, another that way, but all agree about
one thing, never say anything to grown-ups, they're so
dumb.

It's a strange world anyplace—for instance, the boy in
"Aunt's" painting had stood here alive one day. He was the
boy in the painting that hung on the wall in the house where
"Aunt" broke her leg, the "aunt" she lived with when Mama
had her own room with flowers in a vase. The loveliest and
the worst happened in that time, flowers in Mama's own
room, and then Mama died. Ellen can never forget that
"Aunt" nor her painting. A boy, a big boy, fourteen years old
maybe, holds a cluster of grapes in his hand, a cluster of
grapes like the one on "Uncle's" brandy bottle. Such grapes

she had never seen in working-class quarters and never such a boy either as the one in the painting. He was more beautiful than the child Jesus, whose picture hung in all the alleys' houses.

Maybe one became beautiful like that if one ate grapes. Or maybe only beautiful children with black eyes and brown curls got to eat grapes? The boy in the painting had certainly never played with drunk guys, or sworn, or stolen the organ-grinder's two öre that were thrown down from the window. The theft of the organ-grinder's money is a real burden for Ellen to carry. And the cats, of course, when the boys played butchering. The driver's boy was downright dangerous, one time wanting to cut off the finger of a little boy, who was scared out of his wits, saying he could do it so it wouldn't hurt. The driver was so rich, but his boy was a real devil; "Aunt" had said that, for she cleaned for them. The organ-grinder was sometimes drunk and always mean, so taking his two öre wasn't any sin. Why shouldn't one take things from mean people? But his monkey was so thin, so hungry that he constantly trembled. Anyway, the two-öre lollipop wasn't so good to lick that time, and she gladly gave it to the driver's boy who always got it anyhow; she just got to lick it here and there, and then he always took it away from her and ate it himself.

It's a strange world anyplace, a world grown-ups know nothing about.

It's a big house, and the whole day long there's a constant rush and commotion, and there's also plenty of food. Ellen runs many errands, getting many tips, which the cafe owner regularly keeps track of, but Ellen is no idiot—does anyone think she says she gets nothing? Oh, no, only not how much. . . .

Aunt has been to the poor relief board and complained, Aunt and a Salvation Army soldier who knew Mama. She had lived at the Army woman's for two months, but she had so many lice that Mama had moved. "It's sinful," the Salvation Army woman had said to the poor relief board, "you can't have children at a cafe."

"Oh, dear me, with such noise and such talk all day long, kids are ruined," Aunt had said, "and it's my sister's only child. I want to take her. She'll be like one of my own, and she'll have something to do, too, she can watch my youngest." And the relief board had promised to investigate, and the Salvation Army soldier had added, "Remember, the least of my little ones—a millstone around his neck."

One day a man comes and asks about Ellen; "Aunt" of the cafe whispers in Ellen's ear, "He's from the relief board; your aunt wants to have you." Ellen has heard so much about the poor relief board that she's surprised that it's a friendly man who has come, who doesn't even have a saber like the police. He's a very kind man who says that she's a pretty girl and looks clever and well fed, and he asks how she likes it here. Well, she gets food and fine clothes, the man can see she has fine clothes, and when he asks if she doesn't want to go to her aunt's, she begins to cry, sobbing out that she's afraid of Aunt, that she has only black coffee and hard rye bread and that her yard is full of ghosts, and Ellen becomes very pale, and the man doesn't ask anything more.

"Aunt" invites him to have coffee, fine coffee on a silver tray with a cloth and fancy cakes that Ellen rushed around the corner to get. "Aunt" then pours a glass of wine for him and gives him twenty-five öre when he goes. And when he's gone, "Aunt" gives Ellen fifty öre, saying, "Tonight you can go to Norrtull." At Norrtull there's a carnival with a merry-go-round. Oh, joy and happiness, only the big girls have been there, the ten-year-olds. A little shadow comes again as it always does when she thinks about "Uncle's" yard, and she goes back and pats "Aunt's" hand. *Ja, ja,* you go now, Ellen." But she promises herself always to tell "Aunt" how much she gets when she goes on errands.

There's a family in the house she gladly does errands for, for nothing if they asked, just to get to step in and look around while she waits to hear what they want. A drape divided the big handsome room nearly in two, and back of the drape, someone is nearly always playing the piano beautifully. The lady, herself, is so beautiful, so unusual, her hair so black and her skin so white, her eyes, black and shining. She can't speak Swedish, but she is always smiling and offering chocolates from a bowl that is never empty. If Ellen's luck is good, she catches a glimpse of the boy, the young gentleman, who has stepped directly out of "Aunt's" painting far away in the alley, and who now lives in this quiet handsome room where there is always music.

No one tells her to go, and she can stay and look on the mother and her son. Maybe it is a ravenous hunger after beauty in the little girl's gray eyes that touches the woman and the boy who know what beauty is, beauty in music, paintings, homes, and clothes. Maybe they think that hunger in a child's eyes is beauty, too, for she can stay in the room as long as she dares before "Aunt" calls her.

It is a day at dusk, a day of nothing but trouble.

That morning "Aunt" was already angry and shrill, for her husband, the shoemaker, was drunk before Ellen went to school. When she came home at noon to eat, he and both his apprentices were dead drunk, and at five in the afternoon, they lay in the workshop, sleeping. "Aunt" had raged and sweated over the stove the whole day, had given the waitress a box on the ear, and had sent Ellen to the sink to dry the dishes before she'd even had a chance to eat.

On this troublesome day, Ellen now runs in the dusk up the third floor's stairs, rings, and asks if there is any errand. The young gentleman from the painting smilingly shakes his head but holds the door open, and she steps in. Ellen can't resist, for it smells of flowers everywhere, and the boy only looks at her and gently laughs. She gets chocolates from the bowl, gets to follow him behind the drapes, and there the

48

boy in the painting sits down at a big piano, big as the organ in the church, bigger than she believed possible, and plays and plays.

A little lamp shines on the keys where his white hands dance, and the room is full of melodies while the dusk darkens over the cafe yard's trash cans, and the everyday world —school, friends, customers of the cafe, the noise, the smell of beer, the fights disappear, and she glides into a world where everything is peaceful and beautiful, just as the world naturally is for those who don't live in a slum or at a cafe. So those who live in slums always believe.

The little girl sits curled up, looking and smiling and listening while the boy's hands dance, and the melodies fly all around. Sometimes he turns and smiles—white teeth and black eyes flashing, and she smiles back, nodding her head, begging for more music, more, don't stop, let your hands dance. But he finishes playing and comes over to Ellen, who still smiles far off in a happy land, puts his hands on her cheeks, kisses her eyes. Carefully he takes off her dress, her bodice, her underclothes, uncovering the thin white shoulders and breasts, strokes his hands over her skin, smiles at her, and she smiles back. Cups his hands over the nipples of her small breasts as if they were something he wants to cover or shape, kisses her shoulders, his black eyes shining so strangely. Suddenly he goes to the piano, falls on his knees, folds his hands, and prays to God.

Fascinated, frightened, she hastily tries to get her clothes on. Gets tangled up, begins to sob. God, it is dark! How long has she been here, a whole night maybe? And "Aunt"? What will happen now? And what can she do for the boy, lying with his beautiful head on a stool and crying? Everything is so quiet; are there no more people left anywhere? She sobs and tears at her clothes that won't go on. The boy gets up, helps her get her clothes on, and following her into the next room, he empties the bowl of chocolates in her hands and in her apron. Then he kisses her eyes. She

49

stands outside a closed door, and she hears voices and the noise of the wagons in the street again. The world is still there. All is the same as before.

Dreamily she goes with unsteady steps down the stairs and out to the back yard, sits down in the light from the cafe's kitchen windows beside the trash cans, eats a chocolate now and then, thinking over that incomprehensible strangeness that she experiences and never understands.

She is suddenly startled; she imagines "Aunt" to be standing right beside her saying, "You must do the right thing by her, she hasn't eaten dinner—it's been a devil of a day." Then from across the yard comes "Aunt's" actual long drawn-out cry, "E-l-l-e-e-en!"

She calmly goes in without thinking that it's maybe risky, but she can't run away any longer from "Aunt," or from the dishes, or from everyday. It's dangerous to go in without figuring out what she should say, but what pleasure is there in some well-spun lie when reality can be so unbounded, so strangely beautiful, and so dangerous.

"Where have you been?"

"On the third floor running an errand. They hadn't any change. I'll get paid in the morning." The most banal lie, so easy to make up, and "Aunt" is satisfied; her judgment is dulled after a whole day's quarreling.

School is over. School with its everlasting struggle and anxiety. All the centuries that had been written about, all the words about this or that event are as if blown away. And finally exam day, the last exam day. Long, meaningless chains of words ring in Ellen's ears. Then-Karl-died-unmarried-his-younger-sister-Ulrika Eleonora-was chosen-queen-of-Sweden. But she was married to Prince Fredrik from Hessen. A king of Sweden does not run willingly away . . . your ox or ass . . . your worker's ass's foal. . . . Is it the wild hunter who sets off straining . . . chains that one learns by heart from the sheer monotony of the rhythm. And the

50

terrible quadrangular figures that one must exactly imitate with pen and ruler, using a dumb lead pencil like the one "Aunt" writes the beer driver's notes with. Christ on the cross revealed himself also (right among sweating, well-dressed friends and their parents) and the soldier gave him vinegar. What pain there is in that legend of the suffering Christ. It had been really frightening in primary school before one knew anything. Nights full of horrible dreams right up to the burial of Christ, which had come as a relief, his burial in an expensive grave, one intended for a rich man; that had seemed to Ellen the only reward Christ had got for all his misery. God had to be mean to act that way to his son; he'd been worse than the alley's meanest woman, or a drunk man, or the police. He'd allowed the soldiers, the emperor, and everyone to hurt his son though he'd been mightier than the emperor and could have done whatever he'd wanted, and here he'd wanted the worst. Ellen had felt sorry for those who had tormented Christ, for they'd been forced to do something so grim.

The last exam day was no shining one for Ellen. Only one question could she answer, but she alone of all the children held up her hand that time, for no one understood the question that the inspector asked. No one *could* know the answer, for they had never heard tales about odd things. He asked about insects' breathing organs, and Ellen answered, "They breathe through a hole in the skin." She had read about it in a newspaper. The answer was accepted, and the teacher gave a sigh of relief. The inspector couldn't know how things were in that school. Teach the children to read and teach them religion, nothing else is needed—that was the standard advice the priest gave the teacher. And he willingly obeyed it to the letter, for he was also of the opinion that too much learning for poor children wasn't healthy.

When Ellen came home from the exam, "Aunt" said, "You did just fine. You knew what no one else did. You won't get rich off that stuff in the catechism, or from any fly lungs either, for that matter, but it's good to know about things that really exist."

Books, many of Ellen's friends loaned them and got to borrow them; but she, and there were others, didn't get to, for the refrain was always "you need to help here after you come home from school, we're paid so little for you." Now all that lay behind her, even her religious instruction with the priest, a time that was really laughable. The priest talked as if one were an angel. He tried to explain what one should watch out for. What did he know about life's strange things? What did he know about a boy who stepped out of a painting and kissed and cried, whose white fingers dancing over the keys made sounds so beautiful that she forgot "Aunt" and everything? What did the priest know about old men who came with King of Denmark's? What did he know about all the women, her "aunts" who swore and quarreled and fought but who still could be nice to a small child? What did he know about the horror and darkness of a big yard? Did he know any prayers to help against rats? He didn't know anything. She laughed at him behind his back.

The only time she became serious was when he talked about the strange thing that the grown-ups never discussed. "Girls, when you are grown, then you become women and build homes, and you shall not grumble when God, perhaps, gives you a burden of a large family of children. It is your duty to obey God's will."

Quietly and seriously the girls from the alleys listened to these words. Some hid them in their hearts and consoled themselves later with them when their number of children grew, and there were fights with landlords and relief boards. But some thought that God's will was as usual directly contrary to all that was right, was incomprehensible—mean.

Now all of that was behind Ellen. Her life lay ahead, vulnerable, palpably vulnerable, as it always had been for as long as she could remember, but in another way.

Ellen is one of the grown-ups.

Saturdays are the busiest days, and "Aunt" doesn't count the cash receipts until one in the morning when the scrub woman is hard at work on the dirty cafe floor.

The cafe has a little room, opening into the back yard —some wit once called it a "safety valve," but that's so long ago, that now it's just called the "safe." When obstinate customers, bricklayers, brickcarriers, railroad workers, get really drunk, "loaded," as they put it, but at midnight think they're sober and refuse to go, then "Aunt" never calls the police. They're moved into the safe, which has such a thick shade at the window that not a ray of light gleams on the kitchen garden. It's well placed, for overhead is a bathroom and under it the potato cellar. No one can be disturbed by singing and yelling. Someone knocks on the glass. "Ellen, where is she? One glass more." They are singing and playing cards. Ellen has learned to parry wisecracks, learned to put on a businesslike appearance, even imitated "Aunt" a little, "Aunt" who always sends her off to bed at eleven, for after that it won't do for young girls to be among drunk fellows —any religion has its values.

"Wait, Ellen. Wait, damn it, Rosen's going to sing." A good voice begins to sing.

> Then I'll see that I'm the first
> and get to be the stoker,
> then to my great relief
> a brandy distiller I'll be
> and get the devil to drink
> till every day he's drunk
> so there'll be life in hell
> and therefore do I drink.

"Devilish good, that will I be, just that, be a brandy distiller, for in hell they don't keep count. That Bellman was a glad shit, he knew, he did."

"Is that Bellman?"

"*Ja,* sure. Who the hell could put it together so good

otherwise? The scholar Ellen looks damned mad. What'll you get from me? Tips, you'll get, and don't anyone try to pass me up. We're a clean-haired gang that knows what's going on. Jesus Christ, you're like my own kid, as many times as you've run to buy snuff for us before you got so big and uppity."

"That's not Bellman you're singing. He wrote only about Stockholm and Haga and Ulla. He didn't write about hell like in that song, and you can just keep your tips. You can get it in your heads instead that I need to get to bed." Ellen slams the door to the safe and warns "Aunt." "They want more beer in the safe and now it's twelve."

"Aunt" says firmly, "Go up to bed, Ellen, but don't slam the hall door so you wake up the shoemaker. I want to have peace when I come up." ("Aunt" always calls her husband the shoemaker.)

Ellen is out for a walk.

"Aunt" wants her to go for a walk every day if it isn't too busy at the cafe. Sometimes "Aunt" gives her a theater ticket and looks cross. But Ellen knows that on the day after, when it's quiet and no brawling beer drinkers are in the safe, that "Aunt" will prepare a "coffee for three" with soft buns; and they'll sit in the safe, the most peaceful place, and "Aunt" and the waitress will listen while Ellen describes the play, imitating the actors and making comical faces. Sometimes the shoemaker is there, but then the theatricals always end with the walls tumbling down, for when "Aunt" is most interested and saying, "No, but Ellen, you make those ridiculous gestures just like Inga Berentz, I've seen her several times," then the shoemaker opens a bottle and talks, nodding and grinning and gulping his beer, as if "Aunt's" formidable eyes didn't exist. When he pads out for another bottle at a lively point in the drama, then "Aunt" explodes, and Ellen and the waitress rush out of the way. But the shoemaker doesn't come out; "Aunt" locks him in, shrieking that at her cafe no one gets free beer so that day after day not a single krona is earned, that there are ten persons in the house—doesn't the shoemaker know that? Hasn't he taken that in?

Ellen is out walking—with a student.

It is cloudy and dark. A warm wind blows, and two young people, both the same age, walk in the late spring evenings as if they had wings. Ellen wants to go out every night, and "Aunt" begins to question this. "Have you company? Watch out for fast guys. I think you've seen what they're like at the cafe here."

Ja, Ellen would watch out for fast guys. Students weren't like them, and Ellen went on longer and longer walks with hers.

"Aunt" began to spy on her. One night she follows Ellen, sees her turn up at St. John's churchyard, sees the student, sees Ellen and the student on a bench, sees smiles, kisses, caresses. "Aunt" goes over to them. "This is no company for you, Ellen. You, you puppy, keep company in your own circles! Come now, Ellen."

Without a word to the student or to "Aunt," Ellen walks away. She is ashamed, ashamed not for "Aunt," but for the student. What will he think? She had talked so easily with him about books and things she had read, and he had said that she was so intelligent, and both of them had the same opinion about God, that he was nothing to concern themselves with. And "Aunt" comes like an idiot, like a drunk old woman, like a—*ja,* she is shamed to death.

A week goes by. Ellen is terribly angry with "Aunt," and "Aunt" is just as cross with her; both slam and bang the doors and the dishes, and it's miserable for the shoemaker. The waitress, who's been engaged for five years, although no one's ever seen her fiancé, gives her opinion, *"Ja,* I knew Ellen's aunt, boy-crazy before she was married she was, and Ellen's mother was one of those 'kept' women, and she died of syphilis, so Ellen is sure not much to count on coming from such stock. I think you've been too nice to her. I know she lies to you sometimes."

Then "Aunt" is furious. "Ellen is the only one here who hasn't fawned upon the shoemaker, never anytime, not when she was younger either; she never babbled about receipts to him, or any shit of any kind, and if Ellen and I aren't good enough for one like you, then get out! As for the rest, her mother died of TB, so what you said is enough to sue you for libel. Try to keep your mouth shut!"

That evening Ellen gets to go to the movies, and "Aunt" gives her a new pair of gloves, which she had bartered from a customer who couldn't pay for his meals. He was a glove salesman, and vexed that the stubborn woman wouldn't give him credit, he had given her a pair that were too small. But they fit Ellen fine.

"Aunt" talks with Ellen. "No students, Ellen. A bricklayer or a rail worker, but no students. A rail worker can pay for a kid or marry you; most often he wants to marry you. But a student never marries one like you. They can't pay for a kid either, for they have nothing. They don't earn any money, they only take it."

"How do you know students so well?" Ellen is on the point of being angry again. "What do you know about them? They're folks, too, so they are, fine and polite and friendly."

"Well, you can just as well know why," "Aunt" says, eager to be at peace with her again. "I got into trouble with a student and had to marry the shoemaker, and you see how I have it." Ellen had certainly heard talk about the son that "Aunt" had far off someplace. "You've heard, of course," "Aunt" continues, "that I have a son; *ja,* he's at the university now in Lund, studying to be a doctor. That costs money, you'd better believe, and the shoemaker hasn't helped with an öre. I took this cafe when I had been married two years, for I knew then that the shoemaker wouldn't keep a word of what he'd promised. He knew, of course, that he wasn't the boy's father, but he had promised me that it would be all right anyway. But when the boy was born and I was already married to the shoemaker, it was a constant nagging; whole nights he lay and crabbed and was jealous of the boy, and I nearly went crazy. But then I got a hold of this cafe. The shoemaker had a big workshop, and I got entrusted to get it in installments, and I borrowed from one and paid another. I allowed the safe to be used, for I thought guys can just as well leave their money with me and drink beer until they sleep, than to end up on the streets in the middle of the night and follow the girls and get both infected or otherwise, for that's how it used to be when they were thrown out, drunk and crazy.

"As soon as I could manage it, I got a family to take my boy. He was five years old then. I paid well. It was a priest's family that took him. I paid them two hundred kronor a year, and when he began school, double that. This last year he has cost me three thousand kronor. But the day I traveled with my boy to the priest's family, the shoemaker didn't dare to be home, and for half a year, I never spoke a word to him. I worked and worked; I was alone in the kitchen, served, had only a girl to wash dishes. When my scrub woman, Mrs. Bergman, broke her leg, I went with her to the hospital, and she begged me to take care of you, for she had got attached to you, and you were frightened to death of your own aunt, she said. And she told me about your mother, how unhappy she was, a fine woman, who did everything for her child, exactly as I did for mine.

"Then I went to the poor relief board and said that I would take you for half the usual amount. I got it and no one has known it. I don't regret it, for it was a little more natural with a child in the house. You've been treated right. You haven't had an easy time with me, but you haven't been cold and you haven't starved, and you've learned to prepare proper food and keep things clean.

"Now that you're grown and can take care of yourself, you can move if it should be you don't like it here any longer, although it would certainly be empty without you. But don't get mixed up with students or any other shit-fine guys, for you'll get no money from me; every öre goes to him down in Lund, and without some money of your own, you can't marry anyone else than a worker. What you don't know, you can't guard yourself against."

"Aunt" poured two cups of coffee and offered one to Ellen. Then the talk was over.

In the forests of the world, there are many cottages, and each one has its story. The man who built his cottage in this forest lives there still, a little gray, a little bent, but strong and healthy. The apple and pear trees that he planted thirty years ago point toward the sky, far above the chimney of the cottage. He lives alone, tilling his land, harvesting his fruit, helping the farmers get their crops in.

His four young sons are out in the world, and what they're doing always lies behind the newly opened roads, stonewalled canal banks, and empty bottles. One woman, then another is also left behind; pale and quiet, she looks hatefully at the new road, taking instead the old knotted paths. Sometimes she walks on forever, never returning. There are many lakes, many bottomless marshes that newly opened roads lead to.

Sometimes four tall men come, taking the narrow path through the forest to the cottage where they were born, where every log in its timbered walls had been carried on father's back to the clearing, where the cottage lies out of the way because freeholding farmers never sold lots to outsiders.

A long time ago, a great religious movement had swept over the district where, after many years of wandering, an outsider, a giantlike West Gotlander had come. He needed to earn money then to travel to God's land, Utah, but he had

59

stayed on in the village. He had practiced sorcery in his wanderings, the villagers said. They had no proof, but the rumor persisted. He had a hundred kronor and with that he bought a lot between the forest and the swamp, and there he built his cottage. The village had never seen such power, for he carried every log on his long, strong back and sawed every floor plank by hand. The poor land of Mark fostered fierce sons.

The village that was dependent on shoemakers, tailors, carpenters, builders, farm workers, the village whose biggest hero was the gentleman of the entailed estate, and who had so distinguished himself in the war in Poland, that he could ride on his horse right in the chancel of the church without the priest punishing him—the village got to see a man who was horse, architect, carpenter, and above all, something fine, for he planted fruit trees, fruit trees that he walked seven miles to the nearest city to get and then carried home seven miles on his back. Three rows of them he planted before the roof trusses were raised. To plant fruit trees in rows was fine, the village knew that, but when a horse, carpenter, and West Gotlander did it, that was crazy.

There was no shortcut to the cottage; no shortcut is there even today. But the cottage got finished and was painted red. The whole village there was gray. It had taken two years, but now it was ready, and the Visigoth from Mark dressed in his Sunday best one weekday to go court-ing.

There was a woman in the village that he longed for. It was for a woman he had built and planted trees and worked as a hired man. Never before in that district had anyone worked so hard, experienced so many difficulties for the sake of a woman.

And the woman said yes, but her father, the farmer, said no. The woman followed him just as she was, in every-day skirt and kerchief, so thin and little that a giantlike

Visigoth from Mark could easily carry her on the rough path home to the cottage with the three rows of apple trees. He put her down in the cottage and said, "Now I've made a home for us as well as I can, and now I'll work to feed us."

But the woman cried, for she was going to have a baby in several months, and Father and Mother knew nothing about it; she cried for, of course, everything was new here, but so little, so poor, no big display of shining pewter and copperware like at home in the large kitchen, and it was unpainted, but the child . . . she must stay here, and, of course, she liked the big man here; he was different from the others in the village. She didn't understand that love had made him do his giant-work. That brimming love for a woman that forced muscles to do great deeds while the villagers shook their heads, forced him to do months of the heaviest work on the gentleman's farm to get money for materials, for windows, and nails, for no one allowed credit to an outsider. A strong man who forced himself to chew hard bread, hard black bread, bought from the gentleman's driver, forced himself to chew that bitter wheat bread, day after day, until the cottage was ready, and he could fetch the woman he could not live without, and who would have his children. She could not understand. How could she understand the enormity of the sacrifice he who had only his hands and his wits had made? All the sacrifices of needy people seem small to one who has never lacked butter on soft, moist bread.

She was born in the village. There no other books than the Bible and the farmer's almanac were known. In broad terms, she knew something about morals. She knew that she shouldn't steal, nor lie, nor let poor men kiss her, hired men, ones like that. Above all she must be married before she got with child; otherwise father would drive her out and she would have to drown herself. It was wondrously good to have a big fellow who loved her, fussed over her so everyone could see it, always to be the chosen one, never needing to see herself passed over for another. That happened often in the village. Girls went with eyes red from crying because of that. But, if she were not with child, she would have married a farmer's son and had a kitchen as big as the one at home and been a bride in the church and had a big wedding.

The western sun shone over the newly spaded garden, over the small, fine newly planted fruit trees, shone over the plain in front of the mountain, in the western windows, and made the room like a gold cabinet. The new beams, the new, handsawed, planed floor shone like gold, and a happy, strong man took a small, crying woman in his arms and said, "Now life begins, now I will work for bread, never, never will you need to starve."

Now sometimes the four tall sons come, shouting and quarreling through the crooked forest lane, the firs brushing their faces with their plumes, the same ones that swept over their father's face when he carried the logs to his lot, and when he carried home the woman who now rests in the churchyard. Firs don't grow tall in marshland. Like giant carrots they only spread themselves out. Their broad branches unwillingly leave room for those who will not bow their necks and stoop under them.

The old man stays on in his cottage, keeps it in order, for where else should his sons go, sons of her who rests among her relatives by that ancient church?

And four half-drunk young men bring gifts and give them to their gray-haired father, taller than any of them, and the youngest goes out to look at the apple trees that are in bloom, and says, as so often he has before—often when he was little and wanted to hold his own among the village children, says, now grown and half-drunk, "No one has such fine apple trees as ours."

Sometimes the sons bring friends home.

Sometimes industrious men, who, after eating the old man's food and drinking his coffee, rest under his apple trees, and thoughtfully stroking their mustaches, they say before they go back to their waiting spades and crowbars, "This isn't right; an old man ought to get paid for this. It's not right that grown sons exploit an old father."

An old man ought to get paid for board and room. It wasn't right for big strong sons to come home drunk and fighting to a father who had done more than his share of work and didn't have anything else in the world to live for than them. Then the sons, tired from work and brandy, used to say in agreement, "We'll end all this, and next time we'll bring home money so there can be a new roof on the barn."

Then the old man straightened his back and cleaned up after them, took on timber felling and threshing, laying krona upon krona; if there were to be a new roof on the barn, he should surely do his part.

But more often other friends came home with them. Men who swore at him for his terrible lane, who drank his brandy as fast as the glasses got on the table. Men who had lice in their clothes and who did acrobatics in the precious apple trees and made so much noise it was heard all over.

After these visits it took longer than ever before everything was in order and clean again. And then a strange thing happened. The old man sat a whole day under his apple trees without working. One day he locked the windows of the cottage and went away. At seventy-five, he was on his way to Mark to see if a sod house were still there, the hut in the hillside where he was born.

The villagers wondered and shook their heads. The old ones who remembered his exceptional strength when he was building his cottage said, "He's always been strange. He'll not come back anymore, so that will be a rough life down there in the forest with those rail-worker rowdies for sons. Outsiders shouldn't get to buy land, for you never know what you're getting. He was stuck-up, wouldn't even take a nip when you offered him; well, now that's taken care of for him, his sons drink enough for him as well."

It's a long way to travel on the train, many miles through Sörmland and West Gotland to Borås.

From the city the road wound eighteen miles through the forests, through sandy plains of juniper and heather, sixty years ago when a fifteen-year-old, without even the usual bundle of clothes, left the sod house in Mark. The day before, his father had hung himself in the woodshed. The constable had said, "We'll bury your father, and the parish will look after your sister and brother, but you, big as you are, must get out and seek something yourself."

And he had gone out and sought.

Now after sixty years, he was going back over the road where he had herded sheep as a child. Why? He didn't know. Time was getting on. The years alone in his cottage had awakened a strange longing for life. Spring's three rows of flowering apple trees, his shouting, thoughtless, strong sons who let time run like the money they earned, the gray monotony of the village, all had given him a longing that couldn't be resisted. Mark's bare sandy plain, the grim poverty, the starvation in the sod house, everything had at once become so living. Mother had died. Then Father had hung himself the next year. The parish had taken two of the family; the older ones had left long before this. He would see none of them any more. No one would recognize him. Those who knew him once had forgotten him the same day he had left to "seek something" himself. But a brightness lay over the day. The old man didn't remember the misery, the hard work, the long years as much. He remembered the strength, the courage, the urgency for life of the young. And when the strange longing came over him at home under the apple trees, he had to be on his way, to breathe once again the air of the juniper and heather over the plain where he had begun with only a pair of willing hands and no knowledge of life at all outside of Mark's heath.

The stars began their journey over the heath. The juniper bushes seemed to crouch in the sheen of the moon that spread its radiance over the land and then encountered the impenetrable darkness of Småland's forests. The moon shone on a pile of stones in the middle of the heath where only a gooseberry bush and some thistles indicated what had been there. A giant figure outlined itself against the horizon, like some awakened spirit of the heath, as the man stood by the cairn, meditating, wondering. Then he sat down on a stone and let the night pass. The moon and the stars and the hours wandered by, and the juniper bushes looked like a little scattered army on the march.

In the morning the heath's gray, bent son was on his way back. At the station in Borås, he took out his worn purse and bought a ticket back, through West Gotland and Sörmland, home to his cottage and apple trees.

That journey was the first, the only, and the last extravagance in his long life. In many stormy years in his old age, for peaceful old age is given only to those who give in to life, often, often he wondered, stroking his beard, how in the world he could have taken the time to travel and waste so much money.

The villagers said that he had been to his homeplace and inherited something, for otherwise he wouldn't have spent so much money. And they were friendly and interested and invited him for coffee, invited a traveled old man like him for coffee and delicious treats.

But one who was reticent and never invited back was soon left in peace again. And when the villagers saw that he had planted two juniper bushes at the corners of his cottage, they were agreed. . . . Foolish, maybe dangerous?

Spring and summer go, and fall and winter.

Spring is here again. If it is the old one that comes back again, the old spring that was here last year, or if it is a new one, those who are learned can decide in time. Space is time and time is space and nothing thereover. The balance in this everlasting universe is called comparison; without a thing's comparison with another, there is chaos. There is mathematical order in the new religion.

Spring is here again.

Ellen and "Aunt" don't know anything about relativity. Neither do the shoemaker and his apprentices. Thus, everything comes to them as a surprise.

The son in Lund, the son who twice in his life has seen his mother, the mother who has worked like a horse for his sake, or for her idea's sake or however the truth's construed, the son who was to be a doctor isn't one after all.

He marries a doctor's maid and becomes a mailman. It's so easy to forget to share things with a mother. He's already married and established, is happy to have escaped from learning's prison into life. He sits with a neat housewife in a neat kitchen and in a neat mailman's uniform and begins to think about Mother who has always sent money and never enough of it. The priest's wife in Småland had always thought so, too, and he had run errands and weeded the garden, and made himself useful in every way, for there's always been too little money from Mother.

And then the questions in Mother's letters, those difficult questions he has answered just enough to get by with.
Mother firmly believes that he'll be a doctor soon, has written that again in her letter with the thousand crowns that he
used to marry and buy the furniture. He must write to her
that he can support himself now. She'll surely be glad, for
she has to be old now. He doesn't know for sure how old
she is. He'd had the priest's wife in Småland to think about,
and it had been hard to scrape together enough for her
birthdays; now there's an end to all that, God be praised. He
doesn't need to congratulate the priest's wife any longer.

He sits down and writes to Mother that he can support
himself now, is married, a mailman, and asks her to save for
her old age. He posts his letter, and the train whistles
through forests and meadows and cities, bringing the mailman's letter punctually two days later. And the mother
whose son was to be a doctor now hangs in the shoemaker's
workshop.

To hang oneself is horrid. The body looks grotesque.
But she who has done everything each day with one idea in
mind hasn't time to think about her looks after death like
a Madame de Pompadour. A piece of rope one can always
get to catch on something. Always, when the journey is
over, or someone tramples an idea like a cow hoof a puffball,
the rope's end is there. Even in a jail where life is watched
like a precious stone, the rope's end is found. The rope is a
suicide's most accessible weapon.

The shoemaker doesn't dare to live in the house any
longer. He sells everything, lock, stock and barrel. And the
mailman comes for his inheritance from a mother he has
seen twice, the last time when he was fourteen and going to
high school. Now she lies blue and swollen in her casket,
and the mailman's wife thinks that everything is dreadful.

Ellen doesn't get any inheritance and she's out of work.
She doesn't get a work reference either, just a certificate that
Ellen Karlsson had worked at the cafe and that her mistress
had died too suddenly to draw up a testimonial.

A couple of Bellman singers happening to be in the city, sit dejected and quiet in the safe, and drink their beer mostly for old times' sake. It is always distressing when a friend takes his own life. It is like a reflection on yourself; you are in some way deficient, aren't what you meant to be to that good friend after all. In his frenzy the friend can't wait for you to find time to talk to him. Last week Kiruna-Sven put a stick of dynamite in his mouth, and the kind old woman here has hung herself. It is quite incomprehensible. If you could beat up the shoemaker a bit, that might help, but he fusses around and cries and thinks about hanging himself, too. "When the fur is clipped, the lice lose foothold," the bass-voiced driller says, wiping beer from his beard. "Damn it! The beer is even bitter." Ellen is serious, not looking as if she wanted to talk to anyone. No, it'd be best to go back to the construction site again. "We must pay up now, Ellen."

And then another asks to have something to say, "Will you be staying on here?"

"No, the cafe will be closed."

Hmm. The end of these pleasant comradely nights in the safe. *Ja*, life is then an encumbrance. . . .

"Have you a new place then?"

"No, I can just serve and cook, and gentlemen's families won't have a worker at a cafe near them. I'll have to find work at another cafe, although here there's no opening. There are places in private homes, but I've inquired about them, and got no, and I think I won't trouble any more. . . ." Ellen stiffens a little.

"They'll not have you! What's the matter with those idiots? A clever girl like you!" The Bellman singers are glad to have something to fight about in all the sadness, and the "private" families who won't have girls from cafes in their service are thoroughly debated and get a verdict of failing marks. They are worse than *all* the others, for one knows very well how they act when it comes to the point; all who set themselves up are worse than the worst.

"You come with us, Ellen, to the construction site. There's always something available at the canteen there, and you'll get good pay and polite treatment—we'll see to that. No beer or whisky is served there, so folks are sober during the week."

Ellen is happy and thankful to go with them. And the Bellman singers have another round of beer, describe exactly for Ellen the journey to the construction site, and then break up, satisfied that they got to be a part of things.

Ellen is traveling for the second time in her life, the first when she was two, and her mother had come to the city to find work at a factory. Every day she's seen the smoke from the trains, and several automobiles that the richest factory owners are beginning to use. Now it's the first time she's traveling through forests and fields, past towns and villages, thinking the ticket seems cheap for so much pleasure. At the edge of a vast swamp the rails end. Huddled some way out in the marshy ground are four buildings: the barracks, the canteen, the bakery, the outhouse.

The canteen's chimney smokes like a locomotive's funnel, and in the kitchen everything is lively and fast. Ellen is taken on without fuss. "Well, it's good that you're here," a dumpy housekeeper says, and a dark-haired, pallid man says, "Bonjour, mademoiselle." When the coffee is drunk, Ellen needs only to go to her room on the floor above and change clothes; then her life begins again as usual—set the tables, cut the bread, give a hand where it's needed, but no dishes, that the Bellman singers expressly forbid, "for we know Ellen and she must have proper work; to do dishes can make the smartest crazy, we know, for we used to cook for ourselves."

Ellen looks at the big barracks with its bare windows and thinks that guys are satisfied with anything; a curtain could surely be hung, as much money as they seem to have and which they drink up in the safe.

It is quiet in the barracks during the day. The bare windows look like gloomy giants' eyes, turned toward the forest ridges that are etched high in the distance. Behind those ridges the rich live, the rich who stake their money on the railroads through the marsh.

Peace prevails over the barracks' bunks, which are built into the walls. There's no one to make a fuss over a little rat who looks around from the top of a table. It is empty and quiet in the big, drafty barracks. All the men are out at war, at war with the marsh, fighting with axes and crowbars to get firm ground under their feet and the crossties. There's a strange peace over the barracks that shelters tired men every night. Cheap and bare the barracks seem to wait in the marsh, desolate and still, with poverty's ricketiness, awaiting tired and dirty men.

At night all the windows in the barracks gleam. The naked house comes alive. Songs are heard, sometimes quarrels, sometimes fights. At night the high forest ridges close in on the marsh filled with the low-growing bog myrtle. The whole marsh becomes warmer at night. The shadows conceal the barracks' homelessness, conceal the turf where mignonette or peonies never grow. . . . But flowers, who thinks about them, has time for them? In the fall, the camp breaks up again and moves to the next desolate marsh.

Ellen likes the marsh and the open horizon, often pausing to look out over the marsh and wonder what it is like behind it. And in the kitchen she is pleased with all the new and unusual. On that first day when she saw that a man was the chef, she was surprised, a man cooking sauce, cutting pork, frying it, and stoking the fire! Ellen knew about chefs only from the novels she had read, and this one was a genuine French chef, just as in a novel.

The railroad workers had found him in the city, drunk and abandoned, and taken him along to the construction site. In a few days he was lord and master in the kitchen. The old housekeeper, who helped herself to her own pocket flask and was often hazy after dinner, was helplessly demoted, threatening to move every day, but staying on, and explaining to anyone who was willing to listen, "He came here because he was drunk, and you can be sure he'll leave again when he wants his brandy, and then, *ja*, the men will be thankful to have a proper Swedish woman in the kitchen." And she took a gulp from her flask.

The farmers didn't like the French cook. He was too exacting about the meat and potatoes. Before he came, they had got away with selling the fleshiest parts of some worn-out horse to the canteen now and then. The housekeeper had just said, "Bring it here; it'll be all right." And the railroad workers ate "seaman's beef" without knowing that it maybe was an old comrade before the stone-cart that they sat and chewed on. It was lucky for the housekeeper that they didn't get wise to it, for railroad workers here were finicky about food and wouldn't have appreciated eating an old work comrade up, even if it happened to be a horse.

But the cook didn't buy horse meat, and gesturing with both hands, he refused the thin calves whose flesh was as blue as the milk they drank.

The farmers had to deliver the best meat, the best potatoes, the best of everything, otherwise they didn't get to deliver at all. The French cook threatened to take his custom from them. The worst was that they could not take more money for these far superior goods, for they couldn't disclose the motives behind a much higher price, when they already had taken the highest possible price for very inferior stuff, for the housekeeper was never exacting. She sometimes even offered them snaps. That damned French cook ought to be banished from the country, the farmers thought.

The Frenchman didn't mind what the farmers thought, and didn't understand what they said either; he was helplessly in love with mademoiselle Ellen and considered her opinion the most important in the world.

Ellen thought it was interesting to have a chef, and a foreign one, in the kitchen, but in the long dusky spring evenings, she walked in the marsh with a tall young man who confided to her, among other things, that he's going home, must leave here soon to help his father put a roof on the barn.

The marsh was firm for walking while the ground frost held, and the tufts of grass glimmered dark red from the cranberries when the western sun dropped behind the ridge. Ellen had never picked cranberries before. "We should have a basket with us," she said, for the man put them in his hat.

The next evening she took a basket and walked out to the marsh. The infatuated French cook followed her, wanting to help mademoiselle. His eyes darkened with anger when he saw the man gathering berries in his hat. And the man emptied them in Ellen's basket and said, "When I go home after the next payday, for I must go home and help Father with the barn, then you may gladly come, too. This is no place for ladies." Ellen said nothing, laughed a little, but the French cook went sadly, forlornly home.

On the marsh the two came to an agreement. A brandy-loving young worker suddenly found that there was nothing as delicious in the world as a woman's lips, lips shyly, a little hesitantly, lifted up for a kiss out on the cranberry tufts a late spring evening.

When the month had passed and the summer was beginning even here up in the north, Ellen and her young man traveled south to help an old father with a barn roof. The French cook left the day after.

"That he should leave now, when the days are beginning to be fine and warm," the bass driller said, stroking his mustache.

"The grapes are ripening in France, he just got homesick," grinned the pile driver and the best one to tolerate brandy.

"He had to leave to get a woman, you'd better believe," Pelle said, tilting his hat.

"He had to leave to go out with the girls," the young boy who handled the dynamite said seriously and manly.

"And Bernhard took Ellen along." The bass driller, one of the Bellman singers, was thoughtful. "Now maybe that barn roof will finally get done that Bernhard and his brothers have talked about for years. Bernhard's a little unsteady, but Ellen can keep him in line. She can manage him. She's much too good for him." And the driller took a pinch of snuff.

But the housekeeper put on a clean apron, had a drop from her flask, and went to ask the driller for two more helpers in the kitchen, for Ellen had become marriage-crazy and the cook brandy-crazy, she said, finishing her request.

The barracks remained just as before in the day, its empty windows, like eyes, overlooking the marsh far off to the forest ridge, waiting for tired men, working for footholds for new railties out on the cranberry tufts.

THREE

Today it is bright over the whole earth. So the old man thinks in the forest cottage. In that shining June morning all the earth's people breathe in its scents and light.

It is early. The woodcock has just flown up, her wings grazing the bog myrtle in the meadow; she's the June morning's earliest bird. The wood grouse and her brood pluck seeds under the biggest spruce. The fox stalks carefully along the edges of the field on his way to his den, carrying his family's breakfast in his mouth, a little newly born rabbit. On the cottage's narrow well path, the fruit blossoms lie in drifts, and the blackbirds hop around in the sweet scented petals, hunting worms, while the big gray cat watches, her body poised for a single springing movement, preparing herself for a meal.

The morning wind sweeps through the rye field, the pollen whirling in veils, floating down in the clover, already spreading its pithy smell. The sun bathes the graymatted fallow field and the plow, still standing where the farmer and his horse left it after yesterday's work.

A garden snake, its golden dots artfully daubed behind its flat head, has been lured by the sun out of the garden's reeking warm manure pile. Blinded by the sun, rash from the zest of life, and startled out of his sleep, a mouse runs right into the troll power of the snake's dangerous eyes for all mice and birds. The snake has only to swallow, roll himself up, and continue the night's rest.

The morning's fragrance rises with the wind—the smells of meadowsweet, of the new shoots of the firs, of lilac and lily-of-the-valley and dew-wet earth, of the lake, of grazing cattle, of wild rosemary and marsh mud, all sap-filled, teeming life.

An old man holds his hand like a visor over his eyes looking out over the land and is happy. Happy, for in the room that he has always tried to keep in order, keep as fine as his wife did, a young woman sleeps, and in the kitchen, his youngest son, sleeps.

Now his son said everything will be neat and tidy again. He had been sober and he must have been saving, for he had given him a big sum to "manage with," fifty kronor in all. And they both had many packages, and never, not since he was young and out in the world, had he seen such a good, natural, beautiful woman as Ellen. After she had looked around, she had said, "It isn't as beautiful in paradise as it is here. Look at the apple blossoms!" And she had taken hold of him, an old man, and danced around with him, and Bernhard had laughed and said, "Watch out, for Father is as strong as a bear; provoke him, and he can easily give you a birching." And there was no brandy, no bottle in the knapsack.

The sun wanders farther from the east, and he hears the sounds of the farm workers' voices, of horses dragging harness chains, the slack lines stretched to the fields' harrows and plows, and creaking harnesses and jingling chains blend themselves in a morning chorus. He goes in and puts on the coffee, for today he thinks he won't go straight in to work at the manor house.

Happiness can make even an old man a spendthrift.

It is bitter January. At the cottage corner the fox barks his mating cry when he whirls past in burning haste through the snow. It is so cold that the snow shines greenish white in the starlight. Cold and quiet, so solemnly quiet. The firs bide, heavy, dark. The fields lie bound beneath the snow, and the apple trees, stiff with cold, lift their branches to the relentless sky.

The old man stirs up the fire and Ellen looks quietly on. They are alone in the cottage, and the year has given them a whole world to share.

Ellen looks out over the field, looks far over the forests, sees the construction site, the bare, ugly barracks now surrounded by snow, and she expectantly waits. He's there now, her love, he will earn, earn a lot of money, and in the spring, they'll be married. "Stay with Father," he had said, "you don't need to work anymore. Stay with Father, he needs you." And she had certainly wanted to stay in this magical silent forest and in this storybook cottage among the apple trees.

Now that the weather is cold, the old man and she must sleep in the cottage's warmest room, which lies on the lee side of the north. In the other room the walls can easily frost. The old man says, "Undress, child, don't be embarrassed, but don't take off so much that you freeze; it will be cold before morning." And she undresses piece by piece. Her arms gleam white against the dark window, and the fire gives her young face a glowing shimmer, but her eyes look far, far away over the heath and the forest, while she loosens her long black hair and warms her feet at the fire. The old one, *ja,* she doesn't look directly at him, he's so old, he doesn't know—she smiles to herself and brushes out her hair.

But the old one looks and looks, and all of his young man's splendor springs up in his mind. *Jungfru,* a virgin used to be called in the old days. A young woman was called *jungfru* in the old man's time. And here sits a little *jungfru* in his cottage, smiling to herself and combing her long hair and warming her feet by the fire, by his fire in his cottage, the cottage for which he had carried every log on his back. And she, the *jungfru,* late she had come, for now he is old, will soon die, but she had thought his cottage was better than paradise; she hadn't thought it too little, too poor, and she had sung every day.

With his powerful old hands he wants to warm those cold feet. He wants to do everything for her who had come with happiness for his old age. But she looks beyond the forest and smiles; she doesn't see an old man now in that quiet, white winter evening whose splendor nourishes longing and dreams.

He straightens his back. He is proud of his strength and his health, proud of his cottage that lies, low and plain, crouching against the forest and mountain, but now is lustrous with richness, with youth, with memories, with all of life's wonderful power and glory.

Ellen lies down in her bed in the farthest corner of the room and murmurs good night. The old man lies long awake. He thinks of how fast the time has gone since the day in June Ellen had come. How every day has been like a party, how he, a lonely man, has had someone to talk with the whole day. Everything has become so pleasant in the cottage, scrubbed, starched, pressed, the curtains, the linen. And she, herself, is clean and neat. She has told him so much—about the city, the alleys, about her mother she remembers so well, about Aunt and Uncle and the terrible yard they lived in, about the strange "aunt" who hanged herself when she got the letter from her son. "She was certainly proud," Ellen had said, "she thought his being a mailman wasn't good enough." But he had shaken his head and said, "No, she wasn't proud. Don't think that, Ellen. It was something else." But he couldn't explain what it was.

He knew that his older sons were in Norway, and he had vague thoughts that he hardly dared to think through for himself, that they should stay there a long time. He was tired of trouble and cares. He wanted to have a little happiness. And it was happiness that he experienced. It was a joy to come home from the day's work and find her waiting, dressed up and fine, and the cottage, straightened up and shining, and she never tired of hearing about Bernhard, everything he had said and done when he was little, and he has had to tell her over and over again how he had once upon a time, long ago, built this place. And what the villagers had said, and how they had laughed at his apple trees, but now wanted to buy his fruit. One day when he had walked through the village, one of the old women had said to him, "That's a very good and pretty girl you're thinking of getting for your son to marry, Mr. Olsson. I hope she'll only be content now with you." *Ja,* life wasn't bad at all in spite of his eighty years.

The night painted ice on the windows, but inside, the walls stayed warm while the stars twinkled. Ellen breathed lightly in safe sleep, and the old one folded his hands and prayed to God for the *jungfru.* It had been a long time since he had prayed, many years.

The sun shines on a mother and a baby through the western window. Ellen gives her little one her breast. He drinks and swallows and chokes with the effort to get down all he can at once. Then he goes off to sleep, dozes full and content, a little warm bundle in his mother's lap.

Ellen feels she's alone in the whole world with her baby, far from the city, from groping men, from the shrieking and murmuring, alone with her baby and Grandfather, with the sun, with birds, and apple trees. She often forgets that one day she had been up to an old deaf, and she had thought, dumb, priest, and been married to Bernhard. Bernhard, *ja.* He was a little too much for a good time still. Once he had come home drunk, just the day before the baby's birth, and Grandfather had really been angry and given him a talking to. She had heard him through the wall of the little room Grandfather had taken for himself. Then things had been fine for a long time. But he was so far away always. The railroad camp was farther up north, and it was a wild life there. The farther into the forests the railroad stretched, the wilder and looser the morals became. Bernhard was never really sober when he came home, but he was sweet and happy and took a tremendous pride in the baby, and then Ellen was happy, too.

The solitude, nature's beauty and variety had given her a desire for dreams and air castles. Everything outside was magnificent, clean, in harmony. It deeply affected her. She was enchanted by the sunlight through the pines or the moonlight over the snowfields, over leafing birch trees, over flowers and budding apple trees. In her enchantment she thought that everything outside of nature was gray, dirty, diminished. She thought the baby looked imperfect when she stood with him in the garden and looked at the loveliness of the apple trees.

She became too exacting with herself. She washed and ironed constantly. She washed the baby. She washed herself every time she went to the outhouse. She used up so much soap, and Grandfather often wondered why she had the door locked.

Ellen was not conventionally beautiful. She was well proportioned, and motherhood had given her fullness. She was attractive with her thick dark hair and pleasant gray eyes. The excessive care she was now taking with herself gave her charm and freshness. Bernhard became more and more in love with her.

He avoided his friends, looked twice at his money when the beer brewer came, and rail workers gambled for beer. As often as he could, he traveled home, and one day when he heard about a big job only twelve miles from home, he quit the railroad at once and looked for new work. But Ellen's steady refrain was "Wash yourself, don't pick up the baby, you'll get him dirty, let me be, wash yourself, you're getting me dirty." And Bernhard, infatuated and submissive, washed and tidied himself, obediently put on the clean clothes she'd laid out, and found Ellen more and more desirable the more inaccessible she made herself. Burning with love and suffering, he became a perfect lover to his own wife, obeying her every whim. For it was only whim, he thought, as stingy as she was with her love.

The vital physical act that Bernhard's happiness always wanted to find release in was like a horror to Ellen. It was vice, shameful, vile. She saw at once the slum's streetwalkers; she remembered groping hands and coarse shouts and old men with candy sacks. She remembered the alley quarrels, where sexual intercourse was openly derided as the most repulsive thing in creation, she remembered, *ja*, she remembered the boy from the painting, but then her thoughts quieted down, and she dreamed vague, unspeakable dreams.

All the slum's dreadfulness has come between Ellen and her husband.

One night Bernhard cries, shakes with sobs. The baby is sleeping, Grandfather, too. Bernhard's sobbing cuts through the silence, and Ellen thinks that everyone in the world must be able to hear him. "No, Bernhard, no but . . ." and Ellen begins to cry herself. Pressed tightly to each other, both of them crying, Bernhard whispers, "Why don't you like me? I do everything you say, everything I do, but you only say no; I will be rough with you, you are mine, mine!" And he crushes her against himself.

"*Ja*, but I do like you! I only don't want . . . it's so horrid in here where the baby is sleeping. I don't want to, and I don't want to have more children either, Bernhard, not more . . . Bernhard, have you seen how clean everything is outside, the pines and firs and apple trees and stars, everything. You don't understand. I think that what we do is so dirty. Bernhard, I do like you!"

And Bernhard sits up and looks at her, looks for a long time at her, and love gives him the right words, and he says,

"You are more beautiful than flowers and trees and stars and everything you're talking about, and you are my wife. Ellen, be nice to me."

The summer goes and the fall comes. Grandfather often stays home from his day's work, and Ellen goes instead. To bind the grain, or dig potatoes, or pick berries is like an adventure, something she had read about in books after she had served beer the whole day in the cafe. Grandfather and Ellen earn money, proudly showing Bernhard what they have bought while he's been away—a shirt, a breadboard, a towel, a picture.

And the barn roof is put on. A lame old man, Liter-Olle, once a junkman, who lives about three miles away, has helped Grandfather. Ellen and Grandfather had bound the reeds for the roof themselves.

Ja, she can take care of herself now, and something of the self-conscious farmer comes over Ellen every time she looks at the barn roof. She can do things herself in a pinch; she doesn't need to run to the store for everything. There are reeds in the lake, and when the winter freezes it over, she can just help herself to them for a roof!

For the first time in a long while, Bernhard comes home drunk. Before he says hello, he begins fondling and kissing Ellen, without caring if he's hurting the baby she's holding on her arm. Roughly he grabs at her between her legs, and furious with pain, she hits him, and then rushes with the baby in to Grandfather.

Grandfather doesn't say anything. Taking the boy from her, he locks the door, and they sit there quietly. They hear Bernhard swearing, splashing in the water (her blow had struck his nose), throwing the furniture. Then he pounds on the wall, yelling, "Get in here and set out the food! What the hell are you running in there for? What do you have to do with the old man?" Ellen and Grandfather silently wait;

even the baby is quiet. Then they see Bernhard stagger outside, see him stumble, fall, strike himself. Raging, he pounds an apple tree with his hands and head. Then he rushes away.

The tough-needled firs scratch his face as he plunges down the lane. He runs through the village, and beginning to sober up, he takes the main road and slows his pace. He feels sick, the cold sweat runs, and his mouth burns. He goes to the nearest tenant farmer's place. *Ja,* sure, he could get some water, and a drop to drink, a whole liter. In a few hours the tenant farmer and Bernhard are agreed: Women should be beaten when they act crazy, otherwise they'll stay crazy.

The tenant farmer's old woman had one time smashed a full bottle of brandy to bits right under his nose. Right then and there, he had beaten her up so that after that day she never so much as raised her voice more than usual, of course. "There's nothing else to do, Bernhard. Your old woman begins to make hell, just beat her up."

Crazy with drink and with hazy ideas about a great injustice to himself, Bernhard thumps on the cottage door in the middle of the night. Ellen opens it. As soon as he sees her, he strikes her in the face. With a little cry, she falls like a tree. Grabbing her by the hair, he hits and shakes her, the whole time grinning like a madman. Desperately Ellen cries out, and Grandfather, who is already at the door, yells, "What's come over you!" And the old man gives his son a blow that knocks him down. "Dear child!" His big old body is shaking. "Dear child, he hit you!" And he helps her up from the floor.

Bernhard lies where he fell. Intoxication sweeps over him like a black night; he dozes off, snoring wheezily. Horrid, repulsive snores, sounds heard only from the dying or the dead drunk.

Ellen and the baby bed down on the floor in Grandfather's room.

It is a radiant September morning. The apple trees are drooping with fruit, the potato patch is ready to be dug, the scent of asters, sweet peas, and mignonette mingles deliciously, although the frosty nights in the marsh have already brushed as far as the forest edge. Ellen is sitting in the cottage with Grandfather, drinking coffee, good, strong coffee. Her eye and cheek are very swollen, and tears run down Grandfather's cheeks when he looks at her.

He gets the lead water, the only medication in the cottage, except the herbs, of course, that he picks for stomachache and rheumatism. Taking out a soft, worn handkerchief, the only one he owns, and soaking it in the lead water, he wrings it out, and ties it around Ellen's cheeks. And Ellen thinks with such a kind father as Bernhard has, how can he possibly be so mean, that it must be the brandy's doing. Grandfather breaks into her thoughts, "If anyone comes from the village today, you can just say you have a toothache."

"Ja, sure," Ellen says, wanting no village gossip about it either. "But, Grandfather, no excuse will help; either they'll talk or they won't." And Ellen drinks another cup while the baby is at her breast. Her headache begins to leave, and the sunlit day, the brilliant colors of the trees sweep away the night's experience like a bad dream that one doesn't think about anymore. It is impossible to bury herself in thoughts of anger and revenge on such a splendid fall day. And there is work to be done, and Bernhard? Ja, he lies there, still snoring on the floor. The main thing is that nobody comes to call. One's misery ought to be kept to oneself, Grandfather is right about that. Flowers and fruit and fine potato land are all that are suitable to show guests. No lies can be told about them. So Grandfather always says, and Ellen thinks exactly the same.

Grandfather gets a basket, and he and Ellen and the baby go out to pick the fall fruit.

Bernhard's punishment is hardly to be borne. His wife

walks around with a black eye. And *he* had hit her, hit Ellen. Why? He doesn't know. Ellen who is the best in the world, so indescribably beautiful with her black hair and her white breasts. And the baby. There she sits now, holding the boy, and has a disfigured face. He nearly wishes that the Bellman singers, who had been so crazy about Ellen, would come; if they could see how he'd acted, he'd really get beaten up. He's about to go crazy, lying there like a hog and vomiting. And she sits there, giving the baby her breast, smiling at the boy. And then, *ja,* her eye looks so nasty, and her cheek is green and yellow.

She cleans up after him, all the vomit, and says, "Drink coffee, now, Bernhard, and help Grandfather with the potatoes after a while."

Good God and all devils! He had beaten her as if she had been a card cheat or a hooligan in the barracks. Not even streetwalkers get beatings, that he knows. He goes out to the woodshed, the usual place for working off a hangover. The whole day he chops wood and drinks water, sometimes wiping his cheeks with his rough fists, for the sweat runs in the corners of his eyes. Ellen offers him food. No, he can't eat.

"No, they didn't do that in the safe, either; they never ate, just drank," Ellen mutters bitterly to herself.

It is evening, as still as it can only be after a September day in a forest cottage. Bernhard sits alone in the kitchen and looks at the harvest moon climb over the edge of the forest. He looks out over the garden and the field as if it were something new. He has, in fact, never seen this scene before, although he was born here. He has never seen a clear September night over the forest and mountain, because he has never before been so sad, so full of regret. Everything has become so worth striving for, and he thinks that the moon and fields are about to leave him. Everything is so fair outside, and he's here in the darkness alone, abandoned, hated. Ellen is sleeping, and the baby; Father probably is asleep, too. Bernhard sees how beautiful the night and his home are, and at the same time he is certain that everything is lost. For Ellen can't forgive this.

The place lies like a perfect being, letting the moon shine on its nakedness, on its perfection. Only he must sit here, huddled up, brooding, regretting much, so much. Think of just Father! So mean they've been to him always, telling him a lot of lies, bragging, making a dirty mess for him. *Ja*, not since Ellen has come. . . . He sits for a long time, looking out, and he *forgets* in the peaceful beauty of the night. It begins to brighten, begins to ease, feels not so hopeless any longer. He goes slowly in to Ellen, bows over the bed, and says, "Forgive me, otherwise I can't live." And she draws him to her and says, *"Ja, ja."*

While Ellen rests her head on his arm, he lies long awake. Warm with passion he wants to embrace her, wants to say the most beautiful words he can think of, words that he has learned from Kiruna-Sven, who wrote songs and shot himself with dynamite. He feels his passion heighten and his blood pound, but the moonlight shines almost threateningly over Ellen's disfigured cheek, and he clenches his teeth and mumbles, "Damned brandy." Finally he sleeps, sloughing off his day of torment.

Ellen carefully moves away from him. She lies and looks at the room. Everything looks so neat; it feels so peaceful with the baby in his cradle, with Grandfather on the other side of the wall, and Bernhard. *Ja*, his contrition has filled her, radiated through her, with a shining hope. She wants to bless her bruised cheek and her black eye. Now at last maybe there'll be peace. Now at last maybe Grandfather can get some peace, now their home will be calm, the home that Ellen loves like a living person. The slums and cafes won't come anymore to haunt the forests of the night. She becomes more and more wakeful. She gets up, throws a shawl around herself, and sits at the window. The dew drops from the trees. The stubbled field below the forest line looks like a lake with a belt of cotton sailing above its surface. She sees something move in the belt of mist.

Enormous shapes free themselves from the mist. One, two, three, majestically they glide over the stubble and dive in the forest's shadows. They are elk. Fascinated and a little disturbed, Ellen stares at them. It's the first time she has seen elk. It is their month now. It is now the month when last year's elk calf snorts at his father, and the giant animal with its many branched antlers snorts back. The family is breaking up. The young going his way, the old keeping his cow, guarding her, fighting for her.

It is September, the grass-eating elks' month.

So deliciously beautiful and curious everything is. Life is so splendid. Ellen wants to sing, to talk, but no one is awake. Slowly she goes out in the night and steals through the garden. Maybe they're still around. Maybe she will get to see the wondrously magnificent sight once more here alone in the night. Here, when her heart sings with hope and joy.

Bernhard! Never will he drink anymore. She believes that fully and firmly. The elk do not appear, and with a little shiver, Ellen comes to her senses. She is standing only in her nightgown with a shawl on her shoulders. Shaking with cold, she goes into the peaceful kitchen, and gets in the warm, comfortable bed. Sitting awake, she looks at her husband, and bending over him, she kisses him, and lies down near him to sleep.

But the night is bewitched. A violent restlessness comes over her. She feels burning hot, her limbs feel stretched, her sexual organs tighten, and a powerful lust grips her. Grips her so she becomes afraid. Now she is in the middle of something she never understood when it was discussed. She has had a child, experienced love's painful embrace, but passion is unknown to her. Trembling with desire and with something like shame, she longs to get up again, but is drawn irresistibly to the sleeping man. Trembling, frightened, embarrassed, she throws her arms around him. "Bernhard, Bernhard," she whispers. He mumbles in his sleep, "Poor Ellen, forgive me!" She presses herself nearer him, burrows her head in his chest, then feels how her cheek and eye ache. The thoughts come like choking steam: He hit me! He dragged me by the hair! He gave me hell, and I'm lying here now, now tonight, and he did that last night, and there the baby lies, and I, what do I want? What will I say if he wakes up? It becomes a great struggle for the genteel woman who doesn't tolerate blows from a man, a struggle between instincts and pride. For Ellen it becomes in an obscure way a moral struggle.

She is caught off guard, feels herself shameless. Thinking to wake the man there who hit her yesterday, to wake him and be good to him as never before. No, no, it can't happen. Never. Oh, the shame of everything. She didn't know what forces she was struggling with.

The monk and the nun swore before God their vow of chastity, and the skeleton of a child was found under a hundred-year-old rosewood tree by people in a later time.

Morality is a grim god. Grimmer is lust's god.

Lust's god grins with his death skull and says, "Expect nothing from me, I can only kill." Lust's god is a polite god.

Morality sits there enigmatic and threateningly says, "Maybe, maybe." In eternity he sits there with his maybe.

Ellen's convictions are firm as a rock.

The darkness is thick and dangerous, lies sinfully and suffocatingly around the act when a new life comes into being. Such longing, such urges must be choked. A wife ought to be clean, marriage exists for the clean. Her passion, her quivering young body, her womb's eagerness for fecundation are lust, are lowness. Sin must be conquered. That is morality's message. So is it established society's message. The woman is her man's humble servant, the man shall love and honor his wife. How shall a man be able to love and honor a wife who wakes him in the middle of the night for the sake of her passion? Men, accustomed to bought women, want to have a clean wife that they can honor. Ellen, who has grown up in the slums, doesn't want to be like those women without shame. She has seen them at close quarters. Shameless. Double morality thrives undisturbed in the slums. The privilege of love is an unknown thing there: love is lust.

Stealing sun, food, all life's bodily necessities is nothing to stealing love's privilege for the people in the slums. In poverty, love between the sexes becomes lust. The rich think so, and the poor think often as do the rich.

Ellen, growing up in the slums with their twilight wisdom is not one who could break with a thousand years' hypocrisy. She fights her battle between sound passion and morality while the night passes as slowly as tormenting pain.

The morning sun shines harshly on her pale face with its bruised cheek. At the sight, a man, already contrite, is even more humbled. Over and over again he is sure he is worthless. Again he begs for forgiveness, embracing her tenderly and carefully as if she had become holy through his brutal handling.

To his surprise, happiness, and great delight, she throws her arms hard around him, whispering incomprehensible things in his ears. The night darkness is gone, the sun shines, two people embrace each other in passion and love.

Life's richness is no myth.

"I hit you, dear love."

"Ack, I could have fallen down and hurt myself worse. You didn't mean to. We'll not talk about it any more."

The frost comes and kills, but it spares what shall live.

Ellen, smiling, knowing, inscrutable as a Mona Lisa, walks around Appledale with a black eye and love's joy in her heart.

Night after night the autumn stars cross the sky in

twinkling caravans. If the night is cloudy, if the sky is as dark in the evening as the forest of firs beyond the marsh, Ellen still feels the stars glinting behind them.

The days' gray is not noticed. Life is full and whole. A man is won to one of life's many meanings, home and passionate union with a woman.

When the manor house begins logging its forest, Bernhard stays away from the railroad camp. He goes every day with the forester through the silent, untouched forests and marks, measures, and paces out the boundary lines, for the gentleman of the manor house must have money, and now, as it always is, it is the defenseless that will be plundered—the forest.

"It is ripe," the forester says, "it needs cutting." The forester is a faithful worker, wanting only to hear good about his master. The forest is ripe.

Every night Bernhard comes home to his wife and cottage, home to food, drink and cleanness and a crowing little son.

The bed is made, gleaming white pillowcases, everything is clean. He remembers the dirty pillows and black sleeping-bunks in the barracks as a nightmare, as a Monday after a week's drinking.

He is as tender as a child, and he stands with Ellen at night, looking at the autumn sky's stars so long that his neck aches, for a working man's neck often aches when he looks at the sky—he is used to staring at the earth and the mine pits. Bernhard becomes so soft and pliant in spirit that when Ellen and he walk together to feed the pig, he says, "The pig is so happy with us that I hardly want to be around when he's butchered."

"Nor I, but I can certainly see he's fat enough, as heavy as any in the village," Ellen says.

The old man is quite lonesome these days. Little Bernhard is the only one who is still like himself.

There are many descendants, second cousins, third cousins in a family. Frequently they meet, for the country is small, without knowing they are related. Sometimes when there's talk about a bleaching field, a plum orchard, and a drowned relative, they find out that they're distantly related.

Not many of them own land. Most of them are employed, are maids, hired men, housekeepers, weavers, railroad workers, machinists, telephone operators. Someone has a cafe like "Aunt," Ellen's foster mother, many are musicians, some write books, one's a murderer, all have many children, frequently illegitimate, and there are often suicides, but the family grows steadily larger. Mother Sofi's curly blonde hair appears more frequently in the male descendants than in the women, who are often heavy, dark, and melancholy by nature.

Sally is one of the few women in the family who inherited Mother Sofi's light hair and features. By chance it had happened that she had been the only one in the third generation who had got to hear Mother Sofi's story in detail, who had cried over it, had been fascinated by it, and from her southern suburb, had longed for the plum orchard and the bleaching field.

Sometime she would go there, sit under the whitebeam tree, and listen to the purling river.

Ellen walks through the village, a little out of breath. Her hips are enormously broad.

The old mother* of First Farm screws up her eyes when Ellen greets her. She likes to sit on her porch and let people greet her. *"Ja,* look who's with child," she mutters after Ellen goes by. "They never think of the consequences. It isn't good to have too many children."

The old mother's thoughts wander, wander far back in time. She remembered a church decorated with flowers, a bridegroom, very impressive, and a bride, the bride, herself. Deathly pale, trembling, she tried to follow what the priest was saying. There was a child at home, a dead child, a little blue corpse in her loft chest. Three days ago it had been born; she, the assessor's daughter had given birth to it in the attic, and then had smothered it, although the bridegroom thought he was the father. The bridegroom, the farmer of First Farm, *ja,* he thought he was, but he never would have thought so, if he found out it had already been born, had been fully developed. It was Walloon Bruse, the hired man at Vide Farm who was the father, the curly black-haired hired man, who could play the fiddle and who seldom looked at a woman. He was the father, and black as night was the little corpse's hair.

The church swam before her, the fragrance from the flowers was suffocating; she felt a warm stream of blood between her thighs, and she fainted. *"Ja,"* she said to the priest's question, and then she fainted. A farmer who's also an assessor and a rich son-in-law could help a wife and her daughter out a lot. They didn't know about a little blue corpse with black hair though. The assessor's daughter had had a miscarriage in the church went the rumor, such a thing wasn't so exceptional. She was in any case married. But the rumor grew, and then it was said that one day Bruse had demanded a child from the wife of the farmer of First Farm, the assessor's daughter. "Have you drowned the child?" he had asked.

---

*Mother is used to designate the wife of a farmer who owns a sizable farm. She retains this designation after the death of her husband.

The old mother becomes sad every time she sees someone with child. Then she thinks life is hard, that death is
tardy, for she is eighty years old, has no children, and is a
widow, and now she sits on the porch of her cousin's child.

Ellen walks through the village, greeting everyone,
greeting the mother of North Farm, who was once the maid
there. She had married the owner's son, although her future
father-in-law spit in her face when she told him his son was
the father of the child she was carrying. Ellen hails Crazy
John, holding his cap in his hand and bowing over and over
again. She waves to Västby's epileptic maid who had had
seven children and didn't know any of their fathers.

Beads of sweat trickle down her face; the May sun is
hot, and the child in her womb kicks so forcefully that Ellen
sometimes stops and presses her hands against her stomach
as if to make him be still. While she's waiting, the mother
of Östby comes with her maid on the way to the milk pen,
and nodding to Ellen, she says, "You don't have long now,
Mrs. Olsson." And she and her maid proceed to the pen.

The mother of Östby remembers the day, the shameful,
terrible day at the district court, when she had had to swear
on oath in order to clear her rich fiancé of charges brought
by her family's maid who had had a child and challenged the
validity of the banns for her and her fiancé, the only son of
Östby. Near the courthouse was a tavern, and the maid's
friends and followers had liberally treated the son of Östby
to brandy. Late in the afternoon when the case was called
up, the son couldn't be found. She and her family had
hunted desperately for him, but the maid's lawyer, taking
along two of the jury, had found the son sleeping in the
maid's arms at the court's stables. Naturally the maid won
the case, and her baby got proper support, but everyone
knew, of course, that she had been in court and had sworn
on oath that her fiancé was innocent. He went to America
until the worst talk was over and done with, and then he
came back and married her. But the mother of Östby, whose
hair now is gray, also becomes sad, like the old mother at

First Farm, when she sees the most impressive sight Solomon ever beheld. She has no children. But there are always maids at Östby, of course, and the parish gets to bring up many children that Östby's maids come dragging along.

Ellen is afraid of the village. She had heard so much slander, so many lies there, especially in the store. Such nasty things were said there and in the village. One Sunday when Crazy John had come to Appledale to beg a little tobacco, he had said, "You're a rail worker's chick."

"Who says so?" Ellen had asked.

But then Crazy John had blinked and whistled and hopped on one leg, holding his hand over his mouth. "Maybe at Vide they say that," Grandfather had said gruffly. Crazy John had snorted and hissed, then had crowed like a rooster. It was at Vide, one of the largest, richest farms of the village, that Grandfather had found his bride.

Ellen had often noticed how most of the old people in the village fussed over Grandfather, particularly the women, like the old daughter at Ängsbo. She had been in love with her father's hired man who had then been killed on his way to the market, and faithful to her love, she had never married. Old daughter, as she is called, had once said to Ellen, "Old Olsson could dance and was very handsome, but after he started building that house and got married to Anna from Vide, he acted just like somebody who was religious."

It is uphill, always uphill. Ellen is on her way to the shoemaker, to Liter-Olle, the lame old man who had helped Grandfather with the barn roof. She had been in the district so long now that she knows what people are called, knows all their nicknames, and no one has ever heard any other name for the shoemaker than Liter-Olle.

Now at the end of May, when the wild cherry trees are in bloom, she had felt an overwhelming desire to get away. No one seems to mind that she is dressed up, though it's a weekday, and strolling leisurely through the village, not when one is "so far along" as Ellen. Now that she has the village behind her, she isn't sure about the way, although Grandfather had pointed out the cottage one day in late fall when they had been gathering lingonberries. "There's the worst scoundrel hole in the countryside," he had said. Ellen hadn't answered. For the first time she had doubted Grandfather's judgment, for she had happened to meet Liter-Olle's daughter-in-law in the village store, and instantly she had liked her. It is soon six months since that day, but is as vivid to Ellen as if it were yesterday. It is as if she had brushed against something she'd always been waiting for, as if she'd encountered some friend from her dreams, and couldn't remember how the dream went.

The storekeeper had invited Ellen for coffee after the woman from the "scoundrel hole" had left. She had the same opinion as Grandfather, "Ja, Mrs. Olsson, you heard how brazen she was. They owe a lot of money here, and if we take our shoes to Liter-Olle, he won't fix them. You know he's called Liter-Olle because he used to run an illegal gin shop."

Ellen had listened politely, drinking her coffee in the storekeeper's fine kitchen. But she sees there in front of her a woman with big gray eyes, strangely lustrous, light golden curly hair, a mouth that smiles scornfully when she orders "a hecto of the best candy," which the storekeeper obediently weighs up although it's taken on credit. While the storekeeper counts up the herring, kerosene, pork, yeast, and soap, and the hecto of the best candy, the woman says, her big shining eyes indifferently glancing over Ellen's figure, "When I've had my baby, I'll come down and do some day work in the garden for you or help with the spring cleaning, for I haven't any money." Even her voice had delighted Ellen. It was so sad, so rich, and so young. Ellen suddenly remembered her mother. . . . But after the woman had left, and the storekeeper had invited Ellen for coffee, she called all of Liter-Olle's family "a pack of thieves."

"But she was so beautiful and young."

"Beautiful? You can't live on that very well." Ellen had thanked for the coffee, thinking that there are many who live on being beautiful and who don't need to buy pork and kerosene and the "best candy" on credit and pay with work when the fourth or fifth child is born. Ellen didn't know how many children the young woman at Mårbo had. But now Ellen is on her way there to Mårbo, the right name for Liter-Olle's cottage. She had felt such an irresistible longing that she would have gone without an excuse, without the package of worn-out shoes, but it is good to have them for an excuse, for it is hard to come without an errand to folks.

She struggles untiringly up the hill, continuously uphill. The forest ends, and the mile-long clearing begins. Hill against hill as far as the eye can reach, and gray stumps, gold stumps on every hill. It was as if the sea had stiffened after a hard storm, as if all the world's ships had gone under in the storm, and all their rubbish, kegs and tubs had stiffened fast in an eternal swell. On one of the highest crests, with its thousand kegs and tubs illuminated by the May sun, and with the freshest stumps shining like giant spring lilies, lies Mårbo, "the scoundrel hole." Ellen stands for a long time looking at that unusual sight. The smallest cottage she'd ever seen seems tossed up like a little barge on the forest's highest crest.

Suddenly a whining howl from the stumps cuts through her thoughts. Another, then another, the whole place is filled with noise. She listens, a little frightened, although the sun shines. *Ja,* the howling is coming from up there at Mårbo. Now again. What in the name of God are they doing?

Finally she climbs the last hill while the howling continues. There at the corner of the cottage a woman holds a howling, snarling hunting dog by the scruff of its neck, beating it furiously with a strap. The dog is powerfully built, with broad shoulders and a large head, its teeth threateningly bared at the woman with every lash of the strap. The woman is too near the dog, hitting him not more than several times, and the dog is nearly getting the better of her. Fiery red in her face she lifts him by the scruff of his neck high up in the air, as if she were going to throw him against the cottage, almost like a rug that one shakes the dust from. At the same time Liter-Olle limps up, shrieking, "Are you crazy, you damned whore! Are you going to kill the dog?"

The woman catches sight of Ellen. Dragging the dog along with her, she flicks the drunk old man on the face with the strap. Then she pulls the dog to the outhouse where the hook and chain are fastened, leashes him, veering away before he can reach her with his jaws. She strikes the dog again. Liter-Olle limps again to the corner of the cottage, yelling incessantly, "Are you going to kill the dog, you damned whore!" But he doesn't dare to move. He hasn't noticed Ellen. The woman continues to beat the dog. He stops snarling, howling more and more plaintively, and then lies down, rolling and whining. Shaking and nearly crying, Ellen steps forward and calls, "Please, please don't beat the dog anymore!" The woman only looks up at her with glistening eyes and gives the dog another lash.

"Go in, Mrs. Olsson! Go in to my children! Go in to the children!" She slaps the dog again who menacingly snarls at the stranger, and Ellen hurries past Liter-Olle and goes into the cottage.

Nearly stumbling over a big cradle, for it is half-dark in the room in spite of the sun outside, she sees a boy, about four years old, nearly naked with blood streaming from his shoulder and plump little thigh. He is sobbing and stammering, "You damn dog, you—you damn dog, you." A little girl, who looks about six, huddles in a corner, her hands over her face, rocking herself back and forth, and wailing, "Hear how he swears, don't swear, don't swear, then the devil comes and gets you, you know." Neither of the children takes any notice of Ellen, wholly absorbed in the drama they are taking part in.

Putting down her package, Ellen tries to get her bearings. She sees a clean handtowel on the wall and finds some soap and water. "You damn dog, you, you damn dog," the little boy cries over and over. And the little girl rocks more and more despairingly and sobs, "Don't swear, the devil will come in here and get you."

The baby in the big cradle sleeps. At his feet, another little child is sleeping, rolled up like a bundle, and on a bench still another sleeps.

Ellen dips the handtowel in the water, saying, "If you let me wash the blood off, you'll be better right away."

The boy doesn't answer her. "You damn dog," he says when Ellen washes him. The wounds are ugly, and his clothes are torn to shreds. Beginning to calm down, he looks searchingly at Ellen, and making a funny little forlorn face at her, he holds up his knee, "Here, too." He whimpers a bit again. It smarts when the wet towel touches the wounds.

The little girl comes over. "He hasn't anything to put on." Ellen looks around.

"Can't you find something for him to wear?"

"There's nothing, nothing's left. The dog tore everything up."

"You damn dog," the boy says, looking as if he were going to cry again. Ellen feels dizzy . . . the long walk and this upsetting scene. Suddenly she thinks of the thin white underskirt she has on. With shaking hands, she takes it off and wraps it around his chubby body. Sitting down quickly on a chair with the boy in her lap, she asks,

"Will you get me some water to drink?" The girl brings her a dipper full. Ellen drinks and feels steady again.

The girl delightedly fingers the embroidered edging of the underskirt. "Are you leaving this here after you've gone home? Did you bring shoes to Liter-Olle?"

"He's called Grandfather, that's what Mama's said," the boy says emphatically.

"You have such a big stomach," the girl says. "Mama has a big stomach, too."

Accustomed as she had been to the calm of an only child home in Appledale, Ellen wonders how on earth a person could stand it here. So many little ones, just the girl's chatter gets on her nerves, think of all the rest—a crazy dog that bites a child and tears his clothes to shreds, and the cottage so cramped, so dark, built probably for just one person to live in, and the road to this place! Only people with hard natures and feet like leather could live here. How could *she,* the woman, stand it? With a drunk father-in-law that shouts damned whore when *folks* come? How could a person, a mother, a beautiful young woman stand it with things like this?

"Do we get to keep your skirt? Why don't you answer? Say if we can keep the skirt."

"Ja, if your mama wants it."

"She won't want it; she never wants to have anything, but I want it. Bruno is sleeping now, so you can put him down. It's Papa and Liter-Olle, and the fishermen who tease the dog. Have you seen fishermen? They have rubber boots, rubber! The same as they make balls from, have you seen the balls in the store?"

The door opens, and with the strap in her hand, the woman steps inside. Both the women look silently into each other's eyes. The little girl, looking from one to the other, nods her head, her willing tongue unable to find words in her haste, there's so much to explain. "She's leaving the skirt here," she finally says.

Putting down the strap, the woman sits beside the cradle. Silently she looks with sparkling eyes at Ellen. *"Ja,* so you've got tired now, you damned whore!" Liter-Olle yells, fumbling at the door.

"Be quiet, Liter-Olle! We have company!" the girl shouts.

"*Ja,* you'll be a whore, too!" the old man hollers, jerking open the door.

The woman gets up, and grabbing the strap, lashes him in the face. Swearing and crying in anger and drunkenness, he stumbles out. The dog begins to growl and bark again. "*Ja,* now you see, Mrs. Olsson, how we have it here." She sits down again beside the cradle. She is deathly white and can't sit up straight. Ellen sees that she is far along with child. Aching with compassion, she can't reply. The brutal scene when the woman beat the dog—that she understands. She, herself, would probably have carried on worse or crazier if it had been her own child who'd been bitten, would have taken a stick and beaten the hide off the dog. And the old man! "You'll be a whore, too"—he had shrieked to a little girl. That sounds familiar! The alleys and taverns, peep-holes, and rats come back. She is suddenly furious. Maybe it's the vision she'd had of the little barge on the forest crest, the sunny greenness of spring, the solitude on her way here that make her anger so strong now at finding the insults and dreadful ways of the slums up here. She wants to go out, right then and there, and beat the old man. Beat, beat, it would be good. It is as if all the world's shrieking drunk mouths, hypocritically holy mouths, snuff-filled mouths, moralistic mouths with their everlasting "whore" could be choked up, if she were to go out now and beat that shrieking old man on his mouth. Those brandy-fogged brains that shrieked "whore" to a mother and to a mother's little girl, that pious morality spewing out of his brandied brains as it does from all mean and stupid brains and hearts.

(Poor Liter-Olle, the insult had become a custom with him. He hardly gave a thought to its meaning. In his drunken confusion it was the only insult that came to him. Though it didn't mean a thing to him, he had noticed how, surprisingly, people got angry when he used it, and that was the only weapon he had had in all his life, to anger people. No one is so powerless that he can't find a weapon.)

"You were right to hit the old man," Ellen says in a loud voice.

"I don't know," the woman replies, "I don't know if it's right. He's old and lame. Right or not, I had to do something."

They are silent. The little ones breathe heavily in their sleep. Even Edith is silent.

"My name is Sally."

"And mine is Ellen."

"And mine Edith," the little girl says, trying to look as vexed as Ellen had awhile ago. The women smile.

Here is Sally again, Sally from the southern suburb where people died from the "innocent's sickness," Sally from the moonlake, the moonlake that she had floated over in an ox-cart, had floated slowly over, rubbing out everything old, believing the old lay at the bottom of the lake, Sally who had played at the garbage dump, never meeting Ellen, although she had been in that same playground.

And why shouldn't Ellen have remembered her mother the day she first had seen Sally and had heard her voice in the store? Sally and Ellen are children of the third generation of Mother Sofi from the Big Farm.

"I'd better get something to cheer us up, you look so worn out, Mama," Edith says. Sally and Ellen laugh.

"No, I'll set the coffee pot on to cheer us up, for you look all worn out, too, and Ellen certainly needs something to perk herself up."

While the coffee is being ground, Ellen seems to hear again the storekeeper's voice—"yeast, herring, kerosene, a hecto of the best candy," and Sally's voice, that clear good voice she had remembered all her life but couldn't place—"when I've had my baby, I'll come and work for you."

A new Mother Sofi, new clamoring little children, but no Big Farm, no miles of unfruitful land, no cow or calf. Sally is alone. There is no one, no friend—Grandma dead, Father dead, Mother back again in the southern suburb. Sally is in the middle of a frightening adventure, where there are only barren hills and clamoring children that she has to find food for.

Sally opens a wallpapered door, and where Ellen had thought there'd be only a closet, is a little room, the smallest she'd ever seen. It is furnished with a small table and two chairs. A bright rag rug covers the floor. Ellen notices that the rug is not woven. It is braided of rags of many colors artfully sewn together to form a pattern. The walls are papered with old issues of *Witness to the Truth*, yellowed with age. Open shelves, put up every which way, cover most of the walls, and are full of ragged books tied into packets. The only bound volume among all the paperbacks is an old Bible. Under the table and in the corners are big bundles of newspapers tied with string. On a single small shelf below the window stands a little, brightly polished copper lamp, one with an open burner without glass. It looks so peculiarly old, as if it could have been lost by a foolish virgin in legend.

In the midst of the burning revolution of 1791, the French engineer, Argenner, had been busy with an invention for mankind's material illumination, and he had found it to the extent that eighty years later, his Argenner burner with glass had gone over the world. The revolution had become less epoch making, going in for intellectual illumination and daily bread, but at Mårbo there still isn't enough to buy a lamp with glass, nor enough to waste kerosene.

"What a beautiful old lamp," Ellen exclaims.

"*Ja*, and it uses up so little kerosene. I always read and write a bit after the children are asleep. The books here and all the newspapers are my father-in-law's. He got them in the days when he bought up junk, and I've taken them over and arranged them. There are lots of interesting books, newspapers, too, though they're old. I found the lamp in his junk, too. It's too bad you had to hear all that row. My father-in-law's not mean, but he drinks and gets confused. Take a book, Ellen, while the coffee boils." She takes her sleeping boy from Ellen. "Here is my oldest son," she says, sounding as if Mårbo were an entailed estate, Mårbo, which the poor relief board wants forty kronor a year for in rent. "Go in and sit down, Ellen. Choose a book."

"Have you read all of them?" Ellen asks, stepping into the room, which smells of juniper. In a corner an enormous broom of juniper and birch leaves stands in a butter churn.

"*Ja*, sure, the whole lot. There aren't as many as it looks. Do you like to read?"

"*Ja-a*, stories for sure, but I haven't time."

"Time, *ja*, well, I probably shouldn't have that either, but one can always find some time. There isn't much to do, you can see, Ellen, when you don't have anything."

Edith proudly runs with cups and saucers. Putting a bottle of wood anemones on the table, she says to Ellen, "We'll get two aprons from your skirt."

Ellen smiles. "I'll give you a new apron."

"Do you have money? We never have any. Mama has just one apron, but she never puts it on. Come in now, Mama, and sit down. They're all sleeping so it's quiet. Liter-Olle must be, too. He always does that when he's drunk too much, and then he's nice again. Come, Mama, so I can pour the coffee."

Sally brings in a plate of rye bread. Slipping in with a tiny, soiled package and smiling contentedly, Edith unwraps it and with an air of mystery, she puts a dried-up bit of cake on top of Ellen's slice of rye bread. Sally comes with the coffeepot. "You still have that old bit of cake left! Dear child, Ellen doesn't want it! At Appledale they have plenty of everything. You remember how Grandfather bragged when he came from their place. I'll have to let you know, Ellen, she's had that bit nearly half a year now. She got it last fall from the teacher when he brought his class up here on a school trip to the forest. Even over Christmas she saved it,

103

and she's offered it to both the priest and the chairman of the relief board. They didn't want to eat it!" Sally pours the coffee and sits down. Carefully holding her mug with its drop of coffee, Edith sits on a little stool.

Broad through their hips, both expecting new life, the women sit there quietly, blowing on their coffee. Edith is also quiet, watching Ellen intently. "Won't you eat the cake, Aunt? It's clean. I've had it in the paper." The little, bright, flowerlike face, framed with a mass of ash-blonde hair, looks disappointedly at Ellen.

"Thank you, Edith," and Ellen dips the dry, hard cake in her coffee. "You must have a taste, Edith, a little taste; it's so good."

"I have pinched off a bit in one corner. It tasted like oranges. You eat it, eat it all up. Company must have a treat; company doesn't need to share. Mama doesn't want it." Edith looks a little uncomfortably at her. Mama, *ja,* she hadn't really offered her the cake, not during the whole time she'd owned it, but Mama hadn't really ever wanted it, "you eat it," she always had said. Edith isn't completely easy though; Mama should have got to taste it at least, but the company, *ja,* she should see we can have treats here, too.

Ellen chews the dry cake, and her eyes fill with tears. "It must be awful for you, Sally." Her voice trembles.

"*Ja,* it is awful."

"But your man, doesn't he have a job?"

"*Ja,* he's a fisherman, but it doesn't pay much. There are four on the boat, and they've got to be out all the time, and all of them drink. Well, he *can't* be other than what he is. I don't know, everything is so strange. The priest came up here a couple of months ago and preached to me, said that I must baptize the children—he's the one Edith offered her cake to. Then the chairman of the poor relief board runs up here all the time, wanting the rent, for the parish owns Mårbo. Edith offered him her cake, too, but my father-in-law offered him brandy, and he thought that certainly tasted better."

"Have you had the children baptized then?"

"What good does that do whether you're rich or poor? The priest told me that I was a bad woman. 'There is mercy for the worst crimes, for murderers and drunkards, but not for you,' he said. 'That kind of mercy which is so foolish, I don't want,' I said. *Ja,'* he said, 'now I know that everything the decent people in the parish say about you is true. You are a bad woman.' Bad woman—I got angry, Ellen, so I said some bitter things. When he began prattling about decent people, I was furious, for nearly all of those 'decent people' buy brandy on the sly from my father-in-law. 'Bad woman,' I told him, 'that's exactly what the juryman's wife at Lida Farm said to her maid when the maid washed herself and changed her linen—'it's only bad women who fuss like that with themselves,' she said—You know the juryman's wife, don't you, Pastor? You've been there for parties as a matter of fact.' And he said, 'You are utterly shameless, and you're not married and haven't let your children be baptized, but there are laws, there's the children's care committee, and I'll show you that you must have respect for God's law.' *Ja,* that's been a few months ago, and I haven't heard from him. I have enough to do getting money together for a little bread." Sally is quiet.

"I don't like priests, Sally. I think they should just take care of themselves and let folks alone."

"But you have baptized your boy?"

"Ja, we have, of course. Grandfather was in such a hurry for it, though he doesn't like priests either." Ellen defends her highest authority.

"But you slapped the other old man when he tickled you under the chin," Edith puts in.

"Ja, so I did," Sally laughs, "I think you ought to when the chairman of the relief board tickles you under the chin."

They sit there and talk. Sally tells how she tries to do

105

everything possible to get enough for bread, but that children can't live on just bread forever. She cuts rags for housewives in the village, helps them with washing, sews gloves. "I would rather have work that I can do here at home. Grandfather is old. My man is never home, for he is my man, whatever the village and the priest say. And Grandfather drinks, can get drunk just like that, and it won't do to leave the children with him. He has such terrible pain in his leg that I think that's why he drinks so much."

"Do you sew gloves, Sally? I've never heard of such a thing! I've learned to knit gloves, but sew! Please show me." Sally takes out a pair of white gloves made of finespun Swedish wool with red roses sewn on the backs. "You must teach me. Think how fine Grandfather would think these are."

Edith slips out.

"You think a lot of your father-in-law, don't you?"

"*Ja*, he's so kind. I've never met such a wise good man. Everyone's been nice to me since I've grown up. I've had it really good. I wasn't much older than you when I got married. Now Bernhard no longer drinks, comes home every night, and never carouses with the neighbors. I had some worries when I first got married, but now it's so good, I couldn't ask for anything better."

"Things can go better for one than for another. I had three children by the time I was twenty, but that isn't the worst. I can't stand my man any longer. I can't bear him, and I can't get away from here—it's lucky he's never home. Even if he behaved himself, I still couldn't live him, but children there'd be. Maybe the priest is right, maybe I am a bad woman who can't stand her man, who has children, and hardly has food for them. What do you think, Ellen?"

"I don't know. I had a foster mother who lived with her man for thirty years although she couldn't stand him, and they didn't have even one child together. She hanged herself later. It was terrible."

Now they hear Edith chattering to Liter-Olle just out-side the door. As they come in, Liter-Olle says hoarsely, "Well, I heard you had company, really fine company. Thanks, Ellen, for everything when I was at Appledale. Edith gave me your package of shoes. *Ja,* they'll be coming, Ellen. Good to get something to putter with. I was sleeping when Edith brought me your shoes. An old man like me needs to have a snooze the middle of the day, you know, Ellen. Have you got something for us to eat, Sally? Here are a few beans otherwise. Well, Ellen, how did you dare to come up this far in your condition, and a town person like you who's not used to walking up in the forest?"

"She was here when you yelled at us, Grandfather."

"Ja, ja, well, it's a little rowdy up here sometimes. You shouldn't call me Liter-Olle, then I get so mad."

"When you're drunk, I say Liter-Olle, and when you're nice, I say Grandfather," Edith stubbornly answers.

"Then for God's sake, say Liter-Olle, but now let's be happy when we've got company. Ellen doesn't come walk-ing up here every day. Olsson from Appledale, he was a fellow. Well, he isn't finished yet. I wouldn't want to tangle with him. *Ja,* Ellen, you know even before the railroad was built here, everyone who had a hack was on the road to town. I remember when the farmer from Vide, the one be-fore the fellow that's there now—they're only distantly related—well, I remember how he dragged the last sheep he owned on the road in to town to get money for brandy. His cows had long since been sold, and it was then, and still is, the biggest farm in the parish. He was Olsson from Ap-pledale's father-in-law, *ja,* he died then, the old farmer from Vide, and this fellow that's there now bought that big farm. But it was on that trip, when the old farmer from Vide sold his big farm's last animal for brandy, that Olsson from Ap-pledale whipped all the farmers and threw them out of Sand's tavern. He was ungodly strong, Olsson was, and the farmers had provoked him. *Ja,* I'll never forget that trip, for

107

they had fooled me with a blind horse in town. When I unhitched him from the wagon after I got home, he fell on his head in the well which was fifty feet deep. I was called Joker-Olle then, and I lived in Sjöbon on Vide's outlying land. It was cold—twenty degrees—on that trip to town, and my wife had just had a kid, and there I was with my wife and the kids, and just one horse for the wagon that the police would condemn, and the horse I'd just bought in the well. That wasn't a good day for kindness, Ellen. Helpful folks came and threatened me with a summons because the well was ruined for awhile, but there wasn't a whisper about helping me get the cadaver out of the well."

"Drink another cup of coffee now," Sally says, interrupting his torrent of words.

The old man sits quietly and moans, for his body aches. His black eyes, clear and fierce, shine in his wrinkled face. His eyes seem a little too clear, Ellen thinks, when the old man stares at her as if in thought. She thinks he looks like someone in a painting she'd seen—Peter, when the cock crowed the third time. That painting had also hung on many walls in the alleys. Liter-Olle is like Peter, wild, yet humble, startled black eyes, the same carved features, and black curly hair. It is hard to believe that the same man had so recently shrieked those coarse words of abuse. While he quietly drinks his coffee, he stares thoughtfully at Ellen, as if he, himself, wonders why he had heaped abuse on the only ones he really holds dear.

"Poverty—you can either talk it away or swear it away," he says slowly. The others are silent. "You should lawfully marry Frans, Sally, then everything would be better. I was rightfully married, and though I was called Joker-Olle, we held together, my wife and I."

"You shouldn't drink so much, Father," Sally says abruptly.

Liter-Olle thanks for the coffee and limps out.

An afternoon, a milestone, a day that, like a long journey, changes thoughts and views.

The sun is going down in the west, and Ellen realizes that she'd stayed too long, much too long at Mårbo. She hurries home as fast as she can. Edith, Sally, Liter-Olle, everything whirls around in her head. But Grandfather had certainly been unjust to call Mårbo a scoundrel hole. *Ja*, it's some life up there, of course. But think if anyone had come the night Bernhard had beaten her, and Grandfather had protected her, what would they have said then? Everyone has difficulties, and no one needs to be called a scoundrel for that. Poor Sally, not a drop of milk in the house, and the baby had pulled and pulled on her nipples. It had to be just two months left for her to go before she has a new mouth to feed. What does all this misery come to? It's the same in the country as in the city, the same insults, the same poverty. Ellen is already through the village before she comes to the conclusion that however things are now, people always make them better or worse than reality.

Sally is one of the most beautiful and wisest women Ellen has known; her children are well taken care of and well built, whatever folks say. They had certainly gossiped in the slums, too, but there had seldom been any *bite* in the gossip; too many had been poor together.

Bernhard had been ready to meet Ellen when she comes. The table is set—cold meat, cheese, butter, pickled herring. "Dear man, do you have to eat a cold supper?" At the same time, it comes home to her: where she had just been, they certainly would have liked such cold food. "It will do," she adds, "it's not cold out."

"You've been gone so long," Bernhard says. "Father has been like an egg-sick hen, in and out."

"I was sitting there talking. She's a good person, Sally is, but you wouldn't believe how awful she has it. She has to earn money herself for their food. Liter-Olle helps her a little, but he drinks. Do you know her man? What's he like?"

"*Ja*, I know Frans. He isn't married to her, so she can just blame herself."

"He has children by her, and she doesn't want to marry."

"She's only joking. All women want to marry."

That evening in Appledale there isn't time to discuss women's desire to get married. There are things to be done, here, there, and everywhere. Bernhard has to hurry to the village for the help that had been engaged in advance, and the next morning there's a new grandson for the old man in Appledale.

What Liter-Olle remembered

Even an old junkman had once been a child, unbelievable as it seems, a child born to grow up and go around collecting junk, not having a chance to do anything else, for Liter-Olle was the oldest son of the parish's good-for-nothing. With five more in the family, naturally they all had to go out and beg. In those times it wasn't, for that matter, such a terrible shame to go out and beg. It was usual, there was nothing else to do. The entrance to heaven for the affluent was cheaper then than now: a bit of bread given to a poor person, and heaven's door was opened. Everyone had heard the story about the terribly wicked woman who went to heaven because she had given away an onion stalk. Well, she never got there after all, for she was so wicked that she didn't want the other people down in hell to hang on tight to her onion stalk, and God became afraid then of so much wickedness. When he threw down a rescue line disguised as an onion stalk, she kicked and beat her unlucky comrades, wanting to go to heaven by herself on that rescue line. No, God could not be so charitable as to have mercy on such a sinner. She was left in hell.

But what was an onion stalk to a loaf of bread?

The one who gave the bread was sure about salvation.

Liter-Olle and his sisters and brothers walked the parish road, getting a loaf of bread occasionally. Then a new time came, a foolish doomsday time, for the farmers decided that Liter-Olle and his sisters and brothers should go to school just like their children. Two days a week, at the very *least,* they must be in school. Three of them were of school age long ago.

A parish summons was drawn up. Brandy and sandwiches were on the table so the mind could be receptive to salvation, and the farmer of First Farm was willing to give a little food to Liter-Olle and one brother on the days they would go to school, but then they would have to tend his cattle in the summer. The arrangement was clear.

Liter-Olle is ten years old, his brother nine; they wait outside the First Farm's steps for their food before going on to school. It is seven in the morning. On their feet they have pieces of cloth sewn for stockings and wooden shoes. It is cold, is January. The mother of First Farm comes out with a pot of milk and two half-slices of bread, bread black as pitch.

"I don't want you to come in. Drink your milk now so I get the pot back. You can take the bread with you."

That is the food, food for the day.

But the milk is icy and the day is cold. The nine-year-old drinks too much of it, and the whole day he sits beside his brother in school, shaking with cold, never warming up again. The milk has run ice-cold right into his heart. On the way home he lies down, the shivering never ceases. He becomes stiffer and stiffer while the January night gets all the colder, and soon Liter-Olle is left with a dead brother on a desolate road.

He remembers hearing his father curse the Big Farm many times, but Father cursed everything. Liter-Olle never forgets that cold night and his frozen brother. And he never forgets the First Farm's steps, the black bread, the ice bits clinking in the milk, and the mother's fear that they would come in. They had lice, of course.

He remembers being so happy when the message came: "You can eat at the First Farm every day you go to school." He had dreamed about warm food in a warm kitchen. That night his brother lay stiff and cold, dead from starvation and ice milk and flimsy rags. At eighty years Liter-Olle still remembers how thin his brother was when he lay stiff and blue and pitiful on the road. This wasn't the only brother that Liter-Olle saw lying dead on the road. At Christmas, two years later, when they all were out begging, the farmhands on the estate had given brandy to the smallest brother who was seven. He had also died on the road, didn't make it home, dying from cold and alcohol poisoning. Liter-Olle remembers it well.

One summer Liter-Olle tended the cows at the First Farm. One day the farmer of First Farm came out to the field, shrieking, "Drive a cow here! Mother must have milk warm from the cow. Her lungs are hemorrhaging. Quick, quick, drive all the cows together, so we can catch one that has milk!"

But then Liter-Olle drove all the cows away in every direction, yelling, "Your devilish old woman can gladly die, and you, too, you devil!" In his rage he chased the cows through the fields and the village. The mother of First Farm died. She would have died anyway, for sweet milk wouldn't save anyone from lung hemorrhaging, but the village was convinced that she would have lived if Liter-Olle hadn't driven the cows away.

That was the night Liter-Olle became lame. The farmer of First Farm gave him "domestic chastisement," as it was called, and his leg was broken. Father, the good-for-nothing, who knew a little, set the leg as well as he could, but Liter-Olle became lame.

Liter-Olle remembered so much.

All paths are worn.
Only the tree roots lie
like slaves' arms under my feet.
Where is the path where no one has walked?
The corner where no one has cried,
begged, and forgiven?
Where is the corner in the spheres,
where no one cries for bread?

The days go.

How long is a life? The old man in Appledale wonders about this. Life is not, as he believes, a straight line, a row of events like links in a chain. Life is something winding, a tree root, a worn tree root, that grows hidden in the earth and then sometimes winds itself up above ground again.

Life is a circle. The old man finds that nothing is finished. Everything goes back to its starting point. What is so far away comes nearer now, has been near for a long, long time. When he was seventy, he had made a costly journey to reach Mark's sandy plain, to come nearer that curve of life which until then had always seemed farthest away. While the night had slipped by under the stars on the sandy plain, life had turned itself right again, and he had traveled home to his cottage. Life had begun anew.

The old man stoops with difficulty under the fir branches on his way to the village. Long ago he had come through the forests to the village. Now other men had come to the village through the forests, had come with electric lines, with light—a wonder: light on wires, light from water, fire from water. The old myth that there can't be fire from water isn't believable any longer. He had certainly heard of electricity before. The city had had it for many years. But now it was here in the village. Not many in the village had telephone wires fastened to their roofs, but all of them wanted electric light. The old man often goes to the village to see how many now had it.

There's another man who lives there now, one to the old man's taste, a man with an ice-gray mustache and honest eyes. Often they talk together, and sometimes the old railroad worker comes to the old man's cottage, for he's one of the Bellman singers who knew Ellen when she was a girl.

But now the old man is far in the past again, is at the beginning. He hears a voice saying, "You must go out and seek something for yourself!" He is again the young boy who stands on a sandy plain with the whole world before him, ready to go out and seek.

The old man walks through the village. All the old folks are dead. He doesn't know many now. He doesn't see if they wave to him either, for he is so far away; he is in that which had come nearer, digging hole after hole, planting tree after tree, apple trees. Now they yield baskets of fruit sometimes, but the old man only remembers little apple trees, a freshly planed floor, the western sun in a new room, and a woman.

"Go out and seek something!"

Vide Farm's descendants beat with their sledgehammers, sing, dance, fight, love women, and measure the brandy line with their thumbnails. A couple of them wander crazed in the countryside, and people feel sorry for them: "Think, they're so rich and so unlucky," they say. Many of the farm's descendants sit in the mental hospital. It is as if the earth wanted to revenge itself for the overcultivation—for all the digging and plowing year in and year out.

Through the years the turf has been harrowed, cut, and sowed. "Damned clay clods that won't give!" Hard fingers have dug in the seeded earth to see how far the sprouts have come, have pulled out a grain, picking with coarse nails the new sprout from the cracked mother kernel in order to see how it is growing for the brandy keg or baking tray.

115

The fields lie there, aging and graying, and their seeds become shriveled with the years; the fields lie and wait for peace, for groves of trees and clumps of windflowers. No one plows up their roots and exposes the insects and worms to the burning sun. The sun loves color and brilliance. When the earth is plowed and seeded every spring, stripped and defiled every fall, the sun treats it like a whore, gives it no fruit. And the earth revenges itself on men. Gray lines, undefined horizons, mutilated groves, thin, stunted pine forests help her imbue her own tired melancholy into man, deranging him with her own gray barrenness, rooting him out.

Even a wandering workman chains himself fast to the earth, holds it in his hands, buys it, calls it his, plants apple trees and flowers, and waits for the harvest.

Under the thick pine branches an old man sits and sleeps his last sleep, or not the last, who knows?

The old man is dead.

War.

Naturally it is war. What else could there be?

The stores, the cellars, the silos are full. But people have no money. The deduction is simple. People must die. Those who have no money must die. But up at Mårbo Sally is giving birth.

War, pestilence, earthquake—even so there's birth.

The pregnant mother gives birth in the water, in a drowning death. The whale gives birth when she's dragged up on land, and is killed.

The whole universe gives birth to life and no life.

Who will judge the children who are born on the last day? The last day? Those who give birth don't believe in the last day. How strangely everything is made. The Milky Way stretches its wintry whiteness across space, the pains of labor go like a gulf stream through it, the nebula whirl around in burning genesis, and the planets shoot into space like the young from the whale's belly.

Nothing is so simple as fecundating and giving birth. Even so it is life's deepest riddle. A riddle deeper than death. Death is no riddle. We can follow death with our eyes. But where does birth begin? Does it begin immediately when death occurs? We know nothing about it.

Are we embryos that grow in the earth, constantly growing like seed, barley seed, and all the million different seeds?

We are seeds growing in the earth.

Our mother's body is the earth where the seed grows, but it is more; it is the dynamo that receives and regenerates the warm soft energy needed for our species' navel cord to be gently clipped so we can become individuals.

In her little room Sally lies on a bed on the floor, turning and groaning, feeling the inexorable coming nearer. The labor pains have just begun, and though the respites are long, the pains are still longer. She crawls into the other room and puts wood in the stove, for the March night is cold, and the glowing moon gives no warmth, nor do the thin blankets over the three little ones who are sleeping in the room.

Edith is already out in the world. She's in Stockholm at a factory, earning money; times are good, and even fourteen-year-olds earn money. Bruno, the twelve-year-old, who has a scar on his shoulder from the dog's bite, earns money, too, by running errands after school and taking the teacher's dog for a walk every day. Sally arranges these things for her children, thinking that things are better for Edith and Bruno where they now are than here at home. Her man has deserted her; some say that he is dead, but maybe he wanted to earn money when there's a war and times are good.

Liter-Olle is dead. Some days after Sally had let a savage old dog be shot, he hanged himself. He couldn't bear the sorrow, the villagers said.

His corpse smelled of liquor when the constable and the parish deputy cut him down. Groping for something to say to Sally, the constable said, "He's really taken one for the road."

Two women, Ellen and Sally, and the child, Edith, followed Liter-Olle's coffin to the grave. "When your father-in-law was buried, the whole village was there," Sally said.

"Ja," Ellen said, "but Grandfather never fussed over people. I can't understand why so many were there."

Liter-Olle's coffin was lowered beside an ordinary one who had died in his "honorable" bed. The priest read the customary ritual, and Ellen and Sally and Edith put flowers on the grave. On the way home they talked about Mother Sofi. Sally told Ellen about that burial, how her grandmother had only seen Mother Sofi when she was dead, and that she was buried outside the churchyard wall. "Like a dog," Sally said.

"Dogs aren't buried," Ellen replied, "they're just dumped in the ground."

"Will Grandfather never come back again?" Edith asked seriously.

"No, never."

All three silently walked up the road to Mårbo.

"She drove the poor old man to his death," the villagers said. "Surely he could have been permitted to keep that old wretched dog."

But Liter-Olle had often told Sally that he couldn't stand the pain any longer, that brandy didn't help anymore, that he'd soon do away with himself.

The village became sentimental over the old man, although the villagers had shooed him off like a stray cat while he lived. People are made afraid by death; even dogs and junkmen are mourned after death.

Now Sally lies on the floor, giving birth.

She thinks about many things, that she's alone, that she mustn't yell, for then the children will wake up. On a stool beside the bed is the shiny copper lamp, filled with precious kerosene. The flame flutters with Sally's every movement in the little room. Liter-Olle's old lamp is good to have now, for food and light are running out in the world, only the bills are rustling and the cannons thundering.

A new cramp. She hoarsely stifles a scream like one who is dying. The pain pulls in the small of her back, the sweat runs, her body begins to tremble, and she reaches down with her hand—no, not yet—it goes so slowly, so slowly, she groans. Another respite. She crawls to get thread and scissors and clean rags, and lies down beside the bed. Ellen won't be here until morning, not until morning. Now the pain comes again, hell and damnation, help me! She pushes her clenched fists against each other over her belly, braces her feet against the wall, shrieks hoarsely, her chin pressed to her breasts. New respite. With her hand she feels up. It's so close, dear God, and no water coming. She feels the membrane around the baby stretching her vagina. Furious, crazy with pain, she sits up, tearing with her fingers at the membrane. It is tough and strong. Nature is wonderful, protecting its young more carefully than any miser his gold. The sweat runs, her light hair looks like a nimbus around her face, wildly beautiful in its pain. Groaning, not daring to use the scissors, she tears with all her strength at the membrane in front of the baby's head. At last! A stream of warm water blended with blood flows out of her, nearly releasing the baby's head through the passageway. What relief! She stretches herself backwards, waiting for the next pain, pushes her hands under the small of her back, and bears down hard, with all her strength, to free herself from the child in her womb that will tear her body in two. She bites her lips until they bleed, sits up, lies down. The narrow passage won't give. Then, at last, the baby is forced out of her shaking body, followed by blood and mucus and fluid. Life, a new life, shrilly crying, demanding a place. Raising herself, Sally turns the baby over, thoughts feverishly flashing across her mind. You are born with your face to the ground. By your own strength you must soar to higher spheres, and you do, but the earth takes you even so. Maybe the earth itself is soaring to higher spheres.

She cuts the navel cord. Shivering, she carefully ties the cord, that entrance to life or death for a new being, wipes the blood and mucus from the baby's eyes. She sees the sex: a boy. She smiles. He won't need to give birth, he won't need to give birth to a child. She carefully looks him over; everything is all right. He has dimples in his cheeks, for he twists his little face into a grimace. Trembling with tenderness, with joy, she bundles him in some rags, holds him close, and lies down. She closes her eyes, and it seems that the little barge, Mårbo, sails away with her over the mountain, the moon, and the sun, and she sees flat, dark hills and figures like trolls far off, and four children, crying in the darkness over a broken glass stopper for a carafe. She sees Grandma, who has been dead for so long, and Father, who hanged himself in the shell barn of the cannon factory. "Ellen," she mumbles. "You will come, you will come? You promised." And the moon hangs over the stubble fields.

The moon shines over Flander's field, over North Atlantic convoys, over dark cities, waiting for air raids. It shines on children who are born in the city and in the country, in haylofts, huts, stables, and forests. Everywhere women give birth to children, give birth to them one by one. But in Flanders man does not kill one by one; he shoots them in colonnades in Europe just now. The hanging moon shines over Flanders.

It is two o'clock in the morning. The little ones sleep. Ellen will not come until before sunrise. "I must not sleep, do not sleep," Sally whispers. She does not sleep, for the pains are not over. Not until five o'clock when Ellen comes —"for I had a feeling," she says—is Sally freed from her pain.

Nature vigorously prepares a new life for its journey. That which so beautifully in dialect is called "mothercake" and which for nature's unceasing work after nine months is found to be an intricate system of veins and canals for the new life's benefit, is finally expelled from Sally's body.

"Dear Ellen, wash the baby's eyes well," Sally says and falls asleep.

Ellen rouses her, "Shouldn't I get the midwife?"

"No need to. What would she do now that the baby's born?"

"But how can I get you into bed, Sally?"

"I'll lie here on the floor a couple of days until I can get myself into bed. Let me sleep, Ellen. Only a while. Until you get the fire going and the coffee, a whole hecto I've saved until now. Cook good coffee, use only beans, Ellen. Feed the chickens, ch-il-dren, wash the ba-by, dear Ell-en." Sally sleeps.

Utterly exhausted, Sally sleeps, not feeling how her hard bed tortures her sore, tender body. She's released from the gnawing thoughts for awhile, an hour, no longer. Her mind's uneasiness and despair don't allow the comfort of deep sleep. She is startled, raises up. "It is war. I have had the baby, a boy, a soldier, maybe, no, not that." She calls to Ellen who is talking softly to the children, trying to keep them quiet, for the weather won't allow them to be out. They sit on the couch, asking Ellen about something in whispering stammers, wait and stare expectantly at the wallpapered door that Mother lies behind with a new brother Aunt Ellen has told them. Now Mother calls, and they rush to the door which Ellen opens.

The three children stand quietly. It is so strange. Mother lies on the floor with packets of books and bundles of newspapers all around her. They can't see any new brother. Then Ellen picks up a little bundle beside Mother, saying "Such a fine baby. He looks as if he were already a month old. I've never seen such a beautiful newborn baby."

(These are the usual words at just about every childbed, and mothers lying on featherbeds in great imperial beds, or on functional couches, or on the barn's straw, or on a heap of rags with a gypsy father's old coat over them, happily want to believe they are true. The words are said at almost every baby's birth. Maybe they are said too much or too little. Ask the garbage men in cities, or abortioners, or nearly every doctor, or the country's judges. Every mother—maybe this is said too much—rejoices over her child, is happy that he is beautiful or that people say he is beautiful.)

122

Sally belongs to those who are happy that the baby is well shaped when she has had to give him birth. She knows, for she's read about it in hundreds of places in those old books and newspapers, that it's wrong to have children when the earth is overpopulated, and financiers must stir up war for the sake of balance. War. Sally is aware of everything about war—God, so well she's aware of it—and now she's had a child during the war. A newborn child lies now beside her and not a bit of food in the house. Bread crusts? What is that for a child? A child must have food, not bread crusts.

War. Sally had herself helped in the factory's preparations for war. Father hanged himself in the shell barn at the cannon factory. He had got a good job there, the best job he had ever had, and Mother and Sally had helped all they could so he could manage to keep it. He was not used to working at night and sleeping in the day; he never learned to do it. But rather that life than drive oxen, go to the manor house after the oxen, day in and day out. He had been ready to desert the family. Then he had got the good job as a night watchman at the cannon factory. It was the happiest day in Sally's childhood home. That time Sally and her family were moved by the factory's powerful Ardennes cart horses, and the factory wives competed with each other in inviting Grandma and Mother for coffee, and Mother said to Father, "Now you'll get to be done with your organizing! It's the thirty-fourth time we've moved in nine years."

Father thought it was enough; he got out of his union. He did it only on the condition that he'd get the job. Father had good references; he had worked at the factory. The factory bosses chose him to be their night watchman among ten applicants, most of them sons of farmers in the district, but the factory bosses didn't like to have farmers' sons for night watchmen.

Most of Grandma's junk was sold, and new furniture was bought. But Grandma didn't really like it in the small new rooms by the cannon factory's entrance. She became quiet and tired, lying down most of the time, and one morning she was dead. She probably died of old age, for she was eighty-five years old. Even now Sally feels the tears welling when she thinks about Grandma lying dead in her bed, her old brass bed in the kitchen. Sally lies on the floor in Mårbo and mourns Grandma.

War. The cannons thunder, and the mines on the coast-lands explode so they're heard even as far as Mårbo and the village sometimes. *Ja,* there they have food; in the village everyone has food, but Sally doesn't, nor Ellen. For Ellen also begins to feel the pinch; Bernhard takes days off again and drinks and carouses. But Ellen—*she* was well thought of in the village. It was Sally the village didn't tolerate. Ellen was so quiet and shy and willing to help for little pay, always letting those loud mouths be in the right.

Sally couldn't do that. She had traveled around the country, had moved thirty-four times before she was ten years old. She had gone in the cannon factory's shell barn and pulled the fire insurance company's checkpoint clock when Father couldn't, when he had to sleep some nights, for he couldn't get used to sleeping in the day. . . . She never gave in to the loudmouths, she outshouted them, but who cared about that? Sally didn't, but she simply couldn't accept their order of things. And no one in the village had gone into a big, high shell barn during dark nights. No one in the village really knew how man *prepared for* war. No one in the village knew how it was in the southern suburb, no one other than Ellen, and she didn't know it as well as Sally. No one in the village had been in a factory. The village knew nothing about "innocent's sickness."

"They're talking about how there'll be peace," Ellen says. Sally only nods. "Tomorrow we'll try to get you into the bed. I'll take the children home, so you'll have it quiet here. I have Mimmi helping at home."

"I can never pay you anything, Ellen!"

"What nonsense! Will you have a drop of coffee?"

Ja, Sally will have coffee. The door is closed. The children are jabbering outside it. She hears Ellen promising to make pancakes in the morning only if they'll eat the everlasting potatoes and dried herring nicely today—"You can go home with me," she says—and it becomes quiet and peaceful in the cottage.

War, cannons, the shell barn.

"You must go until twelve tonight. Then I'll relieve you," mother says, putting the strap that the control clock hangs on around Sally's neck, and giving her father's old pocket watch so she can fit the keys on the minute. A little hole in the tape for every stroke. Six small holes an hour. Six small holes on a bit of paper a little askew over the tape which is in nine sections. Six for every hour meant that the cannon factory got its insurance money if the factory burned in the night. Father had already been reported about it; he had missed two holes a couple of times.

It is a holiday. The factory with all its different rooms is deserted and quiet, not really quiet; it's never really quiet in a large factory. In the big workshop the lathes and the smaller dynamos lie idle. It smells of oil and waste and men's sweat. This room is not desolate or frightening. The machines stand there like quiet people waiting for working days.

Machines—Sally later had heard machines cursed so often: they took bread away from the poor, from all except a certain few. Had not they who cursed seen that the machines were fastened down with big screws, that they were shackled like animals in their stalls, to be used as beasts of burden. She had seen that. She had always thought that machines were like mute, shackled creatures, who through no fault of their own, drove people from the world, from life. Perfect in shape and form and fitted for all heavy toil, they stood fastened to the floor and stone bases, were cursed, sometimes smashed to pieces. She had read the word "sabotage," knew what it meant. But a machine, its brain from a man's brain—it wasn't right to crush it, as unjust as to crush the oxen who had pulled her beside the moonlake. What a lot she had read in the old books and newspapers from Liter-Olle's junk. Those who had invented the machines shouldn't bear the blame either. But whose, then, whose was the blame? The machines didn't advise that man use them to make cannons with.

It was so simple. Man should not misuse things. The machines reflected the tragedy of things, *misused things.* Sally almost gets up; she wants so much to write that down. She often wrote down what she thought. It was so much fun to read later when she had forgotten it. Man believed that he could take iron from the earth and do what he wanted with it, because the iron didn't have any nerves. The baby whimpers and moves. She puts him to her breast and tries to sleep.

The control clock! She must go to the power station now. The mechanic usually takes a nap there on a quiet night like this. The gleaming mosaic floor, the machinery shining like gold are better than all the tales she had read. She knows what will take place when this or that button is pressed—this dynamo or another one will begin to work, will pull the heavy lift crane or the bellows or the lathes. It is far better than Aladdin's lamp. The mechanic wakes up when she shuts the little key cupboard, *"Ja,* so it's you!"

"Ja, Father needs to sleep awhile." The mechanic lies down and dozes off again.

She steps carefully through the dark forge shop, the cinders crunching under her feet. Her lantern lights up a circle no bigger than a coffee cup. Next she checks the carpenter shop where the gun carriages are made. It's so clean here, smelling of new wood, and she sits down several minutes on a half-finished gun carriage. The strong smell of resin makes her sleepy. She looks at the old pocket watch,

126

only two minutes to go, and then there's the last attraction: the shell barn. In there everything is orderly, it seems so empty, finished, and cold. The moon shines in through the enormous windows that reach nearly to the roof, dizzily high, with iron bars across the panes. The shining shells lie in orderly rows, in pigeonholes like wine bottles in a wine cellar.

The desolate silence in the big room fills her with horror. The shells lie there by the thousands like big cocoons ready to burst. She knows that sometimes they did burst, and then there was a funeral and crying and complaining at the factory. In the spooky moonlight the shells look like big cocoons ready to burst so that enormous insects could crawl out. A key cupboard is at every gable, and Sally, like the night watchman, must check the whole complex which is so big that ten minutes at least are needed for her to carefully grope her way in the gloom. No matter how carefully she walks, her steps echo like thunder in the night. She is sick with fear after every round. Every hour the same round. First the big room, populated with machines—warm, living. Next the fine power station with its kind old mechanic. Then the carpenter shop with its clean wood and its smell of resin, and last the cold, terrible shell barn where one of the factory's products lay in ordered rows. And there, after the third warning and threatened with dismissal, father had hanged himself.

Sally cannot sleep. Her thoughts swarm like clouds of insects weaving around her. "Now the cocoons have burst," she whispers. "Now it is war, now the shell barn is empty, or they're working night and day at the factory." The baby has fallen asleep, but Sally cannot. She is at a crossroad.

She has suffered much pain, but no more than many another. She knows that. She suffers now because she has given birth to a child during a terrible war. She knows some newspapers praise expectant mothers who want to give birth for the cause—they are fearless, they love their country. That makes the thing worse, such glaring lies no one can contend against. Father had hanged himself. Maybe it hadn't been from fear that he would lose his job. Sally remembers that father always used to talk about justice before he had taken the fine job.

Sinking further and further into despair, she forgets her children, feels all at once life's unbearable burden. She feels beside herself, thinks it is impossible to exist in this world, is impossible to live. Tomorrow, tomorrow! Tomorrow I will be alone, alone with this last baby, this last soldier. Never give birth again. Never. Tomorrow, alone, glorious aloneness, away from everything, forever, away to Grandma, to Father, to all who have gone before, to Mother Sofi. Tomorrow happiness and rest will come. For who can live and give birth to a child in cannon thunder and poverty. Give birth while the shells explode. *The shell barn.* Tomorrow. A quiet peace comes over her. It is despair. Paralyzing, despairing peace and certainty, certainty before death. It is Sally's darkest time. Life's misery overcomes her sound instincts. Death will become a victory. Tomorrow, alone. Ellen will take the children with her, all except the baby. He will go with me on this journey, the last one, the last move. Then everything will be calm. No more voices, no nagging, no hunger, no pain. That quieting thought makes her sleep. Restoring sound sleep comes, too. It is as if it waited until this moment to protest. Good sleep, mankind's highest gift next to death.

Sally wakens the next morning to life.

The March sun shines as if she has been paid, the two men think as they struggle up the hills towards Mårbo. *"Ja,"* the chairman of the relief board says, "I don't expect to get any rent from her."

"No, you can depend on that," agrees the constable, "but Sally's going to have to tell me about her fellow's being there on *Maria* last week, that's for sure. That old boat had sixty thousand liters in its cargo, and every fisherman here in the skerries and a couple of farmers from the mainland lay out there drinking all last week with a German. If one of the farmer's wives hadn't got anxious and reported to me that her fellow had disappeared, no one would have been the wiser. Then to further the matter along for us, they let themselves be photographed out there, so the German mate would recognize them the next time he wanted to do business with them. A few days afterwards, the detective took the mate to a fine tavern in Stockholm, and got all the photographs to boot. Then we constables got a composite picture to see if we knew any of them, and I recognized Frans from Mårbo right off, so he's not dead as was rumored."

"Having anything to do with those smugglers is a dirty business. You could be killed straight out," the chairman shudders.

"Oh, you're on your guard, you take care. Officers of the law aren't afraid of any hoodlum."

They're quiet awhile. The chairman plods along, thinking that he could just as well be the constable as the other one. It certainly has more prestige than a chairman of the relief board, where you just got to deal with thieves, wretches, fools of all kinds, defiant fathers who stood there sneering when you wanted them to take on their responsibilities.

"Sally's with child again, so I've heard?"

"Ja, she is. There'll be kids at Mårbo all the time, though they're in short supply on the farms. The farmer of Vide has even wanted to get a divorce because he can't get kids. It's been a long time since there were kids at Vide, or at Östby, in the whole village for that matter. There aren't more than four kids on six big farms. Can you figure that out? Although Sally, well, I don't think she wanted one with Frans, a real smart woman she is, good-looking, too. She doesn't want to take any relief, but I've got to run up here and try to get the rent anyways."

On the last steep rise, the chairman sits down on a

resiny stump, and the constable sits on one beside him. "Can you imagine, that woman says that Mårbo doesn't belong to the parish. 'Show me the paper!' she said the last time I was there, exactly as though I should carry along papers for one like her!"

"Have you any papers though?" The constable lights his pipe.

"Papers, certainly there are papers. Do you think the parish would demand payment without having clear papers?"

"I've never seen any papers that the parish owns Mårbo." The constable gets up, followed by the chairman, who looks disappointed and deflated.

The little barge lies there as always on the forest's highest crest. Though the sun has burned the ground bare all around, a few green shoots are already up beside the stone steps. Mårbo is in the middle of the big forest's broadest sunglade, and the spring comes early up here. The constable looks around a little. "Beautiful up here in any case," he mutters and knocks.

"Come in," Ellen says. When she sees the constable, she looks anxiously at the bed where Sally is lying, a little pale, in Ellen's finest nightgown, and the four-day-old boy at her overflowing white breast. The men stand there quite embarrassed. They hadn't heard about any childbed at Mårbo right now. That Sally was with child they knew, of course, but. . . .

A flaming redness has sprung to Sally's cheeks. "What do you want?" she abruptly asks. They're silent, seem to have nothing to say. "What do you gentlemen want?"

"The gentlemen" look as if bewitched into those contemptuous eyes, glance uncertainly at the downy little head that drinks, drinks as if from pure joy in having taught himself such a great art as eating. There is no further business for the gentlemen. They also know that Sally has a

temper. Moreover, an old tradition lies ingrained: "It is unlucky to disturb a woman in childbed." In a district where
inbreeding has made men and women sterile, such a bed is
a holy place.

"What do you want?" Sally asks again.

Ellen pushes two stools forward. "Please sit down."

"We can come again. This is certainly not the proper
time," the chairman says, not daring to sit down although
he feels exhausted.

"You don't need to come again. The cottage belongs to
Vide Farm, and it lies on public forest land. I have found out
all this and have written it down," Sally says.

The chairman is speechless. He looks beseechingly at
the constable and then at Sally.

"What do you want, constable?" Sally's eyes glisten
more lustrously; her hair, like a nimbus, curls around her
head and her burning cheeks.

The constable fumbles through his cards, takes out a
photograph, and goes over to the bed. "Sally, can you certify
that this is from Mårbo?"

Sally looks at the photograph, easily recognizes Frans
sitting on a pile of cables on a boat deck, his hat on the back
of his neck, an accordian in his hands. She gazes long at the
photograph, looks for an instant at her newborn, then giving
the photograph back, she answers, "I certify nothing."

The constable turns to Ellen. "Mrs. Olsson, you visit up
here; you no doubt can certify that this is Frans."

"I've never seen Frans." Ellen is telling the truth. In the
ten years that she's lived in the district, Frans has been home
so seldom that Ellen has never seen him. But the constable,
sure that she is lying, flies into a rage.

"I'll clean out this nest!" he shouts.

"What is there to clean? The children and I are the only
ones here. Frans hasn't been here for six months, and my
father-in-law has been dead for a year."

"*Ja,* but you seem to manage here even so. You're not so careful about it either. You have fellows here constantly, whole gangs of them. This will be the end of that now."

"Did you hear what he said, Ellen?"

"*Ja.*"

"Did you hear what the constable said, Chairman?"

"*Ja,* but I don't think he said anything dangerous. You hold those damned socialist meetings up here, but the count has spoken out. He sent a petition to the parish that no Russian meetings can be held on its grounds. Russia is Sweden's eternal enemy. You, Sally, have fellows here all the time, and they wouldn't be likely to come here if you didn't sleep with them. A lot of crazy old women come here, too."

"Old women, crazy ones, I leave that up to you. I won't hold that against you. The only thing I'll hold against you is your incurable stupidity in the parish's business. There wouldn't need to be so much misery here in such a rich parish if one like you weren't in power. How can that be? Can you even read a book?" Sally is burning mad, looking as if she were going to get up, and Ellen begs, "Don't mind them, Sally."

Ellen turns to the men. "How dare you! How dare you! She had to lie here alone and give birth to her child without a person to help her, and even now she doesn't get to lie in peace. Not even a gypsy treats his dog so badly!" Ellen is angry. The men feel things have got too hot, quite too hot, inside the cottage.

"Did she have to be alone?" the constable asks. He looks at Sally and falls into thought. What a woman, he thinks. What a woman for a real man. With the others, it's the doctor and forceps and anesthetic, farm wives have become as whiny as countesses. He turns to the chairman, "You must arrange for some provisions to get here."

"*Ja-a,*" he replies, quite letdown.

"Listen, Constable," Sally says, "when you go past Vide Farm, will you please go in and ask the farmer to come up

132

here a week from today? I have an important matter to talk over with him. It's headland business. If you won't, then I'll have to write to him. Will you do that?"

"I can easily do that since I go right by," the constable answers, "but then, Sally, you must certify that this is Frans in the photograph."

"I've made it clear I won't do that."

"*Ja,* there you see what you have to deal with," the chairman says, recovering courage and trying to fume like a worthy representative of his office.

"Ellen, there's a book in the other room. It's lying on the shelf over the cat hole. Please get it."

Both the men are convinced that the remarkable, shameless Sally is planning to read to them from Sweden's laws of the realm. They try to look superior and knowing. The constable, to his credit, has seen Sweden's lawbook once at the district police superintendent's, but he's never read a syllable of it. The chairman has only heard it talked about time and time again ever since he's been born, and allegedly he's often looked up the country's laws, but he's never seen the book in question. Neither of them nor anyone else in the parish had any other opinion than that punishment is intended to bring about a change for the better. Punishment is a just revenge, ordered by God, so simple it is. And punishment through the law lasts one's whole life. That the law is good for all things, for poverty in particular, the chairman knew.

Ellen came out with a big, patched-up, pasted-together tome. Bless me, the chairman thought, the law is so big. That's certainly not the law, the constable thought, but he wasn't sure.

Sally reads loudly and expressively, "Within the precious tent, embroidered with silver and gold and pearls of immeasurable worth, sat the khans from the high wagons and with Genghis Khan from the Golden Horde. They earnestly talked while the night's stars glided away. They discussed the great question if justice with any mercy were possible for the settled population. It would be best, the khans thought, to root out the settled ones, for they are only mold and fungus on the surface of the earth. Their women are nothing but whores, not wanting to give birth to children. If they get sons, they bring them up to despise the horse. Like rats they stay in their holes, generation after generation, and pollute the earth. The khans from the high wagons and the Golden Horde step out from the tent and inspect their enormous camp with its innumerable crowds of mounted men. Mold are the settled ones, the khans say. . . ." Sally stops reading. The men only stare. Ellen, too. She is deeply interested. "Will you go now?"

"Ja—ja, thanks." The constable and the chairman tumble out. Not a word is exchanged until they reach the road to the village.

"Was that the law book she read from?" the chairman asks.

"No." With a dismissing nod to the chairman, the constable goes off to Vide Farm.

"Did you hear, Ellen, 'Ja, thanks,' they said, when they got to hear that they were mold. They're all alike! All of them in power live on mold, venerate mold so much that they give the beggar and his children moldy bread."

"You must rest now, Sally, you talk as if you had a fever." Sally obediently rests. She is tired to death.

But Ellen reads on in the old volume that Liter-Olle had carried home in his junk, and she finds out wonderful things about the world.

Down in Appledale are life and happiness.

Ellen has left Mimmi, the parish's good-time girl, to look after her own and Sally's children. Mimmi sings all the new waltzes and music hall songs that she's learned at the dance hall. Sometimes she dances with Ellen's Sven or Sally's Gunnar, their small feet easily following her sure, rhythmical steps, and they learn the melodies in a flash.

The parish's good-time girl is beautiful; the whole village agrees about that. She has such red cheeks. When it's freezing cold, they're blue, of course, but she's just as beautiful then, the village thinks. A red-cheeked, blooming girl can't really be so dangerously bad and decadent.

Like Julius Caesar, the village mistrusted thin, pale people, particularly pale ones; if they were dark under their eyes, that meant absolute depravity. The parish's good-time girl was neither pale nor dark under her eyes. She had an ordinary, round, smooth face, with very small eyes, a bit like a pig's eyes, but her mouth was always stretched in laughter, and her nature was friendly. She was nimble in work and obliging.

A little loose she was, of course; one knew about that when she worked at Östby. The fifteen-year-old stable boy became sick there with consumption. She treated him badly. Then she had to move, of course, for the mother of Östby caught her necking with her husband. But the mother of Östby always was jealous of all her maids, and the stable boy should have known better than to start acting like a grown fellow. The village had sympathy for the parish's good-time girl. Of course, she was also from the district and related to the farmers. And when her father, the basket maker, died, she wouldn't be left so badly off at all—at least three acres of land, and money, too. And, God, how fast she could work! As for her fellows, well, women always had them as long as they were young. A pity that she should be drawn to that Sally, but Mrs. Olsson in Appledale was another thing. She was an honest person that the good-time girl would have been better off to be with, but she had also begun to run with Sally, just as the good-time girl had done ever since she was little. One knew, of course, how Frans was, how crazy women were about him.

The strange thing is that the good-time girl continues

to run to Sally's although Frans has disappeared. And with a war going on, food is scarce, and she's always taking along a sack of food for Sally's illegitimate kids—that Sally who only reads and arranges those meetings. It's a good thing for the fellows at the meetings that the good-time girl is there. Poor girl, she'll be completely ruined. Think, now there's talk that the tenant farmer at the manor house is going to rob the whole estate and drive away the gentleman himself! But the gentleman and the farmers have shotguns—just let that guy come and try! And the village has the king and God, to be sure! The village can certainly hold its own always!

But Mimmi dances and sings for Ellen's and Sally's children, and the whole time she tries to hold her head just like Sally, combs her hair just like Sally, curling it to get it even more like hers. Sometimes she sits and ponders. Sally has luck with the guys; that is Mimmi's problem.

Sally even has children, is ten years older than Mimmi, but however happy the men are to be with her, they always act like idiots as soon as Sally comes along. At the meetings up in Mårbo, they snap at Mimmi sometimes. It's happened more than once when she's tried to take part in their crazy conversations with Sally. And Mimmi has even slept with a couple of the younger ones. They don't look at her any more, don't even go to the dance hall, dashing around on their bikes with papers and talking as if they were castrated.

Sally doesn't sleep with them, not with any of the men who gather up there—Mimmi knows that. The whole village says just the opposite, but she knows that the village lies, and though she says so to this one and that, there is no one who believes her. *How* she knows it's a lie, she can't even explain to herself. She sees it in Sally, in her way with the men. Sally likes men though not in the same way as she does. What Sally wants with them, Mimmi can never understand.

But Mimmi likes Sally. When Sally gazes into space, as if lost in her thoughts, and puts her hands on Mimmi's cheeks—it has happened a couple of times—Mimmi has felt a shiver of happiness from the top of her head to her toes.

If Sally wanted to stroke her cheeks often, wanted to be fond of her a little, wanted to talk a bit more with her, Mimmi definitely wouldn't care so much about the men. They wanted only one thing and all at once. Mimmi didn't know herself what she wanted from men. It was as if she couldn't possibly be unfriendly to a man she casually encountered. But always it was so uncertain. The friendship often was short-lived, lasting sometimes a week, a month, a half-year; then someone new hurt the old friendship, and she threw herself into new arms, a new embrace, a new delight, just as fleeting.

Now during wartime the men were all the more worthless, had lots of money, drank, and got rough with women. Mimmi didn't really like the men's world any longer. With Sally the world had fragrance and mystery, and Sally could talk about so many strange things, things Mimmi often thought about, but didn't have anyone she dared to talk them over with. With Sally there was no talk about sin, no warnings, no wonder over letting men kiss and embrace one. And then her gentle caresses, Mimmi could never forget them. Caresses of clean sympathy. She scrubbed and cleaned for Sally, fixed the children's rags, got her mail, for Sally got a lot of mail now.

"I can't pay you anything," Sally says. "You shouldn't sit up here the whole Saturday night. Why don't you go to the dance as usual?" But Mimmi doesn't think it's so much fun to go dancing anymore. The dances are so tiresome, so ordinary.

One time a fine man came up to Mårbo. All the tenant farmers were there, too. This fine man talked like a priest, and he called everyone a friend; he even called Mimmi a friend. Sally wasn't pleased with him at all. She pulled him into her little wallpapered room with its bundles of newspapers, and shouted that he had talked just rubbish at the meeting: "It just isn't true that everyone will have enough to eat! It's a silly, dumb, damn lie! Many will not even have enough to survive one day. The world would be served if some died."

But the fine man talked calmly and politely to Sally, and said, "Watch it, Sally, or you'll be a Bolshevik. Then the union that you have organized so well will break up." But Sally really bawled him out, telling him to get his ideas straightened out. Afterwards, they discussed Sally's old bundles of newspapers and ragged books.

"It's my university, brought from the garbage dump."

"For shame, Sally! I wouldn't get all that you have here read in my whole life. Have you read all these issues of *The Social Democrat,* and these *Mission Tidings?* And here's *The Daily News* and *The Alarm Bell,* too, and look here, a history of the world."

"I read it all the time. Well, so you think it's enough if you get your education from a garbage dump—think, a good Christian like you."

He didn't even get angry at Sally, and he mixed with everyone at the meeting and fussed over Sally, though she had her two-year-old kid on her arm the whole time. But Mimmi, who was young, who had neither children nor a fiancé, who was free and willing for love or whatever, he never even looked at after he'd said, "Hello, friend," whatever that meant. But when the stationmaster always said, "Hello, honey"—that was something she understood. And she couldn't figure out why the village slandered Sally the way they did. Honestly, Sally didn't sleep with guys.

Mimmi didn't know that there was a far bigger sin in the villagers' eyes than "sleeping with guys," a sin so bad that both villagers and townspeople whispered it.

"That poor wretch," the wife of the cowman at the manor house said, "that wretch up there in her gypsy hole can't very well help anybody. You get out of that union.

When you've got nine children, you have to side with the gentlemen. She's just man-crazy."

The cowman struck his wife, it was said.

Sally organized the men; they mistreated their wives.

When the war had been going on for two years, Mimmi had her happiest time. Men, well-mannered men, who paid attention to young, red-cheeked women, men with money in their pockets, good at dancing and playing cards, came to the village. Mimmi was embraced and kissed by one and all. Now we have already come to Mohammed's heaven, the men thought. A young woman who never asked for money, only caresses and kisses and hot embraces—something that they didn't expect to be better than what they got. The men from out in the world and Mimmi were in perfect agreement.

Then it was Sally again, for even those men, so unlike tenant farmers, hired men, and farmers' sons, were in a union, and they gathered for a meeting up at Mårbo. Mimmi was there, too, and cooked coffee for them. A couple of them pinched her cheek and gave her a kiss, but most of them saw only Sally with her children.

A few weeks after the meeting up at Mårbo, the best and the happiest had disappeared from the dance hall; only the drunks were left, and the old men who just sat and played cards. The other happy young guys had also gone away on their bikes and motorcycles, distributing newspapers. Sally's mail was a whole sackful now. Mimmi was strongly tempted to go out herself with those newspapers. Sally beamed like a sun on all who ran around with them.

"Sing more," Ellen's Sven said in the middle of her thoughts. And Mimmi sang while she fixed the simple meal from what was available, and they ate the dry "depression herring" and good mealy potatoes, and drank milk from Appledale's own cow, although next week it would be sold. Ellen could no longer afford fodder, for hay was one krona a kilo, and the farmers now claimed all the scrubby slopes that formerly the poor got to harvest for one or two day's work.

The constable sits drinking coffee and brandy in Vide Farm's big kitchen, its walls gleaming with pewter bowls and copper pans. He still hasn't told his errand, and the farmer and Mother Maria, his wife, are very curious. Their old housemaid looks even more inquisitive than usual, for the constable hardly ever comes to Vide Farm.

"Sally wants you to go up to Mårbo next week."

"Sally. Frans' Sally?"

"Liter-Olle's Sally?" the housemaid, forgetting herself, also asks.

"Why does Sally want me? Wasn't it Maria she wanted?"

"No, it was you, and I can tell you what it's all about. She's found out that the parish doesn't own Mårbo. It's supposed to belong to you, and she maintains she's written it all down."

"Well, that will be good, let me tell you, to get that trash up there out!" Mother Maria reasons triumphantly.

"So Mårbo is ours! *Ja,* that was really good of Sally to find that out," the old housemaid says, forgetting herself again.

"Really good of her! *Ja,* she no doubt thinks she can get out of paying the rent now. She doesn't do anything for nothing, that gypsy, but that'll not happen."

"You have nothing to say in this," the farmer says bitterly, riveting his eyes on his wife. Everyone knows that those two fight like cats and dogs. *"Ja,* well that's good," he says, looking at the constable. "Have half a cup, at least. But why should I wait until next week? I can just as well go up there now."

"She's still in childbed, has just had the kid. She even had to be all by herself. I think that's a devilish thing, to put it bluntly. After all, she's a human being. I know worse people than Sally of Mårbo," the constable says, looking Mother Maria straight in the eyes.

No one says anything. The constable drinks his coffee and brandy. Then Mother Maria says, "Well, it's not so bad for one like Sally when she has a baby, one like her." She snickers.

"You should talk when you haven't had one! Shut up!" the farmer snaps.

"It would be better if you thanked Sally for getting you a cottage for nothing," the old housemaid forgets herself again. Neither the farmer nor Mother Maria dares to contradict her. She knows too much, has seen too much of their marriage's misery.

"*Ja,*" the constable says, "now I've told you what she wanted. As I said, she's still in childbed. I don't think Sally has much in the way of food, so you can keep that in mind when you go up to take the cottage from her." And he gives Mother Maria a hard look again.

He isn't comfortable at Vide, gets irritated and angered every time he has any errand there. Maria is a shrew; he remembers her as a girl, a real stuck-up person, rich as a troll. The farmer of Vide doesn't have any happy time of it. You shouldn't give too much away about yourself to a constable if you have any common sense, but that scarecrow, Maria, hasn't any sense. The constable bangs the door when he leaves.

The day after that Ellen comes to Mårbo again. She has a letter for Sally, a greasy envelope with childish lettering.

Sally silently opens it. A little packet of tens and fives flutters out. On a bit of a torn-off sack is written: "The police have nabbed me, and they'd just as soon get this, so I'm sending it to you. I've heard you're going to have a child again. When I come out, I'll be going my own way. You're a fine girl, Sally, and it's been hell for you. Your man, Frans." There were one hundred and fifty kronor in the letter.

The women look silently at each other. Sally gives Ellen the letter. She reads, nods. "So that's it."

They're quiet awhile, each thinking her own thoughts. "Will you go down to the store, Ellen? There's not a thing to eat in the house."

"*Ja*, sure, thanks to this! Thank God for the money even if he's stolen it." Ellen hurries off.

In the store two loud-voiced farmers are vigorously discussing the economic situation. "Seventeen hundred he was offered, seventeen hundred, and he didn't take it, the crazy devil!"

"Who offered seventeen hundred?" Ellen asks while the storekeeper clips all of Mårbo's bread coupons.

"The farmer of Vide, that's who. Seventeen hundred, he offered him for his cow that was ready to calve, but he didn't take it."

"*Ja*, he was probably dumb not to. Prices like that won't stay forever," Ellen says confidently. "They'll soon be coming down to normal."

"What kind of dumb talk is that? What are you talking about? Do you think prices will go down to what they were before? Never, I'm telling you! It'll never be that bad in the country again. Is it too much to ask that farmers get a little money, too?"

"*Ja*, sure it's too much, seventeen hundred for a cow!" Ellen exclaims a bit heatedly.

"*Ja*, you think so! *Ja*, you go with that whore up in Mårbo, she's taught you!"

"Hold your tongue!" Ellen says curtly.

"*Ja*, don't talk politics in here, if you please!" the storekeeper says, who respects Ellen of Appledale, and, to some extent, Sally, after she came one day and paid every öre Liter-Olle owed, wherever she had got the money. For that matter, the storekeeper doesn't care where people get their money as long as they pay. Ellen and Sally spend their money here. The farmers of the village, however, who often go to the city, don't use her store much. She sticks by those who trade with her, and she firmly tells the farmer to stop his prattle on the economy and be on his way. He leaves, the other one following him, and she says, "I have a little butter and a bit of pork, Mrs. Olsson, that you can have at not too bad a price. I'm not a war profiteer, but don't tell anyone about the bargains." And Ellen spends money, lots of money on food, and thanking the storekeeper, she happily climbs up Mårbo's hills. Finally she can fix a proper meal for a woman in childbed.

But up in Mårbo someone else is paying a call.

The farmer of Vide holds Sally's new baby on his knee, saying over and over again, "Such fine children you have, Sally! Such beautiful children you have! But how did you find out that the cottage is ours? How did you? What a baby!" He pauses and looks at Sally. "Out in the car I have both pork and flour. Take it please, Sally! You must have food! I don't give a shit what they say in the village! To hell with them! All of them! I have it so damned devilish at home. All my cows calve, but in my own kitchen, I've got just those old dried-up women gossiping. God, what a beautiful baby, Sally! Yesterday I offered my brother-in-law seventeen hundred for a cow that was ready to calve, but he wouldn't take it. Think of that! He wouldn't take it! I like calves, you see, Sally. They stare so wide-eyed and wobble on their legs, the little weaklings."

The farmer of Vide is tipsy, nearly drunk, but he sits steadily enough on the chair. Sally is nervous, however, afraid he will drop the baby; no, no, he catches him. "What a baby!" he says, and he cries a little. *Ja*, Sally is used to that —drunks who cry—but that the richest farmer in the village should! May Ellen come soon!

"At least I should have a young maid," he says. "How about it? You, Sally, you've got such uncommonly beautiful children, what the devil do you say about a young maid for me? Do you know anyone, Sally? Say that you know someone! You'll see I have both pork and flour for you. Say that you know some young maid who will come to me. I'm so damned sick of those old nagging women!"

"Mimmi wants to get a place. She's a kind and pretty girl," Sally says.

"The good-time girl! Does she want a place! What are you saying? I'll take her on the spot. What a boy! Look so little he is! Mimmi's a fine girl, quick, too. I'm damned if I don't take that maid for myself!"

Sally hears Ellen coming, thank God.

"Look, Sally, at least ten kilos of pork! And flour, wheat flour!" Ellen calls after she had coaxed the farmer out. "If only I had known before I bought expensive pork in the store. And his wheat flour, God, so happy I am, Sally!" Ellen dances around, whistling.

"You're so beautiful when you're happy," Sally says, radiant with happiness herself that the worst worries are over for the moment.

"The storekeeper sent greetings and these coffee beans and, look, some of her best candy. She's a nice woman."

"Ja, she's nice, but what do you think they'll be saying in the village now after the farmer's visit. I'm really unlucky. Maria from Vide will come for sure and take the pork from me."

"Not as long as I'm here," Ellen says firmly.

But that time the village didn't have as much to say about Sally as about the farmer of Vide who drove off his old maid, who had been there for thirty years, and hired the parish's good-time girl in her place. Of course the old maid got one thousand kronor as a gift for good service, but still, the parish's good-time girl! Mother Maria had gone back to her parental farm in the neighboring parish, but after three days she came back, and now the villagers knew for sure that they behaved worse at Vide Farm than at Mårbo in Liter-Olle's time.

And the moon is full again, etching the silhouettes of the spruce trees' sprawling shapes; the frost-white grass rustles under a man's footsteps, and in Vide Farm's kitchen, a young woman walks, crying.

The parish's good-time girl cries, for she is with child. The moon beams upon the big pewter pots and copper kettles that swing on the walls as if to console her, but Mimmi only cries, doesn't see the moon, or the pewter pots, or any consolation in the world, for she is with child. The worst fate, the thing she's always feared worse than death, has happened to her. And people are babbling. "Not until now are they babbling," she sobs. "Oh, how their mouths run. I can't show myself outside, no dancing, no kissing, only go around here." And she cries even more.

There's a little knock, carefully, softly, a knocking on the door. Mimmi opens it. She's embraced, kissed, comforted. As so often before, she is tenderly pressed against his hard chest, his red lips on hers.

Bernhard from Appledale is in Vide's kitchen, stroking the maid's hair. It is the same kitchen where his father in his youth had come courting. Bernhard kisses and fondles her white breasts, whispers senseless words, hot lies in her willing ears. "What will I do?" she asks. "I'm soon going to have a baby, and you are married."

"Do? We'll leave. There's work everywhere; there's nothing to stay here for."

"Ja, but your wife—you're lawfully married; they can send after you."

"Not Ellen. She's so damned fed up with me, she can't stand to look at me. It'll be good to get away from her whining. Nags as soon as you take a drink, but you, you'll be a sweet little girl." He kisses her, gives her his promise.

"Think! how can Ellen not want you?"

"Oh, she wants me, that's for sure. I didn't just exactly show that I did the last time."

Silence. Then Mimmi cries again. "No, Bernhard. I can't do it, however it goes. Maybe Ellen's also with child. Guys are nothing to trust. She has rights to you, and Ellen is nice. I know that. You're telling a bunch of lies!" Mimmi's no longer quiet, cries loudly, shrieks. There's a knock on the door, and the lean, tall farmer of Vide, stooping a little, steps into the kitchen, his eyes alert. There are sad lines around his mouth. Bernhard huddles in a corner. The moon casts deep shadows. The lamp isn't lit.

"What are you crying for?" he asks, not noticing Bernhard. "Why in God's name are you going around here crying?" He takes her in his arms, kisses her, holds her to himself with tenderness and affection. "Don't cry, Mimmi. You know that I'll claim my child. As soon as he's born, he will have my name. Don't you think I have ample means for a child, for more than one! We'll have another after this one. Be happy now. Go to bed; it's late. I can get another maid if you want, so you won't need to work as much now when you're on the way."

"What the hell!" Bernhard yells, stepping forward. The farmer stares at him.

"Ja, so, ja, it's you from Appledale." The farmer hits Bernhard with all his strength, and Bernhard whirls around. "Get out of here!"

Bernhard stumbles out, sits down back of Vide's big hayrack, and thinks he's gone crazy. He isn't really sober, but still? A married farmer who proudly takes the responsibility for his maid's child? Never has he heard the like! And Mimmi! Think, how she stood there, rolling her eyes to heaven, and bawling, "You mustn't leave Ellen." Ja, think if he had been so dumb. Think if they say anything to Ellen! For gossip always gets around. "It's my child," the farmer said. He was proud of it. Bernhard sits hour after hour behind the hayrack, brooding. He isn't the father of the good-time girl's child; he had been pretty sure of that the whole time, but that it is the farmer! And the farmer is

146

so proud of it! A woman with child. *Ja,* poor Ellen. He cries a little behind the hayrack. Think, as beautiful as Ellen is. And she has borne his children, quietly, peacefully. No bawling and yelling like that fool of a woman the farmer's so proud of. Late at night he walks slowly home, knocks on his door at Appledale, and is let in. It's the first time in months he's come home sober. For the first time in months, Ellen gets a little housekeeping money from Bernhard.

But in Vide Farm's bedroom, Mother Maria stands clenching her fist at her husband, asking if he's thinking of driving her to her death.

"Go and drown yourself if you want," he answers.

"What did you run to the kitchen for? The maid must have been there then! She's soon thick as a barrel, and she doesn't know who the father is!"

"Ja, but I know! It is I! I am the father! Now you can go back to your family and tell them it was a lie you spread around that I was unable to father a child. You didn't think I knew! And when you went to Salve-Lotta in Åsbrink, it was because you knew that you, yourself, were unable to have a child. And you smeared yourself with her salves so your belly is still black. But what did you say to your family? Do you remember? What did you say to your brother? *Ja,* that I was no man, couldn't father a child! Go out and look at Mimmi, and you'll see! But not a word to her, not a word, just as I've told you everyday since she's been here. You know how you must act. Mimmi's going to have peace around here!"

Now Maria does something the farmer has never seen her do. She kneels beside the bed and prays to God. Cries and prays. Never has he seen her cry and never has he heard her pray.

"That was good, Maria," he says awhile after her sobbing has ended. "That was good you did that. Now maybe you can keep things a little peaceful in the house. A man wants to have a child when he has as big a farm as I have; God, a father himself, understands that."

Maria begins to cry and pray again. At last she falls asleep, and the farmer goes once more to the kitchen and sees that Mimmi also is sleeping. He draws the curtains, for the moon shines on her face. Then he goes in to his bedroom which is now peaceful.

Not a word had he asked why Bernhard was in the kitchen. It would never occur to him that it was to sleep with Mimmi. "He was probably drunk and stumbled in here where he thought he'd get more brandy. . . ." Even the farmer sleeps at last.

The days go by, tempers calm down, the young begin to be old. The war rages worse than before at the fronts with names too difficult for the villagers to pronounce. In order for them to feel involved, they agree that Germany will win the war.

Although it is December, the rain is pouring down. Stockholm is murky, little lights gleaming here and there in the rain that streams down almost as if it knew its superfluousness, streams over buildings and pavements, hardly appropriate weather for selling woollen gloves. "People won't buy any gloves in this weather," Ellen says unhappily.

She and Ellen stand on the square in front of Central Station, trying to get their bearings. Twenty pairs of beautiful, warm woollen gloves are their only resources. Twenty pairs of gloves sewn from expensive wool are the means that may be able to keep them from going on relief. Has Sally miscalculated? She has counted on a patriotic fervor for the Swedish sheep, on a spending spree by war profiteers, and on people's longing for warm, genuine things in times of easy money, when coins jingle and paper bills rustle.

If Sally has miscalculated, they will have to travel forty-two miles home and go on relief. Maybe Ellen can still manage. Bernhard has work, and in a moment of remorse he may give her some money. He had done that last summer, the last summer of the war, when the madness in the world reached its peak. But Sally has no way out. Everything is used up—Frans is still in jail, and Vide's old housemaid is fixing the last bit of food at Mårbo while Sally and Ellen are away.

At Vide Farm, Mimmi is broad through the hips with the farmer's child, his second child. The farmer of Vide had made his decision. He lives in an infatuated ecstasy with his illegal wife, who now bears his second child. His honor is saved; no one dares to insinuate that he is incapable of fathering a child. His wife, Maria, dares not to call him "not a man" any more. She is quiet and sad. She had made her decision: she refuses to divorce.

The situation at Vide Farm is strange. Both the priest and the constable have been there, but the farmer wouldn't budge. "It is my maid; no one can prevent us from having children together," he told the priest. The law about marriage crime is so old that it is dead; although the clause is there, no one ever uses it, Maria of Vide least of all, for Vide Farm is big, and a married woman has her rights despite everything.

Strangely enough, the two women came to an agreement. When Mimmi's baby was baptized, it was immediately adopted by the Vide family. He became the lawful heir of the farm. When he was two years old, Mother Maria took him with her to a large coffee party, and everyone thought she was his mother, so eager she was to show off his abilities, his amusing sayings, his plump red cheeks and chubby hands. Maria of Vide, who was generally thought to be stingy and mean, became the parish's most remarkable farm "mother."

"She is a wonder of Christ-like mercy," the priest had said at a meeting soon after the boy had been adopted. Everyone began to look with veneration at Mother Maria of Vide. She was invited to the parish's sewing guilds, and when she happened to take the boy along, all the women felt they were associating in some way with the Christ child, born of a virgin, and were in danger of killing the child with sweets and cakes, in spite of wartime scarcities.

The parish's good-time girl was even accepted, considered much better than just a maid. She had, of course, a view to a little inheritance also, and naturally, if anything should

150

happen—for one never knows—she'd become the "mother" of Vide, that was clear.

Everyone thought that what had happened was for the best. Vide Farm needed an heir, and now Vide's Maria was a wonder of mercy, quite as forgiving as Christ, who forgave the woman who had had seven men. It was almost as if everyone were proud of the situation at Vide Farm, proud of so much sanctity. Mother Maria and the farmer never lay now at night and quarreled. The old housemaid said that in former days they hardly ever slept like an ordinary married pair, for they constantly quarreled and even fought.

Everyone in the village had his struggle to contend with, everyone and everything, from the foxes who attacked the henhouses, the cats who fought in their lust, the sparrows who spit corn at each other, the horses who bit each other over crib feed, and last of all, the villagers who fought with each other. The Vide farmer with his wife, Crazy John with his landlady for depression-time tobacco, the priest against sin, Ellen, Sally, and a crowd of others against poverty. Out in Europe, they didn't know whom they fought, they only murdered each other.

"No one will buy gloves in the rain," Ellen says again and looks irresolutely at thronging Vasa Street.

It is good to have a destination in that confusion of streets, houses, cars, people, shouts, clock bells, jingle, and jangle. It is good if you know what stream you should follow, the never-ceasing streams to north, south, east, and west. A little scrap of paper in a worn purse, a paper with some words on it, has their destination. Just then the afternoon papers are hawked, and you incredibly hear the soughing of the autumn wind in the high-crowned forest, have never heard it so distinctly as now in the constant streams of people, have never distinguished so sharply the smells of resin and tar, have never perceived before how red or gray the houses are there at home. Those pictures that the years and habit have etched have never appeared so clearly as now before bewildered eyes. You would rather turn around, get on the train, and travel home, but when you can't, when the last money is a few copper coins or not even that, only some wartime tokens already rusted on the edges, then a little scrap, a greasy scrap with some words, an address, is like a sturdy boat in a storm, like a lull in a thunderstorm. The address is simple—14 St. Paul's Street, first floor across the courtyard. You ask for directions there; a helpful man stops in the midst of the streaming throng, trying to remember. No, he can't remember—at Vasa Street it is hard to remember streets on the south side—but he helpfully stops another in the stream: *Ja,* straight ahead over the bridge, then ask farther on at Slussen. He scrutinizes the two women, lingering on the taller one, blonde, beautiful, a hauntingly beautiful face, looks like some painting he has seen; he lifts his hat. The helpful man also lifts his hat, and the two women struggle against the stream of people over the bridge, ask at Slussen, and come to 14 St. Paul's Street, across the courtyard. God, so peaceful it has become, so pleasant. Here and there a couple of thin trees struggle up in the dusky shadows. A tumbledown house, looking nearly like a cottage, stands inside the courtyard. It is there they will stay. Now everything is well and good; nothing is confusing any longer.

They wait a minute, listening. Someone bellows a song from a streaky window. There's a smell of garbage, urine, and burning rags. That is familiar; the song is familiar, too:

> and to my great relief
> a brandy distiller I'll be
> and get the devil to drink
> till every day he's drunk.

"I recognize that song," Ellen whispers.
"It's a common drinking song," Sally says. "Let's go in now."

An old woman opens the door. "*Ja, ja,* I know, step in. I've made the beds for you, but you'll be wanting to see the sights, it's easy to see. You won't want to be going to bed in the middle of the afternoon, but I have the beds ready. Edith used to come here sometimes to see my girl, and I have beds as good as they come. I have every bed booked. Telephone boys rent mine, fine boys. They're a little tipsy at night, but they don't disturb anyone."

She sits down on a stool, and it's obvious that she's tipsy, too. Immediately forgetting the two women, she hums along with the song that continues somewhere in the house. It *is* the Bellman singers' song, Ellen remembers, and suddenly she sees her youth unroll—youth, had she ever been young? Though life has turned out well: think if she had become one of those in the slums!

"They never seem to find any new songs to sing," she says to Sally.

Looking a little surprised at Ellen, Sally says to the old woman, "You can show us where we will sleep, please."

"*Ja,* sure, sure." Weaving through the kitchen out to a corridor, she opens a door to a room without a window. Two beds are made up on the floor. It looks clean when the old woman turns on the light, and she tells them to make themselves at home.

Now once again Ellen is in the city. Outside the rain beats steadily down, some men sing and shout after their week of work, but only a stone's throw away is the living, cold stream where she feels frozen, lost, and confused. She is happy for a hole without windows, for a bed, for a scrap of paper with an address on it.

Rain, brandy, songs, tumbledown houses—that she is accustomed to. But without forests, fields, mountains, she feels hemmed in by the noise and the straggling thin trees, by the strange stream of people that seem to be pulling her along without any direction. It is so hard to breathe. But she must go out. Now that she's been through it once, maybe it will be better, for her ears are already getting used to the noise. Sally, of course, proceeds directly just as if she were at home, but Ellen, oh, her childhood city becomes so little before this thundering, roaring enormity now!

She sits down on the floor bed. Her face is white as chalk. Trembling, her teeth chattering, she struggles against violent nausea.

"Ellen, you are sick!" Sally tears a piece of newspaper for her to hold to her mouth. Then she runs out into the corridor, and hearing noise through the walls, she enters a room. "A hand bowl, please, my friend is ill."

"Bless me, what a shame! The hand bowls are already taken, and just like everything else, they cost plenty, so I can't buy anything new; a hand bowl costs ten kronor. But here, here's a tin pan we often use to wash in."

"If someone's needing a brandy, just say so," a tall, stubby-bearded telephone worker says, looking with interest at Sally.

"No thanks," and Sally adds distractedly, "she doesn't drink brandy."

"If you're sick, it's the best thing to do."

The old woman trots in front of Sally, clutching the pan, and Sally says, "I must go out now. Will you please take care of my friend? Mrs. Olsson's not very strong, and she's three months along with child, too; that's probably why she's sick."

"*Ja,* sure, sure. *Ja,* I know that well, have had kids, course not any myself, it's true, but I've heard it all, how they vomit and go on in other ways when they're in that condition. Some get, you know, so they steal, too, food and things. *Ja,* sure, you just go along now. I'll take care of her."

Ellen is a little better. She lies on her bed on the floor —one thing stays the same in the city; her bed is always on the floor. She tries to get up when the other women come in, but the nausea comes back at once, and the room whirls. "Dear Sally, what am I doing like this! It must be the train trip. I'm not used to it, haven't traveled since I went with

154

Bernhard to Appledale. Well, there's another reason, *ja,* you know, of course, Sally." Taking the tin pan from the old woman, Ellen vomits with shuddering gasps.

An old woman in a ramshackle house in a courtyard of a city knows a lot, knows nearly everything that is worth knowing. She knows, among other things, just how you should go about selling gloves in bad times when it rains. "God, that's a small matter, just takes a little know-how, of course. You can't refuse a thing that's offered in these bad times. I'm given a hecto of coffee a month. Is that reasonable, I ask you! One hecto for an old person. I can't be bothered to cook it. You can offer some prayers for me; you probably need some yourselves out there in the sticks. How'm I to cook coffee on a hecto that's to last a month?"

"Was it possibly for a week?" Sally asks.

"*Ja,* well a week, it was something like that. It's exactly the same, it is, as a hecto a month. You should just see those sheep turds they weigh up for you. No, I get a brandy from the boys and just say to hell with the coffee. One hecto a month! But now when you want to sell your gloves, genuine wool gloves, you've got to put on a Dalarna* costume. If you want to sell anything in these times, you've got to have something striped and bordered on, you know. Then they'd buy even if you sold little stones. And you must ask twenty kronor a pair for the gloves, nothing less than that. Just put on a Dalarna rig or something striped; you can borrow mine; I've got the blouse, skirt, and apron. The apron you must promise to wear, see, for it's striped. Go to a Gold Crown restaurant; don't be embarrassed. At the Gold Crown restaurants, they buy like crazy from Dalarna women. You look so fine, too. Twenty kronor, at least, a pair. Sing like so a little, and drawl when you talk like the Dalarna women do. No, if you don't put something striped on, something that looks real Swedish, it won't do, not on your life. They'll

*A province in Sweden famous for its colorful costumes.

155

think you've stolen the gloves. But with a Dal rig on, you could even go to the Grand, but don't go there—that's where only the French and Russians live, ones like that, who don't have any money. Go down to Berns—you know where that is—if I had time I'd go along, but I have to cook coffee for the boys to have for their brandy; otherwise they'll be mad, and then there's the poor sick Mrs. here. Do now just like I've told you, and you'll do fine."

With everything Sally's heard about warmongering and the rage for patriotic songs in the land, she knows the old woman's idea isn't stupid. Gold and blue, striped and woven at home. The Dalarna costumes can be bought in the store for one hundred and twenty kronor, of course, and God knows if they're not woven in Germany, Sally thinks as she puts on a wrinkled, heavy skirt, a soiled blouse, like a man's cut-off shirt, that smells of rank sweat, a red vest, and a striped apron. Ellen laughs even though she feels so sick. "It is just like the theater. I went there sometimes when I worked at the cafe. Ugh, what a pain that I had to get sick just now." And she vomits again.

It is surprising what one like the old woman knows even if her "boys' " brandy has gone to her head, for Sally is a real success in her Dalarna costume. And Ellen? Little by little the boys finish their coffee, and the old woman has time to talk with Ellen a bit. She offers her a sandwich now and then, for the nausea that Ellen is suffering from is of the same curious nature as seasickness—the worse her vomiting is, the hungrier she is afterwards. When she's been pregnant before, the nausea has not been this bad; now nothing that's simple and cheap tastes good and everything that does costs too much. But an old woman knows a remedy for everything, an old woman who's lived in streets and alleys.

"One time I lived in the country," she tells Ellen, "and looked after ten pigs a whole year, but then I left. I was glad at first to get a place. I wasn't so old, fourteen years, and I had no other place to be here in Stockholm than in the farmers' quarters, for I had to go out and beg all of my childhood. Then I got too big to beg; *ja,* you had to sleep with the farmers, of course, if you got to stay over night in their quarters and get a little food. They had boxes of food. You never got money. There was a religious farmer who thought it was terrible; *ja,* for he slept with me one night, but then in the morning when he saw how young I was, he said, 'I can't answer to God for this,' and so I got to go home with him and become a pig maid. I was sick the first three months. *Ja,* that's when I got to know the country. I was there a whole year, but I've lived here in the city ever since. Eat these sandwiches now and drink another glass of beer, that's good for you, and won't make you vomit. I have a foster girl who goes around with Edith. Edith's probably your daughter then?"

"No, she's Sally's, the one selling the gloves," Ellen answers, hardly getting a word in.

"God in heaven! Has *she* such a big daughter, then she began even earlier than I did! Do you know what the farm mother said to me when she heard I'd slept in the farmers' quarters? 'You should have had better sense,' she said. 'Who would have taught me that?' I asked."

Ellen eats the good sandwiches—reliable food that the "boys" get on the black market, drinks a little beer, and feels suddenly well and cheerful again. And from an old woman accustomed to city living, she finds out many things, gets addresses. "Only fifty kronor," the old woman whispers, "you can't go there and have more kids in these times, and thin as a pole, you are, too. Now you just sleep. I'll talk to her in the morning; she's always home then, so you can meet her. That other stylish woman will do a fine business so you'll certainly get fifty kronor to take care of this with. Don't worry now; your friend will do fine with the gloves, for I saw how she went about things. Bless me, what a stylish woman and living out there in the sticks. *Ja,* Edith is a beautiful girl, but she's cold, and then the Salvation

157

Army's going after her. Ugh, a thousand women for the Salvation Army! They're always here ranting at me. I can take care of myself. I'm seventy-eight; I've always managed, the boys are good to me, and then I'll go to the poorhouse when I don't have much time left. You can figure out why those Salvation Army soldiers run here for and always when the boys are home? 'A newspaper,' *The War Cry*—God help me—and 'mercy and salvation,' and 'does the old woman need anything'—kiss the old woman—*ja*, I said that. And it was here that Edith came across them, and they talked right in her face. One big hallelujahing hen nearly pecked the poor girl's face, inviting her home and praying for her, and God knows what all . . . Edith didn't come here when she heard her mother was coming; she wrote, think of that, and reserved the room. *Ja, Ja,* she's gotten caught by the Salvation Army, but I've watched out for myself, don't worry about that. They take over when they get their claws in you; they take right over, and then you've got to scrub for some lazy old women who are in such a hurry to beg for God that they don't have time to scrub. *Ja,* you sleep now. Good night, and in the morning we'll arrange about that for you —don't you worry—I wasn't born yesterday. Leave the light on all night if you want."

And Ellen leaves the light on, for she plans to wait up for Sally. Then thinking that time will go faster if she sleeps, she falls asleep, the night passes, and Sally doesn't come.

The old woman is right: stripes and borders are an entrance card, striped, richly colored, nationalistic, but not variegated, curliqued, or flowered; no, the stripes must be lengthwise or crosswise, otherwise they are foreign, dangerous, gypsylike. The costume must have a regular pattern, stripe after stripe, color after color, in orderly rows; then you know where you have people. Those orderly stripes are wholly and simply Swedish.

"We don't want any more hawkers here," the doorkeeper says dismissingly to Sally when she steps in the side entrance and unwraps her package of gloves.

"Hawker! That's a Dalarna woman," a gentleman tipsy with punch says. "Watch yourself," he says threateningly to the doorkeeper. "Watch yourself. She's wearing the Swedish colors. Soon they'll be flying; soon we'll be dancing, and then you'll see this little one. Step in, you woman from the heart of Sweden!" he proclaims, pushing Sally in front of him.

The big chandeliers seem to sail overhead in clouds of tobacco smoke. The crowd's clamor, the orchestra's loud music thunder in her ears accustomed to the forest's silence for many years. A strange, intoxicated gentleman is good to have in this Nineveh, in these circles of noise, light, and strange people. Everyone is happy, exhilarated. They smile at the Dalarna woman, at the beautiful, impressive Dalarnan, see her package of gloves, become interested, something to buy. Something to buy? The Dalarnan sells something—gloves, woollen gloves! Who will not buy genuine woollen gloves? Who remembers that it's raining outside? It's the month of Christmas, and everyone has money, lots of it, doesn't know what he should do with it, clerks, directors, cattle sellers with wallets full of money. There's one who travels to Gotland every week with a suitcase packed with money to buy up animals, everything, big and little, on the black market—coffee, flour, sugar, shoe polish, lingon tea, everything possible, even pinecones. Someone boasts that he made twenty thousand one day on just pinecones. Everyone wants to buy the Dalarnan's gloves!

But the tipsy, happy gentleman waves and wards them off. "Go along to my table," he says to Sally, "just go there, and I'll take care of the business." Soon six, now seven, tables comprise the gentleman's table. He waves to friend after friend; one couple cheers. Sally needs only to follow along with the stream, let things take care of themselves. She still hasn't opened her mouth.

(Fritz Reuter* writes about a man who followed the stream in a town, and landed in jail, for the stream, wouldn't you know, turned out to be captured prisoners instead of ordinary citizens. Though Sally didn't land in jail, the happy gentleman and several others at his table did several years later. They really didn't know why themselves, for they had been helpful to people all down the line. The happy gentleman was a great patron of the arts to boot. Money from lingon tea, pinecones, and soap, he spent on expensive paintings. Artists worshipped him. They sat around his table night after night at Berns or at Rosenbad or Nacka and worshipped him. It was an illustrious time for art, as the painters were aware, but not so for literature, they would say.)

Sally is offered wine, champagne; no, she doesn't want any, for she wants to sell gloves. Food then? Sandwiches? Warm food? Anything? *Ja,* she wants to eat; she hasn't eaten a bite all day. The gentleman holds up a pair of white gloves with variegated roses sewn on them. "Twenty kronor are bid," he says, "twenty kronor!" The din is alarming. Each one shouts louder than the other. The doorkeeper comes, the headwaiter, too, and the former gets a hundred kronor, while the latter gets a thousand kronor note with an order of champagne for the whole company and a hot dish for Sally. "Fifty kronor are bid, fifty, fifty, gone!"

The gloves disappear like butter, literally speaking, for it is a time of hunger and great demand for butter.

The pile of money grows, that of the gloves diminishes. The company drink champagne, and more guests join in. The last pair of gloves is sold for five hundred kronor. The Dalarnan gets the heap of money. Is she married? *Ja,* she is. Children? *Ja.* God, so sweet! Little ones in striped costumes! One man nearly wants to eat the silent Dalarna wo-

*A 19th-century German writer.

160

man. Everyone begins singing, "Our country's rose shall wither. . . ."

A beautiful woman, naked to the waist, sits down beside Sally. "Your man is home plowing?"

"He's in jail," Sally replies.

"Oh, so! Why, my dear?"

"He smuggles liquor, I presume that is why." No one has time to heed that the Dalarna woman speaks quite good Swedish, not dialect.

"Smuggles liquor! Hurrah! God, so romantic! You must come home with me," the beautiful, half-naked woman says.

"I have a friend who is sick here in town," Sally says.

"Alas, there is nothing to do about that now, it is so late. Hey," she shouts to the company, "I'm going home now. Who wants to come along?"

Just the happy gentleman and another couple want to. And Sally goes with them. She has a big bundle of bills; she doesn't dare to count them, for there are thousands of kronor. If they hear how much it is, maybe they'll want some of it back, and she doesn't want to give back any of it to those people who have so much money. A car is ordered and the address is given. Sally and her company leave, driving through a locale where everyone cheers them. Shouting, laughing, they whiz away.

Sunday in Stockholm. Ellen hears the streetcars rattle, hears voices in the courtyard, but she hears nothing from the old woman and her "boys." She doesn't know what time it is in the windowless room; she doesn't know if it is day or night, and Sally hasn't come.

Feeling completely rested, she would gladly come out of her prison, but doesn't know the way and doesn't want to disturb anyone. Not a book, not a newspaper. What should she do? Not even a peephole. And where is Sally? Ellen waits quietly for so long she feels she will scream. And there is no place to move around. She rolls up the bedding and pillows as much as possible. Now she is nearly cross—can't people get up—it surely is the middle of the morning, but she doesn't hear a sound from within, only a car far off; surely it will stop here. Why doesn't Sally come? Has she been run over? *Ja,* that's it. She is frightened, imagining everything possible, just like a child. If Sally has been run over, a message will come, of course. But who knows that Sally is staying here? She decides to go out and pound on the doors, do anything, just to get out of here. Then Sally comes. And what a Sally, looking so fine and well, she could fly. She has a large package under her arm.

"Where is the costume?"

"Here in the package."

"Where did you get those fine clothes?"

"It's a long story."

They sit cozily, comfortably on their big bed bundles while the one tells and the other listens. Sally opens a packet of money. There's a long red note of a value Ellen has never seen. Sally has often seen them, for one time in her diverse childhood she was an errand girl for a cannon factory. "That's one thousand kronor."

"Do you think it's all right?" Ellen asks.

"Ja, it's fine."

The times are such that two working-class women by the god of chance are sitting on two bed rolls in a room without windows, without furniture, counting out nearly three thousand kronor for twenty pairs of gloves.

"I remember so well the first pair of gloves you showed me, Sally. It was the first time I visited you and you beat the dog."

"Ja, the mother of Östby taught me how to sew them. Now, Ellen, we're going out on the town."

"I'm not so well dressed, Sally, and you're as fine as a lady."

"The woman that gave me these clothes discarded them three years ago, she said, and her girl wouldn't even have them, for they're out-of-date."

"Was the lady an artist? Dear Sally, what adventures you have, and such luck! Was her place fine?"

And Sally tells her about it again, but not all can she tell. Ellen wouldn't understand, maybe wouldn't think such things were possible. Sally had read about such unconventional people in Liter-Olle's old books. The lady was an artist who painted eccentric pictures, strange things, lines, cubes, and a giant-size picture of a naked man. "No woman other than I dares to paint like this," she had said. "Do you know why, my friends? It's impossible to find a model. Men are modest; they won't pose nude for a woman. But I have found a model. Isn't he splendid?" And the company had exclaimed, "You are incomparable, Emelie!"—"A gigolo from Paris models for me. I think I'll paint wings on him and call him Gabriel."—"Not here in Stockholm, Emilie, then you'll be sent to Långholmen.* You must do what the trouser painter of Florence did to Michelangelo's *David;* paint trousers on him." Because Sally had read a lot, she could follow their conversation, listen without blushing or moralizing, but to tell everything to Ellen, no, that won't do.

"I felt sick, for the smell was so stuffy—the Dalarna costume, the turpentine, food, and everything. The woman saw how pale I was and asked why, so I told her. I got to bathe in her bathroom and get these clothes. Then I asked if I could lie down somewhere in her apartment, and I did. When I woke up, I left a note for the woman, took a taxi, and rode here."

"God, Sally, you took a taxi! How did you dare to?"

Sally smiles. She doesn't know much about the leather-apron farmer or about genes. She knows that she is like Mother Sofi from the Big Farm—Grandma has said that—

*A large jail in Stockholm.

163

and she knows that Ellen is also descended from the Big Farm. "You are as cautious as some of the farmers in the village, Ellen."

"*Ja,* you get that way when you get rich," Ellen smiles back.

Today is not yesterday, nor is it tomorrow; it is only today, is now. The streams of people aren't bewildering anymore. It is fun to be in them, to go some place, to look at store windows, to eat curious pastries, to drink coffee, terrible depression-time coffee, but still, just to sit and listen to music, for it is a "fine" cafe. Then they will see Edith, for it is Sunday; she is free, and her mother is coming. She should be free a few hours at least.

Edith, like a flower, blonde, slender, soon sixteen, is happy about Mother coming, certainly is happy about it, a young, beautiful mother that even the lady Edith works for had nodded her head to. And she had told her to invite her mother for coffee and Ellen, too.

Edith now has many aprons with borders, with lace; now Ellen could get one from her. Edith doesn't remember that, nor how she cried because her brother swore when the dog tore his clothes and bit him. No, she doesn't remember, but she still cries when anyone swears too much. And Mother certainly swears, and she doesn't believe in God, doesn't want to bear her cross and believe in God. And Edith must tell something terrible to Mother now, tell her that Bruno has run away, and no one knows where he is. And Mother, who doesn't believe in God, how will she bear that?

Edith gives her mother and Ellen coffee in her mistress's fine town-house kitchen, and the coffee is real; the house has been well supplied before the slump. There is no thin cooking here. There's real white bread. Ellen remembers Edith's dry bit of cake hidden in a paper, for today, when she's happy, she believes she remembers everything.

"Have you heard anything from Bruno?"

Edith is silent.

"Isn't he here? Has he run away maybe?"

"*Ja*, Mama, he has run away."

Sally is quiet for awhile. "*Ja*, so, well, he got tired, wanted to try something else probably. I must try to find him."

That is all. She doesn't cry, doesn't swear. Edith looks with surprise at her. Dear God, in books mothers go crazy when their children ran away.

"Can you get off and come out with us? I can treat you to a movie," Sally says, looking comically at her daughter. "You didn't think that of us, Edith, two country wenches from the forest."

But Edith is silent.

"Dear child, why are you quiet? Is it hard here? I thought it looked so reliable."

No, Edith doesn't have things hard here, but she can't go to the movies; that is sinful. Sally looks almost dumb with astonishment, and Ellen is interested.

"Where I go, Edith, you may go, too, but if you don't want to, that's fine, too. Maybe I'd rather not go to the movies either, not because it's sinful, for I don't believe that, but I think it isn't fun. I want to give *you* a treat."

"I'll gladly go," Ellen says, feeling almost sick with knowing how Sally is suffering from the girl's childish zeal.

"Who has told you, Edith, that it's sinful to go to the movies if you can afford to? You know I haven't run to the movies. You know how it is up in Mårbo. Is your mistress religious?"

"No, she doesn't say anything, but she likes that I don't go to the movies, or go to dances, or run out at night."

"*Ja*, that's good, of course. You're too young to run out at night, but you can go with your mother, my girl. Where do you go when you're free, by the way?"

"I usually go to the Army."

"To the Salvation Army?"

165

"*Ja*, Mama, and you should bear your cross, Mama. You must believe in Christ and bear your cross."

"Dear child," Sally just says. Despairingly, she wonders what she should do. The Salvation Army. She recognizes the cant. How often she had listened to them in the yards in the southern suburb; how jubilantly they had rolled out all the sins they could think of that those in the slums were guilty of. And now Edith is one of them. It probably would go over, but Edith is sensitive and introspective; she could go crazy with it. How I manage to stir things up. One child goes into the Salvation Army and another one runs away. I've lain on the floor and given birth to children, am hated in the village, for I'm ungodly and radical and dangerous, and now Edith is in the Salvation Army. "Well, Edith, you do as you wish. If you need anything, money or clothes, I have enough today so you may have some money, a whole lot, if you wish. But remember one thing: burdens exist to be borne."

"There's no way to find Bruno. He's run away. He's probably become a sailor, for I don't think he's gone into the Salvation Army," Sally says bitterly when they're outside again.

"Is the Army really so bad?" Ellen asks hesitantly.

Sally is silent.

"I was there with my mother when I was little; they sang and offered us coffee. I thought it was fun there," continues Ellen. She wants Sally to be happy again, and she thinks Sally gives the matter too much importance. Ellen thinks that those who have the time and inclination can gladly carry on with their psalms and their salvation, but Sally is inflamed as soon as the word "priest" is mentioned. Ellen can't understand this: you want to be free yourself, then you must let others be free.

It is Sunday, the stores are closed, and there's nothing else to do but go back to the room without windows. Maybe the old woman will cook coffee.

166

As soon as the old woman catches sight of Sally, she calls, "Wasn't it just like I said! I said you'd do a fine business. You've bought new clothes! I told you what folks go for!"

"You do what you can, you do what you have to," Sally says.

On the North Atlantic, a sailor, not yet fifteen, is paid like an experienced seaman because of the risks of war. The convoy slips through the mine fields, trying to maneuver its way through with supplies, medicine, contraband, and its men. On one of the ships a young sailor stands, black haired, black eyed, slim, handsome, and unworried about the newly laid strange fruit that rocks around in the sea.

Sally is out on her errands, Ellen on hers, for each has things she wants to do alone.

Sally goes up stairs and down, asks about Bruno, about Edith, getting sullen answers or none at all. It is futile.

Little Edith, blonde, beautiful Edith, who walks in the big city and dreams, who cries when she hears people swear and say nasty words. She has heard so many nasty words, little Edith, who put flowers in a bottle and offered her bit of cake when guests came to Mårbo, who cried when her little brother swore and her drunk grandfather yelled terrible insults.

Edith walks in the big city and cries over ugly words. Little, fine Edith!

Ellen wanders randomly through the streets. There are things to buy, expensive things, and she has money. She should take something home with her—cloth, linens, curtains, costly ornaments, books, everything except food is on display.

Paintings. She stands for a long time outside the window of an expensive art gallery; then she steps decisively in, becomes intimidated by its elegance, and is ready to turn around and go out. A gentleman hurries over to her, "May I help you, please?" The times are such that one is polite even to simply dressed people in a fine store.

Ellen hopes to buy a painting, one with a dark, beautiful young boy holding a cluster of grapes in his hand. She wonders if it is very expensive.

"Do you know who painted it, Madam?"

No, Ellen doesn't know. The polite gentleman looks in catalogs, then telephones. "Is there a dog also in the painting?"

No, Ellen is sure there is no dog in it.

The gentleman rings still another, talking and explaining in the telephone. No, that painting can't be found. He assumes it was no doubt an ordinary oil impression. Ellen doesn't know about that; she knows nothing about paintings, except about this special painting she wants so much to buy. The gentleman holds out his arms and is sorry. Ellen leaves. She goes in another art gallery and asks about a painting of a beautiful boy with black curly hair and a cluster of grapes in his hand. No, the gentleman knows nothing about that painting. If a dog were in the painting, it is likely to be found.

But the "aunt" that Ellen lived with in the alley couldn't stand dogs and had pasted over the dog's head.

Ellen never found her painting.

On the train going home, Ellen and Sally sit quietly while the forests and fields rush past. There are curious things to muse over. They are rich, but they forget that for awhile. Old gnawing worries crop up, can be worked out, can't be worked out. Then comes the new deliverance: money, we have money.

The old woman had gone with them to the station, had tittled and tattled endlessly about her suggestion to Ellen, but Ellen had only shaken her head negatively. Sally's new friend, the artist, had also been at the station. She was elegant, beautiful, wonderful. Ellen had blushed with shyness when she was introduced.

Many at the station had stared at the four women, each one so different. The artist had waved her handkerchief, boldly shouting, "Expect me soon. I'll come, don't worry, I'm coming to paint you, Sally!"

They are loaded with packages. What joy there'll be when they come home. Appledale is closed, and Ellen's children are up at Mårbo, where Vide's old housemaid is looking after them, happy that she still is able and allowed to earn in spite of her wrinkles and crooked back.

"We'll take a lift since one goes from the station," Sally says.

"Whose is that? Do you think. . . ." Ellen hesitates.

"The inn-keeper's."

"Good Lord, he won't drive up Mårbo's hills for less than eight kronor!"

Sally only laughs. It is good to have money, good to get out of carrying heavy packages long miles, good to get home fast to waiting, hungry children and a worn-out old housemaid.

And the villagers talk a little again, but the time moves toward spring. The war is over.

Peace! But what peace? It is not at all as one had imagined. *Ja*, what really had one imagined? That one didn't know.

One, then others, now many thought to go to countries ravaged by war and build them up, for those countries had no men and would be grateful. They could take along horses and plow and sow for them, too; that they'd be glad for— their horses had, of course, gone during the war. The know-it-alls nearly held orgies, for they all had their peace plans. In all honor, of course, they wanted to help, but naturally they should have payment. But the purses of the war organizers were empty; there could not be any reconstruction. The soldiers, the ones who survived, didn't get their pay. Peace was a fiasco, a complete fiasco.

A new war was begun instead. A war of starvation was in full force in Russia. *Ja,* that wasn't any sin though, certainly not, such dreadful people, the Russians! But tempers cooled down here at home, too. Everything became so dead. No one wanted to buy anything any more. As peace came to countries in the world that had dripped with blood, people here at home began to perceive that peace after a world war wasn't quite the same as that after a boxing match. Life seemed to flow as stickily as clay.

The meetings began again up at Mårbo, but it wasn't the workers who met there nowadays; it was the unemployed.

But Sally wasn't the same as before. She explained that she was tired of everything and would travel. The villagers no longer cared about the meetings, nor about Sally. They had enough with their own, for now they were intent on keeping what they had earned during the good times, that could be well enough seen.

The days and the years go by.

A day with Ellen

There's a fire in the stove. *Ja,* of course, there's a fire in the stove, but what good is that when there's nothing to bake. There's bread, but one gets so tired of just bread.

It's tidy inside, too, *ja,* of course. It always is, but that's no fun. Everything's always the same, always tidy, always just bread. *Ja,* sometimes it's fresh, of course, and then it's a bit like a holiday, but still, if it's bread, even fresh bread is monotonous.

Three children, all about the same age, sit on the wooden settee in Appledale's kitchen in full rebellion. It's always the same, never a drop of coffee except on Sunday or when company comes. And when does company come? Never. Not even Aunt Sally from Mårbo comes here. It's just rain, and mud, dark pines, bare apple trees. The snow won't come for a long time, for it's still October. One of the little boys on the settee gets so fed up that he sticks out his tongue at Ellen.

"Mama, Nisse stuck his tongue out at you," tattles his younger brother from boredom, for they usually don't tattle.

"Why did you do that, Nisse?" And Ellen pinches his ear a little, mostly because she feels she should. And she thinks that she should have a little coffee at least on this boring day, but then the coffee won't last until Sunday.

"Mama, we haven't had meat for a whole year, and the

171

war is over now. We never have any white bread and we never get any new clothes like the other kids in the village. If I were big, I could be off."

"*Ja*, if you were big," Ellen mumbles.

And the wind tears in the cherry tree outside the window, and the rain beats down, and the three on the settee are ready to cry. The forest is like a wall around them, the fields gleam with wet clay, and in the cupboard there's only bread. And for supper, there'll be porridge and herring as usual, and bread, of course, if you want it.

And Father, Nisse thinks, if only he had a father like other fathers—well, Frans from Mårbo, but he had deserted a long time ago and was in jail still. But when Father comes on Saturdays, that's the worst of all, for he brings those guys here, and they order Mama around. They drink and vomit, and Father is the nastiest of them all. Up in the churchyard Grandfather rests; Nisse has been there several times with Mama. He begins to cry, and he goes outside so no one will see him; he's the oldest boy home now, and it wouldn't do for him to cry.

Ellen folds an old overcoat that she's trying to make over for Nisse, an old coat, green with age, a hundred years old at least. It was in the pile of clothes from the veterans' reserves that the chairman of the relief board had auctioned off after the war was over. It had cost fifty öre. Ellen tosses the coat in a corner, folds her hands, and thinks, "The day is unendurable, it is impossible."

Then Nisse comes in. "A peddler is coming around the bend!"

Everyone brightens up, Ellen, too, though she can't buy anything—there's no money—peddlers usually pay for food and a night's lodging.

There's a knock on the door. A thin little Jew with a large pack on his back steps in, bows, asks a question in a low voice. Ellen nods and puts the coffeepot on the stove.

The clouds of boredom are blown away at once. Ellen

172

grinds the coffee, sets out bread, butter blended with lard, sugar and cream. The children and the peddler are already in conversation.

A most delicious smell permeates the room. Ellen gives everyone a cup, even the three boys, only a half-cup, of course, for she remembers from her days in the alleys how she was warned about coffee. But what can she do—children need something that tastes good, too.

It's only a half-cup, but what does that matter when they're sitting with company at the table and drinking coffee, real coffee. It can't be raining out any longer; the sun is surely out. Nisse has to run and look. *Ja,* it's raining just as hard; a cherry branch has even broken off.

A man who looks as if he knew and understood all of life's sadness, its everlasting dailiness, its everlasting old rags and black hard bread, feels himself an honored guest fully welcome.

Just awhile ago he had been slogging in the clay and rain, huddled into himself. Not even a little coffee had sold. "You take away work from Swedes," one had said, slamming the door. (If a Swede had come, the door would have been slammed on him, too, with the words, "You should work and not be drifting around on the roads.")

He had walked and walked. At last, not realizing where he went, he came on an old forest path which he didn't recognize at first, for all his thoughts were in Poland, that beloved, grim Poland where he'd been driven away as a boy. Then he had knocked on a door while the rain streamed down and was made welcome.

Now he begins to talk to the children about Poland, about a big angry goat on his father's farm, about how he and his sisters had fled to Sweden when there'd been a war against Jews in Poland, how they hadn't dared stop and bury their parents who had been killed in the strife. And among Jews it's a deadly sin not to bury their parents. Jehovah punishes hard. The peddler looks sorrowful.

The boys breathlessly listen. The uneventful routine vanishes. Here are adventure and danger!

"Did you go to school in Poland?" Nisse asks.

"*Ja*, but is was only religion I learned, and to read and write, of course."

"How do you write?"

He writes several lines of curious letters, and Pelle, who goes to primary school, asks, "Can you read that?"

Nisse laughs learnedly and importantly and says, "Certainly he can read his own language!" He looks at Mama peeling potatoes, raw potatoes—it's going to be a party!

Cheered up by the coffee and friendliness, the peddler digs in his pack and finds three pairs of stockings that should just about fit Nisse, Pelle, and Sven, and he says, "You've been so nice; always when I've come, you've been nice. If I can stay here tonight, I want you to have these good stockings, please."

Ellen takes the thick, good wool stockings and thanks him. "Of course, you can stay the night. Where would you go otherwise." And she looks happy, carefully putting the stockings in the bureau drawer as if they were made of glass.

The boys wait quietly for supper, and Nisse says, "I can go without my egg. Cook it tonight, cook two, I can go without one next week, too." Nisse is used to taking an egg once a week to school, for his friends who are better off often remark about his simple lunch bag. And Ellen sets fine white potatoes, steaming spiced herring, blended butter, and two fried eggs.

There's another knock at the door. A forest worker asks the way to the village. He had stayed too long at his work, and the rain and October darkness have made him lose his way. "It's quite a long way, and wet and dark in the trees. I haven't any kerosene here and can't lend you the lantern," Ellen says worriedly. "Come in. You can stay here until morning."

And Nisse repeats, "Come in, come in. Hang your cap

by the stove so it dries." He looks proudly at the table set for supper; life is full and whole just now.

Nisse had often glimpsed tables set with fine food in the village, and had longed to have such a table at home, one set with fine food for those, frozen and hungry, to seat themselves at and become glowing and happy.

"Please sit down and have a bite to eat. There's more than enough, I've peeled lots of potatoes," Ellen says. Pelle and Sven act as if they had a party every day, and Nisse is full with only well-being.

The men agree that times are worse than before the war. "It didn't help that so many were killed; there still are too many," the forest worker says, and his lined face looks biting and hateful. "There are those who maintain that we make war, must make war, because we're too many. *Ja,* many writers are dumber than a forest worker."

"To kill or make war doesn't make things any better for us. We're not too many, we're too many who are dumb," the other man says.

Ellen asks them to help themselves again and exclaims, "The worst is that people learned to steal and make their own brandy during the war."

"*Ja,* brandy," the forest worker says. While Ellen serves more potatoes, he adds, "I always cook coffee in the forest. There's a bag of coffee and sugar in my coat. I couldn't cook it today in the rain, so you can have it after supper if you want to go to the trouble. Any that's leftover, you can keep. I haven't anything else to pay my night's lodging with."

While the men are eating and talking, Nisse helps to clear, and the coffee's put on the stove again. The forest worker says, "Russian is probably a hard language. Do Jews speak Russian?"

"*Ja,* I speak Russian. It's probably hard to learn, but Swedish is a very hard language."

"Say something in Russian," Nisse begs.

"Sing something in that language," Pelle shyly asks.

And while the coffee cooks, and Ellen dries the cups, they listen intently as he sings in that strange language. The soft consonants and the pleasing baritone voice give them an awareness even if they don't understand the words. Ellen sits down, doesn't clatter the dishes. Nisse doesn't want to exchange places with anyone in the village just now. There's an air of mystery and faraway lands in his home.

"What is the song about? Is it religious or patriotic?" the forest worker asks.

"No, it's neither. It's a Yiddish song, a real Yiddish song, although it's in Russian. It's about luck. To be a king is nothing more than to be born with luck. He who is born with luck can become foremost among men, can become an emperor over the whole earth, and he who is wise says, 'Don't give me money or power, give me luck.' To be poor can be great luck for many. For the one who will get knowledge, for the one who will invent big things, richness is possibly a hindrance. Money must be taken care of. A lot of money takes a lot of work. He who's got a great understanding has luck. That's what the song is about."

Undreamed of possibilities are opened for the children. The forest worker muses and then says, "Ja, the poor can have luck just like the rich, but good sense is always reckoned according to the bank book."

"Ja, but a little luck can also be good," Ellen says, thinking about the business with the gloves five years ago.

The storm howls in the damper, the rain pours down, and the darkness is like a wall outside, but inside they sit, drinking coffee after supper, like a party, and reflecting on life, rich, splendid, difficult, poor, intolerable life.

It had been a tedious day for all of them, so tedious that Nisse had stuck out his tongue at his mother, the one he would walk on thorns for. But unexpectedly, the day ends happily for all of them. Tomorrow? There is time enough to think about it when it comes. Life would be unendurable without its respite, when the table is set for a party with the last that is found in the cupboard, and cold, tired guests are invited to eat, quite as if there were no need to worry about what tomorrow will bring.

Beds are made on the kitchen floor for the company; bedclothes go farther then. Ellen and the boys lie in Grandfather's room. Ellen lies awake a long time, thinking about the new stockings, about the coat for Nisse, which is impossible to sew, thinking about these rainy days when Bernhard can't work and he's playing cards and drinking. Nothing will be left over for us here at home. She must try to get grain for the hens, for eggs are the only thing she has to sell. She must also write to the schoolteacher that Nisse has to have shoes that the parish must pay for. It is so depressing, she has put it off for as long as she could, but the boy needs shoes. Thank God, he has new stockings now; for them he must have whole shoes, for what help are stockings if the water runs in and out—Ellen falls asleep.

The forest worker, habitually rising at dawn, gets up and goes quietly on his way, not wanting to make more work or take anything more from poor people. It was his custom not to take anything from poor people.

At six o'clock, the peddler looks out the window, the rain continues to pour, and he lies down again. He must wait for dry weather or his goods will be ruined. Ellen and Nisse come into the kitchen. "The grounds are so strong we'll get good coffee. I can't send Nisse to school today either; he hasn't any coat."

The smell of coffee fills the room, and they drink it cheerfully. The peddler is also a fine tailor. He takes the old coat, green with age, turns it inside out, and the material looks like new. He puts a belt in its back, presses and sews, and Ellen tacks and stitches pockets in the lining. Nisse gets the best coat of his childhood. His old coat is now made over. Pockets are set in front to cover the frayed places, a collar big enough to cover the ears is cut from scraps of the

177

green-aged coat, and Pelle is also given a new coat. Nisse says, "We have luck, 'Uncle.' Think, stockings and coats at the same time. When you get such luck, then you probably can keep it."

"You wanted to give me your eggs; often you must buy your luck in that way. But people buy worse goods for dearer prices, people are so strange." Nisse doesn't understand, but he has learned the melody to the wonderful song, and he's trying to put Swedish words to it. When the sun begins to shine and the peddler shoulders his pack, he already has one verse finished.

The sun shines the short October day, and inside the cottage, everyone is happier than in a long time. Ellen thinks that maybe she can begin again, that things will go all right, if she doesn't lose courage. Bernhard is kind and sober for long spells; his friends and brothers lead him on. And the workers' jobs have been terrible. She is ready to forgive, to excuse, to begin anew.

The worst was the time they gossiped about Bernhard and the parish's good-time girl. Then she didn't care if she died. She wanted to be free, wanted to manage by herself with all that money that poured in by luck, poured in thanks to a soiled Swedish costume and war fever, the money that went so fast, for debts, for a few provisions, for expensive, but cheaply made clothes. But Mimmi didn't bear Bernhard's child; the rumor was a lie, and life became light again. Later it was dark many, many times, but never as much as then. Now she wants to begin again, devise some way, get started with something. Little Bernhard is already out earning and helping her like a grown man. *Ja*, it's certainly going to be all right.

Then fate steps in. Crazy John brings a letter to Appledale.

Ellen tears open the envelope and reads the signature: "Nilsson, engineer. Your man is seriously injured, but is expected to live."

Everything becomes gray as it had been. Everything disappears, except a marsh with frozen cranberries and a happy young man with berries in his hat, and an orchard with apple trees full of blooms on a day in June, and a kind old man. Everything else disappears, only the short day of happiness is illuminated, and her heart swells with tenderness, with love.

Nisse runs up to Mårbo. Mama must borrow traveling money. Father is hurt. Sally has money; she's never without money now. Bruno is said to send money, and the union, and the fine artist. No one knows what Sally thinks. No one dares to interfere in her affairs anymore. She has cut her ties in every direction and takes care of herself. They say Frans murdered a liquor smuggler. No one knows for sure, but he's still in prison.

Now she hurries with her last child, the only one she has at home, down to Appledale. Nisse runs on ahead.

"How is he, Ellen?"

Ellen is combing her long black hair (Sally has cut hers), and her mouth is full of hairpins. She hands the letter to Sally.

"May I borrow some money?"

"What a question, Ellen, of course you may." Sally gives her a hundred kronor.

"Has Bruno sent money again?"

"Ja."

Ellen distractedly puts her clothes on. "I don't need so much money. Well, maybe I'd better take it. Maybe Bernhard will get to come home with me, and I'll need it. Think, Sally, that Bruno earns so much! What does he do? He's grown up now—he's twenty or more, isn't he?"

"He dances with elegant women at a fine restaurant in Paris and gets paid for it." Sally looks a little scornfully at Ellen. But Ellen is putting on her clothes, buttoning and snapping, and she perceives neither the scornful look nor the strangeness of women paying beautiful boys to dance with them.

"I understand," she says consolingly. "I understand that well, as handsome as Bruno is, rich ladies would gladly pay to dance with him. Think of being able to do that."

Ellen doesn't see the big tears in Sally's eyes, Sally who rarely cries, and if she saw the tears, she would never believe that they are for Bruno who is doing so well, but for her sake and for Bernhard's.

In isolated districts, surrounded by forests, where the villages are thinly populated, petty hates and ignorance become evil specters who lay threads over dark forest paths to ensnare wanderers, and laugh in the darkness when they hear crying or swearing from those who stumble.

Sally's children, Ellen's children, all mothers' children trip in the darkness over invisible threads. Most of them get up and try to get off the dirt and the stains, try to heal the cuts they get, pat their pale faces with rouge, and continue on their way. Each one tries to catch hold of the thread he tripped over without success. Who has laid the snare? Everyone shakes his head. No one knows anything, but everyone stumbles.

The next day Ellen is already with Bernhard at the hospital —he will live, but he has broken his back; he will never be able to work anymore.

After months Bernhard comes home to Appledale again, comes at the same time as the spring and the larks.

Maria of Vide Farm who has some of her old nature left says, "Have you heard, he gets fifteen hundred kronor a year for doing nothing!"

The farmer of Vide, big and vigorous, says roughly, "For nothing! Are you crazy, woman! He has broken his back. I wouldn't break my back for fifteen million kronor, and National Insurance can surely do something!"

Ja, here could Ellen's story finish and here could it begin. Peace comes to Appledale, and never has a forest's horizon, the sun, moon, and stars been so loved as by the paralyzed man in Appledale, who brushed against death's icy bitterness, which now is forgotten in his joy that he lives, breathes, speaks, hears voices, smells the air, feels warmth, sees his children, and his wife.

The doctor has said perhaps in a year he can move his hands.

His home wins Bernhard forever.

The village had lived through three epochs: railroad, telephone, electric light. Three different generations of capable men had passed through the village, sung, laughed, drunk, played, and above all worked.

The village wanted to be left in peace now, had wanted that all along.

The fourth great wonder came very discreetly to the village. One hardly noticed it. No singing, working men left lonesome women behind them. Everything looked as usual.

One day a rusty old car stopped at Vide Farm. A man in goggles and leather spats stepped out, carrying a box under his arm. The whole world was in the box.

The village had come so far now, and the times had progressed so much that the whole world was held in a little box.

In a few hours a small mast is raised on Vide's roof. In the big kitchen, folk tunes, waltzes, polkas, and jazz with a saxophone blare out to the good-time girl's indescribable joy. The cats hiss and their hair stands up on their backs when the "nightingales" sing in the box; the dog barks and growls when people just laugh. The cats and dog soon get used to it, and the man with the spats and car drives off again.

Often in the evening Mimmi dances with her children in Vide Farm's big kitchen, and the farmer keeps time with his foot while the music pours out from all over the world.

Mother Maria slams the door to her bedroom, crying, "Oh, for all the sin and wickedness!" But on Sundays she sits and listens to sermons, and then she says, "This is truly God's voice. Now his voice is heard over the whole world."

Everywhere in the village more small masts appear on the roofs. The young people put them up themselves. No strangers need to come and help the village anymore. The young people know how to bring the world's voices from outer space.

The village is part of the world community.

Sally

The stars shine, the moon shines, the snow crystals shine. The marsh, called the slough, is like a sea of blue-starched lace curtains. Over the excavated channel, which winds through the slough and never freezes, hangs a cloud of mist, black in the moon's brightness.

Sally stands at the edge of the forest and looks out. She must go over the slough to the store, mail her letter and shop. She must go out in the blue-starched seascape where all the lanes are obliterated. She stands and gazes at the splendor that the forest concealed until she is numb with cold. The scene is like an endless movie set of unreal beauty. Then she strides out into the drifts, plowing slowly through them.

On the other side of the marsh the village is a little dark mound, for what can a few lighted windows do on a winter night compared to the radiance of the universe. Warming up, she stops far out in the drifted marsh to look at the moon and the stars and is almost proud of her solitude, feeling as if she were arranging her own enormous movie set. But she begins to chill—it is twenty degrees—and she continues her plowing, tramping down the snow as much as possible to make it easier on the way home. Down by the misted channel her zigzag tracks cut across a fox's elegant straight tracks, which look freshly made, used but once, but mark the fox's path to water for several days since the last snowfall. She pauses, reflecting on the lithe fox, on the beauty of everything. It is so far to the sky, and the stars are even farther. She would like to have someone to talk with, most of all with someone from that world which has conjured up this display of grandeur.

At last she stomps out of the last drift onto the plowed road that leads to the village store. It is filled as usual with people, a new generation, boys who hardly know Sally, who talk about going to the city and earning a little there shoveling snow.

The storekeeper politely asks what Sally wants. Well, she wants only to mail a letter, but she will have something —a little sugar, kerosene, but she has no can, a bit of cheese, some rusks, yeast. The electric light shines severely on the packages and on Sally's face. "A hecto of candy, too, the best"—*ja*, that the storekeeper knows, it's always the best; and Sally says it so curiously, the storekeeper thinks. Maybe Sally will travel, maybe marry and this time get a good man, for that Frans was only misery; that was youthful imprudence. The storekeeper gives good overweight in the sack of candy.

The villagers look quietly on while the notorious Sally gathers her packages together and says to the storekeeper, "Good-bye. I won't be coming back for a long time."

"*Ja*, well, whatever you do now, good luck, good luck," she says.

One of the young boys who's been sitting gets up and holds the door open for her. The boys know she has a long unmarked way to go, and trouble and work are something they know about and nearly the only thing they respect, the boys who are thinking of shoveling snow in the city.

The hard-packed snow squeaks ominously on the village road in the frigid beautiful night. At the last farm in the village where her way bears out in the drifts, she stops again to enjoy the magnificence of her imagined film set which the healthy, young farm boys want to leave behind when they shovel snow in the city. She is the last to wonder about them. She wanted them to get courage to leave, knowing well the tediousness of their lives and now their impoverishment; an unemployed young man can't find much pleasure in a snowy marsh's beauty be it ever so splendid, not for many years, not before he has sought adventure and found that it was nothing.

Life's compensations are hard to find. Sally enjoys the beauty and peace of limitless space. She believes that every star exists for its own sake, that a person ought to seek her own meaning, meaning that she exists. Certainly all people exist for their own sakes; otherwise the longing wouldn't be there among old and young, the longing to find themselves.

She strides out in the drifts again. Then suddenly something is revealed that she nearly has forgotten in the winter night's splendor: life's daily bread, the daily bread that the farm workers long to get away from, that prevents them from finding beauty in their fields and stars.

The farm's barn door opens with a great hullabaloo. A little wobbling bull is led out, its stomach swollen from the thin, unnourishing winter fodder. A scrubby, freezing cow is also driven out, followed by a woman and three chattering children. The cow tries to go back in the barn, seeming afraid of the moonlight; the farmer slaps her ribs. The bull has now grasped what is wanted of it; the moonlight relentlessly exposes the excrement streaming down his loins as he strains to impregnate the cow. The children snicker, and then they all disappear into the barn again. The cow stumbles, then slips and falls on the threshold, excrement running down her loins. The farmer swears, slamming the door again.

Sally stands there, staring as if she beheld trolls. She has a vision of a murky, blackish brown sky, flat-topped, bare hills, and far-off dark figures like specters on the road. She almost hears the children sobbing over their broken bottle stopper. She suddenly remembers so much. Plowing along in her tracks without seeing the night's beauty any longer, she remembers Scandinavia's smallest lady, "twenty-six years old, twenty-six thumbs tall!" Sally had pulled her once on a sled when father was at the cannon factory. The dwarf had wandered around the factory the whole day, selling pictures of herself. Exhausted she had stumbled in Sally's path just when she, tired and depressed, came dragging a sled in the slushy March snow. "Will you pull me a little ways to the circus?" the little lady asked.

"*Ja.*" The circus was a quarter of a mile from the factory, but Sally said she could pull her a part of the way. The lady sat astride the sled, and Sally took the road outside the factory, out into the country in the dusk. Maybe she'd get to go to the circus free, she thought and pulled for all she was worth. Sometimes she turned around and looked at her rider. Sally felt a bit creepy—the body was so little, the face so big. It was getting darker. Sally saw only a face now, shining white. "I can't pull you any farther," she suddenly said. "It's only a little way left."

The little lady got off, gave Sally a picture of herself, and thanked. Then Sally had to trudge home again in the dark with a picture of Scandinavia's smallest lady when she had hoped to go to the circus.

Now the stars and snow don't furnish Sally with a film any longer. She herself is living the film. The slough is only a slough that's hard to cross; the moon is only the moon, and it is sparkling cold.

She walks in the cold and snow and makes a decision. For years she has thought about it. She will leave, get away from everything. Frans might as well be dead, off there in the prison. All the children have jobs except the youngest, and he can stay at Appledale, Ellen and Bernhard have promised that.

First she will go to Paris to Bruno, who sends money,

lots of it home to her and the family, who dances with elegant ladies for money. Sally knows all of his letters by heart. "There is no danger in my work, ma chère mère, it is no worse than anything else. The rich ladies want to dance and pay to be fair to me; it's no different from paying me for serving them a meal. You used to understand everything, ma chère mère; try to understand even this, and don't write such bitter letters to me."

It's been six months since he last wrote. Maybe he's sick. Rich ladies, elegant ladies certainly don't care about sick dancers, and Sally has saved every öre he has sent, saved out of her work earnings, saved from her big sum for the gloves. She can well afford to travel now. She definitely makes her decision, half-formed when she'd spoken to the storekeeper. She must get away from the village, from gossip, from the dark, brooding forests, out to different sights, out among crowds of people. When she has found her son, she will settle in the neighborhood of the Big Farm, near the river where the bleachfield lay, the bleachfield where Mother Sofi, who had fifteen children and managed the Big Farm, lay one November day, drowned. Sally can't understand that, to have food for her children and still drown herself.

"She married so she could keep me, for I was illegitimate," Grandmother had said. Maybe Mother Sofi grieved over that through all the years until at last she took her life, grieved that she didn't get to keep her first child. Sally thinks so. Soon she will travel to the Big Farm. She knows it's gone, but still it was there Grandmother was born, and a person must have a homeplace; Sally calls the Big Farm her homeplace.

She climbs out of the snowdrifts to the narrow tramped-down path up Mårbo's hills, hurrying up their steep ascent. Small pines and firs, hardly a meter high, stand there with white hoods, casting elf shadows in the moonlight. The whole mile of cleared forest is peopled with forest dwarves in white-peaked caps. She has to stop, her heart pounding—it isn't good anymore to rush up this long path, rush along and finish herself off. The vital blood pump under her ribs cautions, "Go carefully; you aren't young any longer; you have strained me hard enough." Her heart pumps blood in waves to her head, so it seems, and the snow shines red in the moonlight.

She will pack tonight, she decides, as she slowly walks up the path. It seems like a mile from here to the cottage. Feeling so tired, she turns around and looks down at the marsh. Pack, what need to do that? She must go home and lie down, sleep deeply, then she can travel. The thought refreshes her, but she still stands there, looking out over the marsh and the fields. Down there lies the village, and she can see the boundaries of Vide Farm from far up here. Vide Farm. *Ja,* it's likely to be at the mercy of the wind now. Mother Maria of Vide is in the hospital, and the villagers whisper something about cancer, cancer of the stomach, incurable, she'll never come home again. No one says it out loud, of course; it's just whispered. They're afraid of death in the village.

But Mimmi is again the parish's good-time girl. She goes again to the dances every Saturday night in knee skirts and silk stockings, dancing from one pair of arms to another's, a kiss here, a hug there, her round red face smiling at every partner. The old housemaid is back at Vide Farm again, in spite of the gift of money for service and the medal for faithfulness and her seventy years, hushing as well as she can the rumor that Mimmi's last baby is not the Vide farmer's. It is said that the farmer himself washes and dresses his children in the mornings and sends the oldest off to school. And it's said that Mimmi wakes up in the mornings in Vide's farmhand quarters. So much is said. Sally doesn't know what is true.

During the years that have passed since Mimmi went to Vide Farm, neither she nor the farmer has been up to

189

Mårbo. But someone else from Vide Farm has been there several times, one that Sally least of all expected, the mother of Vide, Mother Maria, she who's now in the hospital, dying.

Several times Maria has taken the difficult path up to Mårbo, pretending that she wanted to see the animals in the mile of forest, but sitting most of the time at Sally's. Silent and constrained, thin, pale yellow, she sat there for hours, her pointed nose and suspicious eyes unremittingly focused on Sally. Sally made coffee for her, showed her large flock of chickens, her handwork, even read a story to her.

The last time Maria came in the morning and stayed the whole day. Sally found it almost unbearable with the woman staring intently at her in the low quiet cottage. It was in the fall, a rainy day with fog over the forest. Maria ate the dinner Sally gave her, and when she finished, she said, "That is the first meal in a long time I have dared to eat that someone besides myself has fixed. They poison my food at home. I get sick every time I eat." Then she sat silently, staring as before.

It came at once to Sally how tragically life had shaped itself for Maria of Vide. How endlessly and bitterly her days must pass. On the outside everything looked as usual just as it had before she went to the hospital. "You probably have a stomach illness, Mother Maria." Sally's voice was low and shy. But Maria just shook her head and continued to stare at Sally. "Is there anything special you want of me, Mother Maria, or why do you come here? You know we've never been together. You've never tolerated me. Why do you come up here like this and look at me as if I knew something you wanted to know? I don't want you to come here any more. For that matter, I'll be leaving here soon." Sally was disturbed, almost afraid of the strange woman.

"Why did you advise him to take that hussy for himself? I know it was you who advised him to, he told me so himself. Why didn't you lie with him yourself? At least you take care of the children you bring into the world. The last

190

one the hussy had at Vide, he's not the father of, he only thinks so. And I think he knows he isn't its father. Why didn't you take him yourself when he wanted to have children? He came up here to you. He certainly must have been as good and handsome as that gypsy you have at Långholmen. Why did you send that hussy to our farm? Oh, all of you who can have children, what a pack you are, so important and devilish! You can get kids from whatever cat's to be found. You're not any better than cats. May God damn your offspring!"

Mother Maria raged and cried, and Sally silently listened, filled with horror. So clear and sordid and bitter had everything become in the silence of the forest. *Ja,* why had Sally advised the farmer of Vide to take the parish's good-time girl for himself? Sally had known exactly how it would be. He had sat just there by her bed with her newborn on his knee, and had cursed himself, had sworn that he wanted to have children himself. Thoughtlessly Sally had thrown out the suggestion. Or had it been so thoughtless? Hadn't she been enraged, full of hate and revenge against anything and everything, above all, against the village?

A man, one of the village's foremost and richest had sat by her bed and begged, held her new baby, and longed for children. He had been envious of her, Sally, that he'd come with food to, the only food she'd had for a long time. Hadn't it been from revenge and bitterness that she had advised the Vide farmer to take Mimmi? In his fantasy he had only seen a woman with a child in his own kitchen, crazy as he'd been from drink and the rumor his wife's family encouraged that he wasn't able to father a child. Hadn't Sally been a reason for Mother Maria's suffering? But Mother Maria, why should Sally have to shield her? Hard, stingy, mean, she came now and put the blame on Sally. Why should Sally need to guard the villagers' morals? Who knows what might have happened if Mimmi hadn't gone to Vide? Murder maybe. For seven years, Mother Maria has been the parish's saint; how could she have been that without its good-time girl? Poor Mimmi! No one could say that she set her heart on being farm mother at Vide. Now when Maria lay dying, Mimmi danced as she had before. Or perhaps Mimmi never thought. Perhaps she lived in the now, lived for the moment, without the ability to think and plan, whether for her own sake or for her children's. It was lucky her children had the farmer of Vide for their father. But Sally hadn't inflicted the pain on Mother Maria. She had brought it on herself; she had loved a man without a thought for the man himself, had lied, called her man impotent. And now she sat here and blamed Sally.

"You're going crazy, Mother Maria, I haven't anything to do with your sorrows and difficulties. I have enough with my own. Haven't you sometimes had a hand in my difficulties, Mother Maria? If you don't want to have Mimmi in your house, you can probably get her to go away legally. Whatever you do, I don't care. You are farmers. I am, *ja*, what am I, Mother Maria, that you come here and want to get help? People always want to get help from the ones they accuse."

"You could have taken him yourself. He was as good as Liter-Olle's son, and I would have been spared from having that gang of whore's kids at the farm!"

"Do you mean that I should have lived up here at Mårbo and had children with the Vide farmer! Are you crazy or aren't you! Maybe you mean that Vide farmer's children ought to have been starved to death as soon as they were born?"

"You sent the hussy to Vide, you did that! You should have taken him yourself!" Mother Maria raged.

Sally had made her get her coat on and followed her down the hills of Mårbo in the fall rain, and Mother Maria had cried the whole way.

The scene with Maria, sick and despairing, unreeled for Sally when she stood in her loneliness among all the moon's shadows and forest's white treetops, looking out over her surroundings.

The village! Like a hunched-up fiend it lay down there now. When the cold weather leaves and the ice thaws, the fiend will rise up and assault it. Winter sleep is sweet. Sally must get away from everything now while the spring sleeps! Away!

There, away from the village lies Appledale. Good, faithful Ellen. Sally's youngest, that the farmer of Vide had once held newly born on his knee, and cursed his own fate, is there now in Appledale. It is so lonely up here that he often sleeps over with Ellen and Bernhard where there are playmates.

Travel. She is freezing, numb with cold. Her teeth chatter as she climbs to the little barge tipped on the forest's highest crest.

A shimmer of light blinks through the window.

Sally doesn't like to come into the cottage in the dark. She's afraid of darkness under low ceilings. The little copper lamp holds up its flame over the worn-out watching things, over books and bundles of newspapers, over poor men's cheap furniture, dragged home in the junkcart, over the bright rag rug, over the weathered beams, and over a shiny, new suitcase. Sally had bought it some time ago. For two years it has been standing here in the papered room beside the butter churn—the blue painted churn that had been thrown out by some rich farm mother. Now in the winter cold when all beautiful greening life sleeps or lies under the snow blanket, sprouting and waiting, the churn is filled with stiff, dark green pine branches that hold up their fruit like candelabras their flames. Light shimmers out in the lonely forest, light that barely is visible in the moonlight.

A tall, lean man who had climbed up Mårbo's hills, sees the flicker of light and steps in. When he finds only the little lamp, he sits down to wait. She can't be very long, the lamp is here burning, he thinks. A little flame can decide a man's fate. A friendly flame shining on poor things in a low cottage can give a man courage to wait. A man sits in Mårbo and waits for Sally. It is the farmer of Vide.

A man in the cottage, a man in a cottage she thought was empty. A voice that talks. How everything is changed! The new suitcase is standing there, shining. Travel.

"Will you come down to Vide, Sally, and take care of the house? I'm alone now."

"Mother Maria?"

"She won't come home anymore. She can't live the week out, the doctor says."

"Mimmi?"

"She has run away with the hired man. He's related to you here in Mårbo, he's Liter-Olle's youngest son."

Sally is quiet, busies herself with things, stirring up the fire, putting on coffee. She is cold.

"It's cold. Will you have coffee?"

"*Ja*, it's cold. You're freezing, Sally, I'm freezing, too. I think I'll never be warm again. Will you come, Sally? Remember it was you who advised me to take Mimmi. Now I have three children and only an old worn-out maid to depend on. The whole family has turned against me. Will you come and take care of the house and the children?"

"When I advised you so badly, you ought not come again and take advice."

"You didn't advise me badly, Sally, but now I must have a mother for the children. Will you be that? I can tell you, if you care to listen, that Maria, herself, wanted you. She wants us to marry. She lies there, dying, and imagines that we will marry. Women, Sally, are so strange! They are either crazy or wise, no words can be found for them."

"I also have children, both small and grown. You know

194

how the times are. If they lose their jobs, they'll need a home. Do you mean that I should make them homeless? I'm thinking of traveling to my homeplace now and buying a bit of land, for I have a homeplace, too, you know. I'm tired of the village, of everything, I want to have peace. Don't you know what life would be like for us in the village if I came to you now at Vide?"

"The mother of Östby has advised me to come here. The old maid has begged me every day to come to you, and for myself, I want nothing else than to have you live with me, Sally. Nowadays no one says anything else but that you are a fine and clever woman, Sally, and—a—beautiful woman. You should talk with people more, and you'd hear that no one thinks you are crazy or bad. Your children will have a place at Vide. There's plenty of uncultivated land. And if you don't want to stay with me, then you can leave. But come now, come tonight, let Vide be your homeplace; there are small children who don't have a mother. How can you say no, Sally?"

A man and a woman walk down Mårbo's hills.

The cold is as sharp as before, the moon shines, the snowy fields and forest surround them. Walking with accustomed steps, they talk easily about ordinary things, this or that field, that meadow, a forest over there. And the man says, "You know everything as if you were born here. You don't need to look up your homeplace."

"I thought I'd go to my son, but I'll write to him instead."

The moon shines on the snow, and the man strides through the drifts in recently made tracks. The stars come nearer, the world becomes narrower, can be perceived again. Sally follows behind the man.

"Someone has gone here before, so it isn't such heavy-going now."

195

"*Ja*, I was here. I plowed up the track with my feet as much as I could."

"I took the roundabout way when I climbed up to Mårbo, but you went straight ahead, Sally."

"No, I often go crookedly. Here's one who goes straight ahead and doesn't waste time." And Sally points to the track that marks the fox's water way.

Many winding miles away in the country, at the boundary of a fertile plain where the paths to thin woods and dark mountain tops begin, stands the Big Farm's whitebeam tree, still there hunched down over the river, purling and murmuring in solitude.

The plum orchard is long since cut down, the bleachfield ploughed. The mossy apple trees, where the suitors hid themselves in the moonlight, are gone. A new house, new people. A sawmill and a brick factory are in the valley. Only the whitebeam tree is left, for even the river for long stretches is new, is a wide canal where the swirling water spins around in the turbines.

There is a bench under the whitebeam. It looks new. Maybe there still is someone who longs for something in solitude and moonlight and built a bench here.

One day a tall blonde woman and a tall lean man sit under the whitebeam. "Now I have done as you wanted, Sally. I have followed you here. Now I am asking you for the last time: Will you marry me?"

Sally looks up in the whitebeam. The smoke from the fire that warmed Mother Sofi's bathwater a long time ago has been washed away by the rain, rains of a hundred autumns, and says, "Do you really want to marry me? Have you considered that Mimmi might come back, and that Maria hasn't been dead a year yet?"

"We'll soon be old, Sally, both you and I. I want a wife

after my own nature on my farm before I die, and I want to marry you. I will have a proper wedding for you, have a big party. I want to honor you in some way, Sally. Don't you understand that? You said that you wanted to travel here first, and then you would decide. And I followed you here. Answer me, now, you're used to knowing what you want. You cannot want to leave my children, and your own have a home also at Vide."

Sally sits quietly. Marry the farmer of Vide! She had never really thought he was serious. He was fickle and woman-crazy. But was he? Mimmi. *Ja*, a man is very strange, too.

"It isn't very good land for farming here. Vide is surely better, Sally?"

"*Ja*, Vide is better."

"Will you have me, Sally?"

Sally delays with her answer. Then she smiles a little. I have Mårbo, she thinks, I can marry, marry lawfully. It's the only thing I haven't tried. If it doesn't work out, in spite of the big farm and plenty of everything, then I still have Mårbo which I am used to. She looks at the man, a handsome man and a good man, truly. She felt not the least distaste at the thought of marrying him. Why not marry? It was certain she'd be going back there in any case. And then she had promised Maria, but Maria . . . Sally wasn't sure. Maria certainly hated her; it looked that way sometimes, or Maria was certainly crazy. One promises a dying person just anything, too. *Ja*, that's probably not right either; one shouldn't make worthless promises like that. But mother of a farm, and of Vide, in the middle of the village, the village that knew so well how it used to be at Mårbo in Liter-Olle's time!

"*Ja*, I will marry you," she says happily and decidedly.

"When does the bus go to the station? If we can get home in the morning, then it is Friday, and I can give the order on the banns!"

"The bus goes in an hour," Sally says, and she smiles at the man.

The Big Farm is gone. Mother Sofi's bones are left in the earth, and the moon goes its round as always among heaven's stars.

Afterword

Moa Martinson's first novel, *Women and Appletrees (Kvinnor och äppelträd)*, was published in Sweden in 1933. Sweden's working-class readers were already familiar with the essays and serialized stories she had published in proletariat journals. *Women and Appletrees* secured their devotion and enlarged Martinson's audience in Sweden's then hierarchical society. Critics could not ignore Martinson's remarkable first novel, but this largely male bourgeoise literary establishment was clear in its consensus: *Women and Appletrees,* while realistic and poignant, was undisciplined, muddled, hastily written.[1] In her varied succession of novels, short stories, and poems, Moa Martinson paid no attention to critics; neither did her readers. Even after her death in 1964, her immense popularity in Sweden hardly diminished. In 1973, her publishers began reissuing her novels, *Women and Appletrees* appearing in both hardcover and paperback in 1975. A new generation of readers and critics warmly appreciated her vigorous, inimitable style, which combines her witty, deeply felt response not only to life's almost intolerable burdens but also to its limitless joys. That The Feminist Press now makes *Women and Appletrees* accessible to readers outside of Martinson's native Sweden is just cause for celebration.

Although Martinson begins her novel with Mother Sofi's generation in rural Sweden in the 1840s, it is chiefly her own, from the 1890s to shortly after World War I, that she depicts through her autobiographical characters, Sally and Ellen. *Women and Appletrees* is a novel about women's struggles to endure and overcome the poverty, brutality, and loneliness they suffered in the slums of industrial Norrköping and Stockholm, and in the farming villages between them.

The experiences Martinson relates, her own and those she had heard from others, particularly her mother and grandmother, are exuberantly vigorous, for she writes as if she were telling them to an immediate audience. The novel, thus, is written in a flexible, conversational style, one story following the other. Martinson only interrupts the flow of the stories to intersperse dialogue, growing out of and enhancing them, or to universalize a specific happening, offering choric commentary about life, nature, war, and society. Her use of this convention is perhaps didactic and may be somewhat jarring to modern readers as they move from her fictional creation to her commentary or interpretation. It is here that Martinson's time clock—her shifts from the present to the past, or to the historical or eternal present, when the text compels them—must engage closer attention, or the novel might seem to lose artistic precision. That it does not (anymore than a dexterous use of stream of consciousness) shows her skill.

To sustain the sense of immediacy that she depends on, Martinson uses repetition, gives hints of future action that spur the reader's attention, inserts details that might seem irrelevant, but which evoke time and place, compelling her listener-reader to identify with her intensely personalized characters. The rhythm of her sentences is that of spoken Swedish, the sing-song music of this tonal language.[2]

Dialectical words and contractions for colloquial speech catch her conversational tone, as well as her employment of the ever-present Swedish *ja* and idioms such as "that's to say." She uses oral devices for contrast and emphasis, beginning sentences with "and" or "but," and inserting "and so" as the binder between clauses. She employs repetition in various ways as a storytelling device. Sometimes she repeats a word, a phrase, or a whole clause, as "She's too good for him," when Martinson wants to stress Sofi's importance in the village before she married the mean ruptured farmer. Or she focuses on the descriptive "soft hands" of the farmer and the "leather apron" he wears to hide and protect his scrotal hernia, or she reiterates his "paralyzed mother" or Sofi's "illegitimate child." This repetitive device is skillfully used throughout the novel to fix characters in the reader's mind, to give special emphasis to a point, and to sustain a conversational tone and mood.

The opening section of the novel illustrates Martinson's ease with the technique in her portrayal of the friendship of Sofi and Fredrika, the solidarity they share, as they tenaciously bathe together every Friday. The childless Fredrika's life with her stingy, syphilitic husband is as miserable as Sofi's with her monstrous farmer and her fifteen children. Although Sofi had to get married, she, like Fredrika, thought she would then become wealthy. With mordant irony, Martinson shows how neither woman's dream is fulfilled. For explication, she gives pertinent background detail, effectively and economically, of women's work on the farm, and maps its buildings, including the washhouse with its bakehouse inside. The celebration of Christmas begins on the thirteenth of December (St. Lucia's Day) and continues until the twentieth of January (Canute's Day).[3] Hence, the farmer's amazement that the washhouse would be lighted and heated when the Christmas baking would long be over and the pantry still well supplied. When he calls Sofi and Fredrika "whores," he is echoing a commonly held belief that only prostitutes bathe, and is outraged that his wife is carrying on in this manner with her friend *and* in the Christmas season. He has never seen his wife naked. Sofi has a small, thin figure, and the description of the nude, full-bodied Fredrika is especially forceful in this context; the farmer thinks he has indeed gone mad.

In the oral tradition that Martinson uses, symbols have even greater importance in the novel's construction. The title she chooses—*Women and Appletrees*—immediately elicits a sensual response; the image, elemental, evocative, has a wondrous simplicity. Martinson uses the apple tree in each of its seasonal changes—mossy greenness, flowering beauty, burnished glow, bare sturdiness—to emphasize her main characters' strength and imagination to endure their hard lives and triumph over them.

The symbol of the journey has structural significance in *Women and Appletrees.* Of the four journeys, two of them, the first and the last, are made by Sally, Martinson's most fully autobiographical character in the novel. Sally's moonlit, ox-en-driven ride from the city to the country, when she is seven, is the first. The journey binds the generations in the novel together: Martinson uses it to identify the link between Mother Sofi and her illegitimate child, who is Sally's grandmother, and to illustrate through meditative commentary the harsh life they share.

Ellen, the other main character who is also Mother Sofi's descendant, makes a journey from her home, Appledale, to Sally's home, Mårbo. By means of Ellen's walk through the village, Martinson relates the grim childbearing experiences of its women. Thus, she visually constructs the village and countryside, and psychologically supports one of her main themes, that of the woman as survivor.

Ellen's father-in-law, Mr. Olsson, the only entirely admirable male character central to the action, journeys to his homeplace for a symbolic rebirth. He is the outsider the villagers ironically and suspiciously view. Clearing his tiny holding, he plants apple trees for the hope they inspire in him of life; he builds his cottage and names his place Appledale. Though he tries to be, and is, a good husband and caring father, his wife thinks she married beneath her, and his sons exploit him. Late in his hard life, he goes back to his birthplace, his juniper heath, seeking the urgency of life he felt in his youth. Then he returns home to Appledale. After his son marries Ellen, the old man becomes a grandfather, an intrepid counterpart to Sally's grandmother. His apple trees have nourished and fulfilled his dream.

In the last chapter of the novel, Sally makes another symbolic journey. Trudging through the snowdrifts from her home, Mårbo, which lies on the crest of the forest's steep hills, to the village store and back, she reviews her life. She decides to return to her roots, to the Big Farm and its bleach-field. There, long ago, Mother Sofi, her great grandmother, had dried her weaving, and there Sofi's body had lain after the neighbors had pulled it from the river. Martinson symbolically ends her novel at its beginning; Sally's journey ends in renewal and affirmation of life.

Through this recurring pattern of symbols and oral conventions, Martinson shapes her novel. In her need to define her characters through her own experiences, Martinson also turns to metaphors to establish essential links. One such significant metaphor is her comparison of Sofi's body to a rune stone: "The touchingly thin body . . . resembled a curious living rune stone. . . . Her stomach was one single scar, knot against knot, scar against scar, with big, broad, shimmering streaks here and there."[4] As Swedish critic Ebba Witt-Brattström perceptively comments, "Moa Martinson lets mother Sofi's body narrate her entire life."[5] In her realistic portrayal of a woman's body, exposing the scars of bearing fifteen children, Martinson differs markedly from her contemporary male writers' characterizations of women. They either dreamed up an idealized progenitor, as Moa Martinson's husband, Harry Martinson, did, or they drew the rudimentary, over-simplified woman of Artur Lundquist's *White Man (Vit man)*. Moa Martinson's naked Sofi differs sharply from the portraits of "chubby young bathing nymphs" popularized by Swedish male writers and artists at the time.[6]

An image that is psychologically important in Ellen's

characterization is that of the painting of a curly-haired boy holding a cluster of grapes. In Ellen's eyes, the boy is "more beautiful than the child, Jesus" (p. 46). The painting hangs in one of Ellen's foster homes in the slums of Norrtull near the tollgates. Amidst the dreadful circumstances that Ellen endures—always hungry, always sleeping on a bundle of rags on the floor, receiving beatings and then obscene teasing for wetting her pants before she could make the frightening trip to the outhouse, and, worst of all, suffering sexual abuse—the painting symbolized to the miserable child the world's possible beauty. After her mother's death, when Ellen becomes the foster child of a woman who runs a cafe and rooming house, the painting comes to life. Ellen runs errands for a beautiful foreign boy and his elegant mother who live in rooms above the cafe, rooms that are filled with flowers, books, chocolates, and a large piano that the mysterious pair play. After an especially hard day of work in the cafe, Ellen, seeking respite, goes to these enchanting rooms. The boy is alone, and inviting Ellen in, he first plays the piano, and then after slowly undressing her, he tenderly fondles her small breasts and body.

Martinson conveys the immediacy of the experience from a ten-year-old girl's perspective—Ellen's poignant remembrance of the painting, the reality of the boy's physical presence, her joy in his music, her unquestioning, smiling acceptance of his caresses, her frightened alarm when he abandons her, her sense of the timelessness of the experience, her feeling of the world and herself as an illusion until she hears the familiar noises from the cafe and street below. This singular experience of beauty tangled with the boy's sexual distress, venting itself in his weeping and praying, confuses Ellen. Later, when this memory is entwined with her earlier sexual abuse in the slums, Ellen regards the sexual act as immoral in her marriage. She equates sex with ignorance, filth, excrement, drunkenness, brawls, obscene jokes and language. The sexual act gives her only revulsion and pain. Cleanliness becomes a fetish. She cannot keep her house, her baby, her own person clean enough. The world of nature—the sky, the forest, the apple trees—symbolizes purity and beauty for her. Bernhard, her husband, does not understand Ellen's problem, and lacking perception and inner strength, he takes out his frustration and confusion by drinking. He wants to be a sensitive lover, but she refuses, rebuffs him. At a climactic point in the novel, he drunkenly, brutally, beats her. Not until Ellen comes to grips with her own aroused passion, can she resolve her moral scruples and find sexual pleasure in her marriage.

A major theme running through *Women and Appletrees* is the hypocrisy of double standards reflected in the attitudes of men toward women, of women toward each other and themselves, of the church, the state, and society toward freedom of ideas. Through her main characters—Sofi, Sally, and Ellen, Moa Martinson illustrates the injustices that established society inflicts on its people, particularly its poor.

Sally grew up in poverty, but she has none of Ellen's gentility. Like Martinson herself, Sally is self-confident and self-educated. She is as imaginative, independent, and charismatic as her creator. Into Sally's characterization, Martinson poured her own strength and humor. Neither of Martinson's marriages—the miserable one that ended in her husband's suicide, the compatible one that ended in a divorce she did not want—embittered nor diminished her.[7] She was sure of her own identity, realizing early that though she might not control her circumstances, never would she meekly submit to them. She fought. Just as Sally gives birth alone, so did Martinson several times in loneliness and poverty. She was tough, like the dandelion, the whitebeam, and the apple trees she uses as metaphor in *Women and Appletrees.* Moa Martinson is like her fictional Sally, spirited and mettlesome.

As a child, Sally had perceived and experienced life's unfairness. She has no illusions. When Ellen reflects that she could not ask for anything better now that her husband no longer drinks, Sally dryly responds, "Things can go better for one than for another" (p. 106). Clearly discerning the hypocrisy of established society's double standards, she refuses to conform. Although she has six children with Frans, a handsome, hard-drinking fisherman, musician, and smuggler who ends up in jail, she does not want to marry him. "I can't stand my man any longer. I can't bear him, and I can't get away from here—it's lucky he's never home. Even if he behaved himself, I still couldn't live with him, but children there'd be" (p. 106). Sally would rather endure the cruel taunts, the threats of the church and the state's poor relief than to make a meaningless marriage.

Sally bravely struggles against the hypocritical moral standards and the economic disparity between rich and poor in her rigid class society. She tries to organize a union of farm workers, holding meetings at her cottage, but her daring attempt is unsuccessful; the workers yield to pressures from the landowners and other villagers. Nearing the crest of the high hill where Mårbo lies, Sally, on that moonlit, cold winter night, surveys the countryside, its big farms and their landowners, sharecroppers, and *statares* (landless farm workers). She thinks about them and their wives, as she looks at the village, for they and the priest, constable, chairman of the poor relief, and storekeeper nearly all live in the village in manor houses, cottages, or huts: "The village! Like a hunched-up fiend it lay down there now. When the cold weather leaves and the ice thaws, the fiend will rise up and assault it" (p. 193). When the constable and the chairman of the poor relief come to threaten her, and she reads *Genghis Khan* to them instead of Sweden's Laws of the Realm, sure that neither man knows the difference, her shrewd tactic works. Cleverly, she dismisses them, and then angrily tells Ellen, " '*Ja*, thanks,' they said, when they got to hear that they were mold. They're all alike! All of them in power live on mold, venerate mold so much that they give the beggar and his children moldy bread" (p. 134).

Sally's instinctive sense of life's injustices, particularly to the poor, to the defenseless, informs her most deeply felt experiences. Martinson creates an unforgettable image for Sally's anguish: "She has a vision of a murky, blackish brown sky, flat-topped, bare hills, and far-off dark figures like specters on the road. She almost hears the children sobbing over their broken bottle stopper" (p. 186). Sally is recalling an early childhood experience, when she decisively assured the oldest of four outcast children, poorer even than she, that his precious glass stopper would not break if he hit it against a stone. She sees this vision when she gives birth alone to her sixth child; and again when she makes her decision to go to her homeplace. The vision is as arresting as Ingmar Bergman's Dance of Death in *The Seventh Seal*.[8]

Moa Martinson's life, like Sally's and Ellen's, was a struggle. She was born Helga Maria Swartz, November 2, 1890, in Vårdnäs, a suburb of Norrköping, in Östergötland, Sweden. Her father, a soldier, belonged to the upper class; and it was then unthinkable that he marry beneath him.[9] After his sudden death the same year of his daughter's birth, Moa lived in foster homes, and her mother in rooming houses near the textile factory where she worked. Her wages were too meager for her daughter to live with her. Moa's foster homes and her mother's rooming houses were always in the slums. When Moa was seven, her mother married a ne'er-do-well; because of his drinking and quick temper, he never could hold a job—farm hand, lumberjack, stevedore, factory worker—for long. Moa's childhood was nomadic. Her mother always worked, either in factories or in homes as a scrubwoman.[10]

In her most famous and artistically her best novel, *My Mother Gets Married (Mor gifter sig, 1936)*, Martinson describes her own and her mother's experiences through the character of Mia. She writes, in a new preface to that novel, "Though the fathers and children starved, the mothers starved even more. . . . In the course of my life [my mother] was my best and most trustworthy friend who possessed that cultivation and experience which never can be learned in schools or the university, only from life in its bitterest form."[11]

Moa worked first as a maid, and then as a waitress, moving to Stockholm, where she became a cold buffet manager (a special class of restaurant worker). In 1910, she married Karl Johansson, a farm worker who owned a small cottage between Ösmo and Sorunda, small towns south of Stockholm. She lived here the rest of her life, ironically referring to her cottage as "Moa's castle" ("Moas slott").[12] Her life was hard and lonely. Her husband was even worse than her stepfather, a brutal, shiftless drunkard, often away from home, who killed himself in 1928. Of the five sons they had in quick succession, the two youngest drowned in a lake near their cottage. Moa was devastated by grief.

To support her other sons and herself, Martinson wrote articles urging better pay and living conditions for farm and factory workers, publishing them in Socialist newspapers, *Fire (Brand)* and *The Workers (Arbetaren),* and signing them simply "Helga." She also organized the farm workers, holding meetings in her cottage, began study circles for them, and worked to get a library for her parish neighborhood. Largely self-educated, she read hungrily, widely, and astutely.

In 1927, Martinson changed her name to Moa, after the main character in Johannes V. Jensen's novel, *The Glacier (Jökeln),* a woman who "gives birth, plants seeds, gathers crops, holds everything together."[13]

Through the help of Elin Wägner, a well-known Swedish novelist, feminist, and pacifist, Martinson attended Fogelstad, a woman's school, in the spring of 1928, and wrote articles for the radical feminist weekly, *The Epoch (Tidevarvet).* Her first attempt at a novel, *Pigmamma: A Novel from a Working Woman's World (Pigmamma: Roman ur arbetarkvinnornas värld)* was rejected, then serialized in *Fire,* 1928–29.[14]

Moa married Harry Martinson in 1929, supporting and helping him in his writing. While he and other distinguished Swedish writers, such as Eyvind Johnson, left their working-class background, Moa Martinson never left hers, "the domain where I felt at home. Poor people's still not mapped-out domain."[15] Harry Martinson divorced Moa in 1940.

After *Women and Appletrees,* Moa Martinson wrote fifteen novels, three volumes of short stories, one of essays, and one of poems. Like her first novel, all that she wrote addressed the needs of the working class, especially the women, who never gave up their struggle to support themselves and their children, and to better their lives. Martinson knew what she was writing about; she had lived their struggle. She was their trusted and beloved articulator until her death.

Through her books, articles, radio talks, and speeches, Moa Martinson became Sweden's "public person, an institution, loved and hated—and always only Moa."[16] She voiced her anger toward a society that permitted or seemed to ignore poverty, child abuse, and the dangers of atomic weapons. She praised Russia during the Cold War as the "ideal" society, insisting after the Soviets' takeover of Hungary in 1956 that there was a "difference between Russia's power politics and the communist ideology."[17]

Writers, artists, opera singers, actors, actresses, farm and factory workers, political figures—all came to her cottage. She had a large correspondence. Her letters, those that she wrote, and those that she received, show how her humor and charm drew a warm and caring response.[18] Among her letters are ones from the acclaimed Danish writer, Martin Anderson Nexö, who admired her work; Elise Ottesen-Jensen, the feminist journalist who first helped and encouraged Moa to publish in *Fire;* Marika Stiernstedt, writer and chairman of Sweden's Writers Union, whose favorable study of Moa's novels appeared in the prestigious *Bonniers Literary Magazine* in 1946; the actor, Karl Gerhard; Prince Wilhelm of Sweden; and Tage Erlander, Sweden's Prime Minister and Chairman of the Social Democratic Party for twenty-three years, from 1946 to 1968.

Sweden's literary critics, however, largely dismissed her novels as limited and undisciplined.[19] In her updated preface to *My Mother Gets Married,* Moa quotes a critic who ridiculed her novel as "food for the dump."[20] Another critic more generously echoed the opinion of his fellows in his assessment of her novels: "a gaudy splash of color" in the "thirties' naturalistic *statare* school of romanticists."[21] This attitude has deservedly and fortunately changed. Her novels have been praised by critics in books as diverse as literary histories and anthologies of radical working-class writers. This criticism is especially true of her autobiographical trilogy, including the already mentioned *My Mother Gets Married, Church Wedding (Kyrkbröllop,* 1938), and *The King's Roses (Kungens Rosor,* 1939).[22] Moa Martinson's most perceptive critics have always been women. Annie Löfstedt in *Figures against a Dark Background (Figurer mot mörk botten),* published in 1943, saw that Martinson's achievement could not be limited to a particular "school" of writers, that she had far larger significance.[23] Maria Bergom-Larsson's valuable, detailed overview of Martinson's life and works appeared in three illustrated articles in Stockholm's famous daily, *The Day's News (Dagens Nyheter)* in 1976, and in expanded form in her book, *Women's Consciousness (Kvinnomedvetande).* Ebba Witt-Brattström has written discerningly about Martinson's artistry and development, and Barbro Backberger's comparison of Martinson's novels to those of the aristocratic Swedish writer, Agnes von Krusenstjerna, is sensitive and provocative.[24]

But the readers who would have the most significance for Moa Martinson would not come from the literary establishment but from the general public.[25] Now, to a still larger audience of readers throughout the English-speaking world, Moa Martinson's stirring first novel, *Women and Appletrees,* compassionately shows the brave endurance of women, strong and beautiful as the apple trees.

MARGARET S. LACY
University of Wisconsin at Madison

NOTES

1. Virtually all information on Martinson's life and criticism of her works are available in Swedish only. All translations in this Afterword are this writer's. For an overview of the male attitude that once prevailed about Martinson's artistry, see Maria Bergom-Larsson's three articles in *The Day's News (Dagens Nyheter)*, Nov. 2, 4, 6, 1975, reprinted in expanded form in her essay, "Moa Martinson—Her Work and Her Love," ("Moa Martinson—arbetet och kärleken") in her book, *Women's Consciousness (Kvinnomedvetande)*, Stockholm, Rabén & Sjögren, 1976, pp. 72–97. For particular criticism that reflects this patronizing view, see Knut Jaensson, *Nine Modern Swedish Prose Writers (Nio moderna svenska prosaförfattare)*, Stockholm, Bonniers, 1943, and *A Swedish Literary Dictionary (Svenskt Litteraturlexikon)* Lund, Gleerup, 1970, pp. 364–365. Two estimable and interesting exceptions to this view should be noted: Victor Svanberg, "Moa's Kingdom" ("Moas rikedom") in his book of essays, *Praise for the Present Day (Till nutidens lov)*, Uppsala, Lindblads, 1956; and Axel Strindberg, *People between Wars (Människor mellan krig)*, Stockholm, Kooperativa förbundets bokförlag, 1941, pp. 295–298.

2. This translation of *Women and Appletrees* strives to catch the singsong rhythm of spoken Swedish, in order to make it congenial with the mood, tone, and visualized experience of the original.

3. "Dance Christmas out on the twentieth of Canute" ("Dansa 'julen' ut på tjugonde Knut") marks a celebration that ends the Christmas season.

4. Moa Martinson, *Women and Appletrees*, p. 11. All subsequent references to *Women and Appletrees* are indicated by page numbers in the text.

5. Ebba Witt-Brattström, " 'Life's own runestone'—Moa Martinson and Realism's Dead End" (" 'Livets egen runsten'—Moa Martinson och realismens döda vinkel"), *Periodical for Literary Scholarship (Tidskrift för Litteratur Vetenskap)*, ed. Urpu-Liisa Karahka and Magnus Röhl, Stockholm, 1983, pp. 276–277. Her essay has perceptive criticism especially on Martinson's development as a writer.

6. Witt-Brattström, p. 276.

7. Glann Boman, *Moa in Letters and Pictures (Moa i brev och bilder)*, Stockholm, Askild & Kärnekull, 1978, p. 14.

8. See the photograph in the Museum of Modern Art Film Stills, Archives, New York, or the reproduction in *Encyclopedia Britannica,* 1976, 12, p. 537.

9. See Franklin D. Scott's discussion of social classes in *Sweden: The Nation's History,* Minneapolis, University of Minnesota Press, 1977, pp. 334–351.

10. For biographical details, see Bergom-Larsson and Boman.

11. Moa Martinson, *My Mother Gets Married (Mor gifter sig),* Preface, p. 5. Martinson's preface to this new edition, Askild & Kärnekull, 1973, has no date.

12. Boman, p. 173.

13. Witt-Brattström, p. 277. The Danish novelist, Johannes V. Jensen, won the Nobel Prize for Literature in 1944.

14. Bergom-Larsson, p. 74; Witt-Brattström, p. 277.

15. Moa Martinson, *I Meet a Poet (Jag möter en diktare),* Folket I Bilds Förlag, 1950. Harry Martinson and Eyvind Johnson shared the Nobel Prize for Literature in 1974.

16. Bergom-Larsson, p. 74.

17. Bergom-Larsson, p. 75. See also Martinson's correspondence with Marika Stiernstedt on this point in Boman, pp. 92–107. Stiernstedt writes in a letter dated March 13, 1941, "So is it also with *communism.* I think nowadays it is simply dumb. We have seen what it did in Russia, where it had *all* unparalleled chances, unparalleled! . . . You *imagine* that you have to be so terribly 'proletariat'! That's a mistake, Moa, you are not one, you have neither the bent, manner, or their way of living now" (pp. 96–98). [All italics are hers.] Moa replies, "I have nothing to do with the official communism in Sweden, but I do not believe that communism will disappear if it becomes forbidden. . . . I belong to the world's proletariat class, the gifts that I have I will always put to its service" (p. 100). Martinson and Stiernstedt were always close friends.

18. Boman. All the letters, including those mentioned in the text following the note, show this response.

19. Bergom-Larsson, p. 91.

20. Martinson, *My Mother Gets Married,* Preface, p. 5.

21. Bergom-Larsson, p. 96.

22. Barrie Selman, "Moa Martinson—Depictor of Women's Oppression," (Moa Martinson—Kvinnoförtryckets skildrare"), *Our Writers (Vara författare),* an Anthology, no editor, Stockholm, Kulturfront, 1974, pp. 154–169. Sven Wernström, "Moa Martinson," *The Writers' History of Literature,* ed. Lars Ardelius and Gunnar Ryström, Stockholm, Författarförlaget, 1978, pp. 202–210.

23. Annie Löfstedt, *Figures against a Dark Background (Figurer mot mörk botten),* Stockholm, Bonniers, 1943.

24. Barbro Backberger, "Class Society and Women's Lives—A Study of Agnes von Krusenstjerna's and Moa Martinson's Works" (Samhällsklass och kvinnoliv—en studie i Agnes von Krusenstjernas och Moa Martinsons författarskap," *Women's History of Literature (Kvinnornas Litteratur Historia),* ed. Marie Louise Ramnefalk and Anna Westberg, Lund, Författarförlaget, 1981, pp. 368–397.

25. Martinson's novel, *My Mother Gets Married,* was made into a seven-hour television series in 1980, which was very popular in Sweden. *Women and Appletrees* was made into a charming, gripping, successful play, which premiered in Stockholm's Lilla Scenen, Jan. 26, 1978. The translator saw this production in September 1978.

.

The **Feminist Press** offers alternatives in education and in literature. Founded in 1970, this non-profit, tax-exempt educational and publishing organization works to eliminate sexual stereotypes in books and schools and to provide literature with a broad vision of human potential. The publishing program includes reprints of important works by women, feminist biographies of women, and nonsexist children's books. Curricular materials, bibliographies, directories, and a quarterly journal provide information and support for students and teachers of women's studies. In-service projects help to transform teaching methods and curricula. Through publications and projects, The Feminist Press contributes to the rediscovery of the history of women and the emergence of a more humane society.

FEMINIST CLASSICS FROM THE FEMINIST PRESS

Antoinette Brown Blackwell: A Biography, by Elizabeth Cazden. $16.95 cloth, $9.95 paper.

Between Mothers and Daughters: Stories Across a Generation. Edited by Susan Koppelman. $8.95 paper.

Brown Girl, Brownstones, a novel by Paule Marshall. Afterword by Mary Helen Washington. $8.95 paper.

Call Home the Heart, a novel of the thirties, by Fielding Burke. Introduction by Alice Kessler-Harris and Paul Lauter and afterwords by Sylvia J. Cook and Anna W. Shannon. $8.95 paper.

Cassandra, by Florence Nightingale. Introduction by Myra Stark. Epilogue by Cynthia Macdonald. $3.50 paper.

The Changelings, a novel by Jo Sinclair. Afterwords by Nellie McKay and by Johnnetta B. Cole and Elizabeth H. Oakes; Biographical Note by Elisabeth Sandberg. $8.95 paper.

The Convert, a novel by Elizabeth Robins. Introduction by Jane Marcus. $6.95 paper.

Daughter of Earth, a novel by Agnes Smedley. Afterword by Paul Lauter. $7.95 paper.

The Female Spectator, edited by Mary R. Mahl and Helen Koon. $8.95 paper.

Guardian Angel and Other Stories, by Margery Latimer. Afterwords by Nancy Loughridge, Meridel Le Sueur, and Louis Kampf. $8.95 paper.

I Love Myself When I Am Laughing . . . And Then Again When I Am Looking Mean and Impressive, by Zora Neale Hurston. Edited by Alice Walker with an introduction by Mary Helen Washington. $9.95 paper.

Käthe Kollwitz: Woman and Artist, by Martha Kearns. $7.95 paper.

Life in the Iron Mills and Other Stories, by Rebecca Harding Davis. Biographical interpretation by Tillie Olsen. $7.95 paper.

The Living Is Easy, a novel by Dorothy West. Afterword by Adelaide M. Cromwell. $8.95 paper.

The Other Woman: Stories of Two Women and a Man. Edited by Susan Koppelman. $8.95 paper.

Mother to Daughter, Daughter to Mother: A Daybook and Reader, selected and shaped by Tillie Olsen. $9.95 paper.

Portraits of Chinese Women in Revolution, by Agnes Smedley. Edited with an introduction by Jan MacKinnon and Steve MacKinnon and an afterword by Florence Howe. $5.95 paper.

Reena and Other Stories, selected short stories by Paule Marshall. $8.95 paper.

Ripening: Selected Work, 1927–1980, by Meridel Le Sueur. Edited with an introduction by Elaine Hedges. $8.95 paper.

Rope of Gold, a novel of the thirties, by Josephine Herbst. Introduction by Alice Kessler-Harris and Paul Lauter and afterword by Elinor Langer. $8.95 paper.

The Silent Partner, a novel by Elizabeth Stuart Phelps. Afterword by Mari Jo Buhle and Florence Howe. $8.95 paper.

These Modern Women: Autobiographical Essays from the Twenties. Edited with an introduction by Elaine Showalter. $4.95 paper.

The Unpossessed, a novel of the thirties, by Tess Slesinger. Introduction by Alice Kessler-Harris and Paul Lauter and afterword by Janet Sharistanian. $8.95 paper.

Weeds, a novel by Edith Summers Kelley. Afterword by Charlotte Goodman. $7.95 paper.

The Woman and the Myth: Margaret Fuller's Life and Writings, by Bell Gale Chevigny. $8.95 paper.

A Woman of Genius, a novel by Mary Austin. Afterword by Nancy Porter. $8.95 paper.

The Yellow Wallpaper, by Charlotte Perkins Gilman. Afterword by Elaine Hedges. $3.95 paper.

For free catalog, write to: The Feminist Press, Box 334, Old Westbury, NY 11568. Send individual book orders to The Feminist Press, P.O. Box 1654, Hagerstown, MD 21741. Include $1.75 postage and handling for one book and 75¢ for each additional book. To order using MasterCard or Visa, call: (800) 638-3030.